# THE FAT OF FED BEASTS

# THE FAT OF FED BEASTS

*Guy Ware*

CROMER

PUBLISHED BY SALT
12 Norwich Road, Cromer, Norfolk NR27 0AX United Kingdom



Printed in Great Britain by Clays Ltd, St Ives plc

Typeset in Sabon 10/13



ISBN 978 1 78463 024 9 paperback

1 3 5 7 9 8 6 4 2

*For Sophy*
*And for Frank and Rebecca*

"What reinforcement we may gain from hope,
If not, what resolution from despair."

MILTON, *Paradise Lost*

"I have often thought upon death, and I find it the least of all evils."

BACON, *An Essay on Death*

# I

THE OFFICE IS not empty, or it would not be an office. There are desks and chairs and computers and some paperwork that hasn't been filed, and there are coffee mugs, some of them clean. On D's desk, there are two or three self-help books for managers, which D isn't. Plus he's beyond help.

But there are no people.

I am here.

There are no other people. Work is for once not hell. Which is ironic – or a coincidence, anyway – given what we do here. I should take advantage.

Not empty, then. But quiet. I am not working. I do not disturb the air around me. But the computers hum and trains still rumble past our third-floor window.

Peaceful, though: an unanticipated bonus in the middle of a working day. It is Monday, so Theo will be at Riverside House. Perhaps. We believe that is where he spends each Monday morning. Rada went for an early lunch; she had to go to the bank, she said. D has been working at home. This is not like D, who has not been himself recently. Just as stupid, obviously, but more focused, somehow. He is up to something. Whatever it is, it will be drivel.

The windows in this office do not open.

I should make a telephone call.

Specifically, I should call Gina Spence. Theo will be expecting *progress* – you would think, at his age, he would know better – but I have nothing to report. I have not spoken to her. It's not the suicide that's the problem. I don't mind suicide; you might even say it's my speciality. But some suicides have mothers who are themselves not dead.

I roll a cigarette, but do not light it, even though the office is empty.

Unwelcome sunshine smears the room. My desk is sticky with it. For a moment I wish I could open the window. But I know it is hotter outside than it is in here, and more humid. There is no breeze. It is June but seems to think it's August. I cannot open the windows because the windows in this office do not open: the office is air-conditioned; the air conditioning does not work. The meeting room this afternoon will be unbearable.

(We will bear it.)

I realise I am squandering the unanticipated tranquility of an almost empty office. Soon Rada will return from the bank. D will foul the already fetid air with testosterone and stupidity.

I should ring Gina Spence, but I won't, not today. I have written up two reports – one up; one down – and that will suffice. Someone commits suicide every thirty-six seconds. This is a job, not a vocation.

For the Ancient Egyptians the heart was the seat of the soul; when you died it was tested in the scales of Maat. If your heart weighed no more than a feather, you made it into the fields of peace. The heart is a meaty organ: tough, dense and muscular, the size of a clenched fist. An unequal deal, then? A long shot? Apparently not. There is no Egyptian Book of the Dead in which the applicant fails; crocodile-headed Ammut waits to eat the hearts in vain; Thoth, who invented writing, records the same verdict every time. Our system is more realistic. Or at least less certain.

Rada has not yet returned from the bank when D arrives, wanting to talk to me. He does not want to talk to me in particular – indeed, he would probably prefer to talk to anyone but me – but I am the one here. Before he can begin I raise the telephone to my ear. With my free hand I signal that I am occupied. Then I pretend to listen. D walks over to my desk anyway. He hovers. He does not sit down at his own desk six feet away and I hate him more than ever. He has thick black wavy hair that falls forward over his eyes and he pushes it back all the time. He could just get it cut. He tosses something small up into the air and catches it. Spiritually, he is whistling. I nod and say Uh-huh into the silent phone. I roll my eyes and pretend to slit my throat as if to indicate that my interlocutor is boring me to death. D tosses whatever it is into the air again – it is a memory stick, I can see that now – and catches it. He does not leave my desk. I accept the inevitable. I put my hand over the mouthpiece and say: Mothers. Fuck 'em.

D nods, says: Dads are just as bad.

I had not expected this. I wonder if he is talking about his own father, which would be unlike D. I probe: Worse, maybe?

Yeah. Quieter, but way worse.

*Way worse?* What has D been reading now? In my disgust I forget to pretend to say goodbye and just hang up.

D asks me who it was.

No one.

D looks confused. He can't work out if I'm telling the truth (which of course I am), or if this is a joke at his expense.

He flips the memory stick between his fingers, attempting to roll it around his knuckles, but drops it. His hair is sleek, like oil on a stranded seabird. As he bends down to retrieve his toy I see traces of some unguent in the roots at his parting. He has come from the shower at the gym. I despise him. But my day is clearly ruined, anyway, so I ask him what is on the memory stick.

He smiles, savouring the moment.

He says, My future.

It's empty, then?

Ha-ha. It's Likker.

I know who Edward Likker is – was. I say, What kind of a name is Likker?

He's my ticket to glory.

D says this, in those words. How old Kalenkov spawned both Rada and this fart in a suit defeats me.

He says, You want to know why?

I am all ears.

D looks around, as if the office might have rearranged itself since Friday, then walks over to the flipchart stand in the corner. He drags it towards my desk, the extendable legs catching in the carpet. It leans towards him like a teenage drunk and the fat marker pens slide onto the floor. He straightens the stand, tightens the screws and bends down to recover the markers. His suit jacket rides up and I am presented with his stairmastered arse in broad chalkstripe. Truly the Lord is bountiful. He tests the pens until he finds one that hasn't dried up. It is green. He sketches a two-by-two matrix and writes "Complexity" along the bottom axis, "Value" up the side. He writes "Low" at the point of origin, and "High" at the tip of each axis.

I watch, a familiar weariness gathering in my bones. I say, How are you measuring value?

There's a formula.

D flips the matrix over the back of the stand and begins to write again on a blank sheet. He runs out of space and has to go onto the sheet beneath. He flips back, tears off a sheet and holds it up next to the stand so I can read the whole thing:

$$CLV = GC \cdot \sum_{i=0}^{n} \frac{r^{i}}{(1+d)^{i}} - M \cdot \sum_{i=1}^{n} \frac{r^{i-1}}{(1+d)^{i-0.5}}$$

And this helps how?

With his free hand, D points to each element of the formula in turn. The lifetime value of a customer equals the discounted gross contribution they make minus the discounted cost of retention.

Value to whom, D?

To the company, of course. OK, we're not a company. We don't have customers, as such. But surely you can see how it applies?

I can – it's obvious when you think about it – but so what? He's still not getting Theo's job.

I say, So where does Edward Likker rate?

D grins like a hyena.

Likker's perfect.

I know what he means. What he means is not perfect at all. He means complex. High value. He means a great white dead whale, amongst dead minnows. A death worthy of the scales of Maat. For a moment I am almost jealous. Then I remember this is D and he will fuck it up.

## 2

THE MAN IN front of me who would not do as he was told and get down on the fucking floor when everybody else got down on the fucking floor moved slowly; he didn't always seem to notice when somebody had finished and stepped away from the cash machine and the queue shuffled one step forward. There would be a pause. A gap would open up and I would feel the pressure growing and the impatience of the people waiting behind me. I felt it myself, the desire to speak up, to tell the old man to get a move on, even though his hesitations made no real difference to the time it would take us all to get our money. I thought about saying something, but nobody speaks to another person in a queue. To be clear, this was not out on the street where sometimes you have to pause and allow a gap to open up to make space for pedestrians who are not waiting for the cash machine or having anything to do with the bank or building society, or whatever, but are just passing along the pavement to somewhere else. It was indoors in a sort of open-plan foyer area of the bank where there were seven machines you could use to withdraw cash or to pay in cash, or cheques, with a queue at each, and there were no actual cashiers. It was cool in the bank; after entering from the humid street, customers would pause to adjust. Some of us would sigh, or surreptitiously adjust our clothes, allowing the refrigerated air to dry our skin. There were two bank employees in a sort of low-key uniform standing to the side of the queues waiting to help anyone who had trouble with the machines, plus one hovering near the door, a chubby woman with a neat blonde bob who had said hello to me when I entered the bank maybe six minutes earlier.

It is hot now in the meeting room, which is up on the fourth floor and has a low ceiling. It is just after four p.m., and the heat has been building up all day. We cannot open the windows because the windows do not open in this building; there is air-conditioning, but the air-conditioning does not work. It is June and there will most likely be a thunderstorm before long; since lunchtime, since the events I am reporting, the sky has turned a sleek mackerel grey. If we could open the windows, the noise of the trains, which pass just below us on elevated tracks, would be impossibly distracting. There are four of us in the room, seated around an oval mahogany table. The table is richly polished and, from where I am sitting, facing the window, the sunlight turns its surface liquid. Briefly, I imagine my crisp pile of closely-typed pages separating and floating on the table like lily-pads.

The man was old, I could tell, even from behind. He had probably been quite tall once, but he was now a little stooped, leaning on a walking stick, his head pointing somewhat forward from his shoulders, not straight up, and the skin above the collar of his shirt was dry and yellow; the hair above the skin was white and clipped short against his neck.

At this point in my report, I stop reading to acknowledge that there is some question, which might become relevant later, in the event of any reprimand or even disciplinary action being deemed appropriate, as to whether I was technically off duty, or not. I was at work, in the sense that it was a working day. I had spent the morning in the office listening to the kind of maddening and distracting fossicking about Alex chooses to do when he should be researching a claim or typing a report or whatever but is actually too unfocussed to stay on task for more than five minutes, without spinning his chair or throwing balled-up timesheets at his computer or trying to start a conversation with me. I took lunch earlier than usual, partly so that I could go to the bank for some cash and to pay in the cheque Gary's mother sent as a present for Matthew, who will be eight at the weekend. I had thought it possible that Gary's mother was the only person left in the world to still use cheques, but the presence of machines there in the bank this morning, machines which existed only for the purpose of depositing cheques, suggests otherwise. As there were no actual cashiers, I realised I was going to have to queue twice, for separate machines, and decided to get cash for myself and for Matthew first on the grounds that the queues for cash withdrawal were longer and I prefer to get the queuing over with as quickly as I possibly can.

Theo says not to think about reprimands right now. I should just concentrate on my report. The *right now* merely confirms my anxiety. I am in trouble.

The old man with the white hair and yellow skin and the walking stick had reached the head of my queue and, after a brief hesitation, had moved right up to the machine, and was hunting through his wallet for his card, when I became aware of an increase in noise and a sense of urgent or flustered movement around us. I turned and noticed that there were now three men in the bank who had not been there when I entered seven minutes earlier, and who had guns. The men were dressed in black; they wore Kevlar stab-proof vests and artificial fibre balaclava helmets. One of the men was short; strands of reddish hair or whiskers curled around the edges of his balaclava. Two of the guns were pistols – Beretta 8000-series Cougar semi-automatics – and the third was a much larger sub-machine gun. The men were shouting that everyone should do what they were told and get down on the fucking floor, which I did.

One of the men pushed some sort of stick through the polished aluminium handles of the double entrance doors. The stick was about a metre long and had a shorter element jutting out at right angles near the end, as if it were a handle; the whole thing may, in fact, have been an extendable sidearm baton of the type used by police forces to control situations of perceived or anticipated civil disorder. The handle of the baton caught on the handle of the door and effectively prevented anyone from entering the bank from the street. At this point one of the men said they were police, although this was not the first thing they had said and I wasn't sure I believed it, or not, but I also wasn't sure it made any difference to my getting down onto the floor in any case, or not, given that they were armed as I have described. The floor was covered in a kind of thick linoleum in the bank's corporate colours and was mostly red. The air-conditioning in the bank was so effective that even today, in this weather, the linoleum felt cool against my cheek. I was quite prepared to observe, and mentally to record any detail that might later prove helpful, or relevant, to whatever claim or claims might arise, but I was not going to not do what I was told by men with guns, even or perhaps especially if those men were not policemen. Neither were the bank employees (who were no doubt governed by bank protocol and training for just such an event, and would have practised) or any of the other customers, except the old man in front of me, who, having finally found his card and inserted it into the machine, ignored the shouting and began entering his Personal Identification Number. I thought the man might be deaf – although he would have to have been profoundly deaf not to have heard anything of the commotion behind him – and perhaps not blessed with the best peripheral vision, or to have been blind, even, although his stick wasn't white and there was no sign of a dog or anything, because most people, I thought, even if they were concentrating on pressing the right buttons and maybe making the right choices on the touch screen, would notice when everyone around them, which was perhaps a dozen or fifteen people, not including the men with guns, dropped suddenly to the floor.

One of the men shouted again and pointed his semi-automatic pistol at roughly the point where my head had been before I knelt, and then lay down, and I thought the old man was going to get shot. I recall thinking it would be a shame and something of a waste and a tragedy for a person to get shot just because he was deaf and maybe didn't have the best peripheral vision. I reached out my right hand. From where I was lying, face down on the linoleum, I could just touch the old man's foot. He was wearing brogues in thick, tan leather with the depth of shine that I knew, from having watched my father clean his shoes, and mine and, later, D's, every Sunday evening until I was fourteen years old, came only as a result of repeated polishing over many years. I pinched the turn-up of his right trouser leg between my first and second fingers – I could not quite reach it with my thumb to get a better grip – and tugged, as best I could, to attract his attention and alert him to the danger he was in. He lifted his foot without turning, and shook it, as if shooing away a fly. When he put it down again, the heel – which I noticed was rubber, although the shoe had a leather half sole which was nearly new, or at least not worn – landed heavily on the first two joints of my index and middle fingers, and I could not help shouting out, even though I was trying not to, on account of not wanting to attract the attention of the men with guns, and possibly get shot.

When I shouted the old man, who was evidently not deaf,

turned, and at the same time bent down towards me. It is still also possible that he was deaf, and, feeling something under his heel – a pen, or even a wallet, perhaps – had turned and simultaneously bent down to see what it was that he might be stepping on. Whether it was the sound of me shouting or the sensation of obstruction, or some combination of the two, he turned and bent at precisely the moment when the man with the gun pulled the trigger. I thought it was likely that the old man still hadn't realised what was going on around him and I closed my eyes, involuntarily.

Here I lay the page I've just finished face down on the pile to my right and, before picking the next page from the larger pile in front of me, I take a moment to point out that although I am a trained observer, I was not on duty. Even if I had been, I would not have seen everything because the decision to close my eyes was not conscious; it would not have been a dereliction of duty, even if I had been on duty, officially, because my unconscious mind anticipated the horror and traumatic images it would not be able to eradicate easily and took over control from my trained, conscious mind, despite the training, and I doubt that, honestly, any of you would have done any differently. Theo, perhaps, could have kept his eyes open; but not you, D, and not Alex.

After which I continue.

When he turned around I saw that I had allowed myself, from the stoop and the slowness in moving forward and perhaps even the idea that he might be deaf or in some way visually impaired, to generate an image in my own mind of a man older than he really was, which was perhaps, I now saw, only mid-sixties, seventy maximum, about the same age my father would have been. I observed this before I closed my eyes and consequently missed the moment when the bullet, as a result of his bending down towards me at the same moment that he turned, missed his face by what could only have been millimetres, judging from the angle of fire I observed when I reopened my eyes, by which time the bullet had passed through a laminated "Cash Withdrawals" sign, through the plaster board and red-painted skim wall to which the sign was affixed, presumably by some sort of industrial polychloroprene adhesive, and through into the office or meeting room or interview room where it must have hit a person I judged from the pitch of the subsequent screams to be a woman, possibly a female bank employee who was in the office or interview room at the time. This woman had not been in the public area of the bank since the entry of the gunmen, and so would obviously not have seen them or heard the instruction to get down on the floor – or, more likely, given the flimsiness of the dividing wall – she may have heard the instruction indistinctly, or may have heard it clearly but simply not understood it or realised that it applied to her, given that she had no visual or other context in which to interpret the instruction as a threat to her own well-being, and was therefore still upright, her head at approximately the same altitude as that of the old (but not ancient) man who I could now see had once been tall but had lost an inch or two to age and gravity, and was thus – the woman – in the (albeit probably deflected) line of fire for no reason other than sheer bad luck/incomprehension.

Jesus, Sis, can we just cut to the chase?

D has a memory stick in his hand. He has been turning it over and over, tapping one end then the other on the thick varnish of the meeting room table. He would have started off trying to listen, I know, albeit not very hard and not for very long. After a while his concentration would have drifted; his eyes would have lost focus and I know that by now he will be timing the gaps between trains, again, counting seconds under his breath. Our meeting room is in a building up by where the railway crosses over into the station. The sound-proofing is good and you can't really hear the trains through the sealed windows, although you can see the aluminium frames vibrate slightly, if you look, and especially if, as now, there is a fly caught in a web in the top right hand corner of the window. As usual, I have chosen the chair facing the windows. I do this to reduce the potential for distraction in my fellow team members, D especially. While I am confident of my own capacity to concentrate, my brother has always lacked focus; he has always been unable to stay truly present – in a room, or in a conversation – even when it is clearly in his own interest to do so. Right now, he will have given up on my report, and – since Theo has recently confirmed that he will not be with us much longer – D lacks even the primal motivation of not aggravating the boss too much that seems, up to now, to have restrained more overt displays of dissatisfaction and boredom.

D says, I mean, this only happened this morning.

He is speaking to Theo, not to me. Theo says, What is your point, D?

D makes a noise like there is something stuck a long way up his sinuses. He says, My sister can't go out for a pint of fucking milk without falling over something. She can't go to the bank like anyone else and get some cash – pay in a cheque, whatever – without running into three armed men and a couple of murders.

I have mentioned only one possible murder so far, and that not conclusive. Theo speaks mildly, in a tone that, whether he knows it or not, is guaranteed to provoke D. I'm certain Theo knows what he is doing.

D says, That's my point! She's been reading for, what, eight minutes? EIGHT minutes, and we're maybe ONE minute into the actual event. It was only this morning. D turns away from

Theo, back to face me. When do you even get time to *type* all this shit?

Theo has taught me not to allow myself to be distracted. I say, The details are important, D. We all know that.

OK, but Jesus, Sis. You're face down on the lino. Some civilian's dead and you're waiting for what I'm assuming here is the subject to get shot in the face. Right? Can you not just tell us: is the old guy in or not?

It is Monday and despite the heat Theo is wearing the herringbone suit. He also has on a white poplin shirt and an anonymous, but possibly regimental, tie with a thin green forty-five degree stripe on a broader red stripe on a darker green background. He has trimmed his beard, which is silver. Not long after D started, Theo took him aside and gave him the name of the tailor who had made this suit; D wrote it down but hadn't actually visited. Recently D tried calling Theo OMT, short for Old Man Theo. Not to his face, obviously; but in the office, when we were supposed to be working. It was OK in emails or texts, but when you said it aloud even D had to admit it wasn't that snappy and it hasn't stuck. Theo would be about the same age as the older man in my report, the man in the bank.

Theo says, Allow Rada to report the incident in her own manner. He always says that. We won't know what's important and what isn't until she has finished. God is in the details.

D knows this; we all know this, but D is still impatient. Can't we just take it from the point where the old deaf guy gets shot and dies and turns out to be someone we're interested in? Please, Sis?

I hate it when he calls me Sis, especially at work. He knows this, of course, which is why he does it. We have discussed this, at home, more than once. At work, I always tell him, we should be professional. D generally says that's a joke, on account of how he's the one trying to drag the place into the twenty-first century. The memory stick he has been fiddling with contains his position paper on calculating Lifetime Value, which, according to the written agenda Theo circulated at the start of the meeting, D will present when we're through with the reports. He must know that interrupting, and calling me Sis, is not going to make me get through my report any more quickly. It never has.

Theo nods and I lift a new page up in front of my face and begin reading again.

I saw the man who had fired his gun take his eyes for a moment off the older man who was still standing, who in fact was straightening up from where he had been bending down to look at me. I saw the gunman's eyes beneath the balaclava helmet; they were grey and looked clouded. The older man must have realised by now that something out of the ordinary and severely threatening to himself and other people was going on, but he did nothing, other than to straighten up. He stood, apparently waiting for the man with the gun to turn back to him and resume his threats. It occurred to me then that perhaps the older man was neither deaf nor visually impaired and might not have been absorbed, in particular, in correctly punching in his Personal Identification Number, but was perhaps more of the absent-minded professor-type with fully working senses that were nonetheless overwhelmed (in terms of neurological stimulation and the kind of messages capable of reaching and attracting the attention of his conscious mind) by the contemplation of some abstruse and potentially world-changing mathematical formula or theorem or whatnot, and that was why he seemed not to have noticed what was going on around him and to get down on the floor like everybody else. But it then occurred to me that if that – the absent-minded professor thing – accounted for the older man's initial lack of awareness, or response, at least, to what was going on and being said, or shouted, it would not adequately explain why, when he had turned around and could plainly see the man with a gun no more than six feet away from him, and could see the people around him, including me, lying for the most part face down on the floor, and must have heard the shot that had missed his face by no more than millimetres, and could, like the rest of us, hear the continuous or rather pullulating screams emanating from behind the partition wall through which the bullet had passed, why, given all of that, he did nothing but stand and wait. It must have been obvious that he was caught up in a robbery or some kind of siege or even terrorist situation. At this point I had not been able conclusively to dismiss the claim made by one of the men with guns that they were in fact policemen, although none of them had actually shouted *Police!* or even *Armed Police!* as their first action on entering the bank with guns in the way that I imagine, on the basis of watching a number of films and TV shows, they would have done if they had in fact been policemen, or at least would have been supposed to do by protocol and legally-enforceable guidance, although I'm pretty sure that in some of the films or TV shows I've seen the failure of the police to shout *Police!* or *Armed Police!* was the subject of much discussion and dispute amongst the various characters – who often had differing memories and interpretations of the events, not to mention differing motives and interests – and was, in fact, the principal plot-point driving the drama, and it was likely that such dramas were based to some extent on reality and that such an omission might occur also in the excitement of real-life events. It was therefore still possible that the older professorial man might have believed himself to be involved in a robbery or siege or terrorist situation in the process of being interrupted and thwarted by the forces of law and order. But even if this were the case, it still did not explain adequately why, when faced by a man in a balaclava helmet with a gun he was obviously prepared to fire and who had told him to get down on the floor like everybody else, why the older man didn't, but stood there, apparently oblivious to the gravity of the situation, the only person in the public area of the bank without a gun still upright, waiting for the man who had fired his gun and missed him by millimetres to re-focus his attention, waiting, in fact, for all the world like a professor who has asked his seminar students a fundamental question to which he of course knows the answer, or at least an answer, but has no intention of letting his students off the hook by answering before at least one of them has worked it out for himself. Waiting, in other words, mildly, as if to see what would happen next.

It occurred to me then that the theorem or formula or whatever might not have been important and world-changing but rather otiose and ultimately fruitless, and that the moment when the professor-type guy was withdrawing cash irritatingly slowly, at least to those waiting in the queue behind him, and ignoring the instructions of armed men in a frankly thoughtless way that might just get us all killed, was in fact the precise moment when he realised that the theorem he had been developing was not important and world-changing after all, but was actually otiose and fruitless, and that he had wasted the last five years of his professional, professorial-type life, and that he now faced ridicule and retirement having achieved nothing of substance since his initial, prodigious breakthrough at the age of twenty. In the nihilistic mood this realisation had engendered, he might not care what happened to him and might, in some way, even welcome the possibility of being shot and killed. But such despair did not seem to tally with the expression of mild interest and even curiosity that I had detected on the older man's features and which I felt was inconsistent with suicidal depression. I will defer to Alex on this point, but my initial assessment was that it was not possible both to wish seriously to be dead and to be curious about what the future might bring, in my opinion.

Alex nods in agreement, but says nothing. As usual, he is sitting across the table from me, not actually looking at me, but at the wall to my left (or my right from his point of view), leaving D and Theo to face each other across the full length of the mahogany oval.

For his part, the man with a gun first turned not to the older man, but to his colleague with the sub-machine gun, a Heckler and Koch UMP45 with flash suppresser and vertical forward hold. Without saying anything, he gestured towards the wall where the bullet hole was clearly visible in the Cash Withdrawal sign, and from behind which the high-pitched screaming continued, albeit with gradually diminishing intensity. The second man moved in the direction that the first had indicated, picking his way between the frightened bodies of those lying on the floor. He was tall and walked with an awkward, high-stepping gait in an attempt to avoid contact with the victims and potential witnesses, but still managed to step on the hair of one woman whom I judged to be in her early thirties. The woman's hair was long and loose and covered her face and spilled out around it, on the floor. When the gunman stepped on her hair, the woman squealed, then quickly muffled the sound. The man continued towards a door, which was set in the wall some way along from the cash machine at which the older professor-type man and I had been queuing. He tried the door, which was locked and had beside it, set into the wall, a metal plate in something like brushed aluminium with a button and a small grille that was probably an intercom, and a keypad with the usual twelve small buttons in four rows of three, including all the digits from zero to 9, plus C for cancelling entries and either * or # – I could not see which – and which was either redundant and included purely for symmetry, or was to be pressed after the correct numerical code had been entered, depending on the manufacturer (of which I was, at that point, and for obvious reasons, unaware). Confronted with a locked door, from behind which the sound of screaming could still be distinctly heard, the man took his right hand from the trigger and, allowing the shoulder strap to bear the weight of the sub-machine gun while he steadied it with his left, drew back his right hand and punched the key pad. This was not a punch in the way that we might normally talk about punching a code into say a telephone, or a cash machine, where there is in fact no actual punching involved but only touching, poking, or at most prodding with a single, usually index, finger. The man was dressed all in black, like the other two, with a balaclava over his face. He had formed a tight fist and hit the keypad precisely, his four larger knuckles landing simultaneously on the 3, 6, 9 and * or # buttons. As the first joint of each finger was held perpendicular to the flat back of his hand, and the second and third joints were curled tightly into the palm and the thumb tucked over out of harm's way – as, in other words, the gunman had made a perfect flat karate-practitioner's fist – there was a realistic possibility that the remaining nine buttons were also pressed at precisely the same time. After hitting the keypad twice, he rubbed his knuckles briefly against the biceps of his left arm before trying the door again and finding it still locked.

During this time – probably no more than seventy-five to ninety seconds since the shot had been fired – the probably female person in what was presumably an office or meeting room or perhaps an interview room in which employees discussed the prospects of the bank loaning money to customers, had continued to scream although by now the intensity of the screaming had reduced to the level where it might more accurately be described as wailing, or keening. Even at this level, however, it was obvious that the sound was exacerbating the already considerable level of fear and general anxiety amongst the bank employees and customers lying on the floor in the public area, although not, apparently, that of the older man who, as previously stated, showed no evidence of fear or anxiety but only mild interest bordering on curiosity. I judged that the screaming/wailing was also likely to have increased the tension and stress levels of the men with guns, with the attendant possibility of reduced rationality in decision-making and the consequential increased risk for those of us on the floor. The first man, the man who had fired the shot, now pointed his gun at a woman lying near the door, not the woman with hair over her face which the second man had inadvertently trodden on, but another, older woman with short, neatly cropped hair that tapered to a point at the nape of her neck in a way that I often think looks attractive in women, although usually in younger women than this one, who was wearing a dark blue blouse in some synthetic sweat-inducing fabric with red piping around the collar and cuffs, and a dark blue skirt and flat shoes that my mother might once have described as 'sensible' in a way which indicated that she – my mother – would never have been seen dead in them, before she died, and which, together with the blouse and the skirt clearly indicated that the woman was an employee of the bank. The second gunman told her to get up and open the door without doing anything stupid, which she did; and then, not knowing what else to do, she sat and then lay back down on the floor. The second gunman went through the now open door and, seven or eight seconds later, the keening or wailing having increased in intensity until it was, if anything, louder than it had been at the start, even allowing for the fact that the door between the person screaming and the public area of the bank was now open, the screaming was followed by a second gunshot, and silence.

Outside, people were still walking up and down the street, looking for lunch or a dry cleaner. A few had tried to enter the bank, but finding the doors surprisingly barred by the stick or baton one of the gunmen had stuck through the polished aluminium handles, and which was presumably visible through the glass doors, had shaken their heads and walked on. I assumed that the people lying on the floor of the bank, and the people standing over them with guns, were not visible through the glass doors to those frustrated customers, perhaps because of the glare of the bright June sunshine out on the street. I could hear trains rumbling in and out of the station, and traffic in the street. In the corner of the public area another woman began to cry quietly; a man began murmuring rhythmically in what I assumed was prayer.

Alex now interrupts to ask me if I had thought there might be more than one person in the office or interview room behind the partition wall. He says he means before the gunman went in there, obviously.

This is a surprise. Alex doesn't speak much in meetings and never interrupts me. D thinks this is because Alex never listens to anybody else, ever. When I say perhaps it is only D that Alex doesn't listen to, and that really he – D – is the one who never listens, D says this is only because, if he did, he would quickly realise he could have done the job better himself, and life would be even more teeth-grindingly frustrating than it already is; whereas Alex, he says, doesn't listen because he genuinely doesn't give a shit.

Now D says to Alex, Well, d'uh. There's a woman with a bullet in her brain. She's not going to be screaming like that for a minute and a half, is she?

Theo says D is jumping to conclusions. He points out that I had not said the bullet was in the woman's brain, but, even if it were, it is still possible that she could have been the one screaming. He says stranger things have happened at sea.

I know it is precisely because Theo says things like *stranger things have happened at sea*, amongst other reasons, that D's actually pretty glad that Theo's finally going. The other reasons include the fact that D thinks Theo's departure will create an opportunity for him to be promoted, which promotion he believes to be long overdue, irrespective of the fact that he is the most recent recruit to the team, and only got the job in the first place because I felt obliged to help him out when the dot-com start-up that was going to make him a billionaire went bust. If D thinks he has not made his desires and expectations perfectly clear to the rest of us, not excluding Theo, then he is wrong.

Alex says, I was just wondering what you thought at the time.

D sighs, so loud that we cannot pretend not to hear. He says, Christ. As if she isn't giving us a blow-by-blow of every minuscule thought process she's ever had.

Alex ignores him. Only, if there's just one person, a woman, who's been shot in the head and was hideously wounded, and she's screaming in pain and fear of dying, then that's one thing. So then the gunman goes in, he sees blood and bits of brain stuff up the wall and the woman lying on the floor or slumped over a desk or whatever, and she's wailing and practically begging him to put her out of her misery, and he does, that's like one thing, right? That's going to play out with you and the others in the bank, and even the old man you say isn't really taking much notice, that's going to play out one way, yeah?

D says, And?

Alex continues to ignore him, talking now to Theo. But if there's two people? If the woman who's been shot was a bank employee and she's talking to a customer, maybe turning down a loan or trying to sell the customer a mortgage or something? And if she was and the customer – and we're assuming the customer's another woman from what Rada said about the pitch of the screams – the customer was on the point of signing up to a mortgage deal when the bullet comes through the wall and hits the bank employee right in front of her, and there's blood and brain and stuff on *her* as well as on the walls, then that's different, isn't it? Then she's screaming and wailing and whatever because a person's been shot right in front of her with no warning or context or anything, and she's traumatised and just hysterical with fear and confusion, and the gunman comes in and shoots her just to shut her up. That's going to be different, isn't it? In the first case there's an element of humanity – of sparing a woman her unbearable pain – which would be pretty horrific and difficult to process for the people in the bank, especially the people without guns who aren't used to that sort of thing and have probably never heard or seen a person die before. But it's a whole different order of things from hearing an uninjured but just deeply traumatised woman executed, basically, just for making too much noise. Different in the way it plays out with the other customers and employees and the professor-guy?

I can see D twitching with impatience. He is staring at Alex in disbelief, his mouth open and his fingers spinning the memory stick. I don't suppose he even knows that he is doing it. D probably thinks that Alex is trying to suck up here; showing off to impress Theo now that Theo is leaving and his job is going to be available. If D thinks that then it is not surprising that he looks so uptight and confused because, for one, that's just not the way Alex behaves, or thinks, and two: if Alex is suddenly changing his spots and undergoing some sort of character-transformation, then D will have some competition that he wasn't expecting. For all that D talks about competition as the spur to innovation and the survival of the fittest, he would obviously prefer not to have to compete himself in any field that is not rigged to demonstrate his own superiority. D is my little brother: I've known him all his life.

Alex has been here longer than D, but that isn't the point. Alex has been here as long as anyone – as long as me – as long as anyone except Theo, of course, who I suspect has been here from the start, although he never actually says so. Alex has a way of being in a meeting and not being there that is different from D's way of not being there. Alex follows his own thoughts while hearing just enough to get by without getting angry or impatient.

But now Alex is saying, Am I right?

Theo says, You may be. Let's hear Rada out, shall we?

I know now that Alex will not say anything more, and I resume reading.

# 3

BY THE TIME I returned to the office I was even later than I'd said, and my back was killing me. I'd been at HQ with the year-end and had told Karen I'd probably have lunch with one or other of the Directors, if any of them were still talking to me. But it was almost three by the time I walked out of the lift and swiped my pass onto the Finance floor.

Karen looked up from her screen as I approached. The clatter of nails on keyboard stopped a moment later. She said, "Good lunch?"

"Bad traffic."

She laughed, but then said, "Traffic?"

I shouldn't have said that. I said, "What have I got?"

"Other than the Losers' Group?" – it was my own fault she called it that; I'd said it first, back when HR set it up – "Nothing."

"What about Peter's appraisal?"

"Uh huh. He came by while you were out and asked me to postpone it."

Peter Thomson knew I was a Loser: they all did.

"What did you say?"

"I told him I could put it back to Thursday."

Thursday was the 30th of June. We both knew that if she put it back any further, it wouldn't happen at all. Peter Thomson knew it, too.

In the office I closed the door. If nothing else, I'd miss the view. In 1961, when I was seven and had no idea what an accountant was, this building had briefly been the tallest in the city. Even now it stuck way up above everything around it, a vast modern stake hammered into the heart of an untidy nineteenth-century suburb. From there I could see right back down the river, past HQ, past the government buildings and the palace, right up to the bridge. I could see most of the route we'd taken, though I couldn't make out the massive snarl-up that had cost us the best part of forty minutes and was the reason I was late. Moody had printed out the route – 7.4 miles, 23 minutes with traffic, she read: which was never going to happen in this city, in the middle of the day – and she was sticking to it. I told her we'd be better off heading south and following the river, but she didn't listen. In a way, I was glad. It had given us something to talk about on the way back that wasn't what had just happened.

Usually I'd feel much worse by this stage. After all the planning, after weeks of meticulous surveillance, of anticipating every risk; after getting into uniform and into role; after the hour of the job itself, when everything would go as planned, and if it didn't I'd improvise instinctively, fluidly, every nerve alive, every muscle light, and time itself would slow; after all that it's no surprise that I'd crash, my vision dull and the world grow weary, stale, flat and unprofitable, so to speak. I'd learned to manage the cycle. The money helped, but not as much as I'd thought it would at first, and less each time. What really helped was work: I'd learned to have the next job mapped out before the current one was done. That way I had something to look forward to. This time, though, I just felt numb.

I was clearing emails when Karen cracked open the door. She didn't come in, but leaned through to say that DI Jenks was here for the meeting. She pushed the door wide and stepped back to let him through.

"You can go in. Would you like a coffee, Detective Inspector?"

Bernie winced at the title. He said, "Three sugars, please."

Karen closed the door behind him. He crossed the office and sat in one of the heavy uncomfortable chairs across the desk from me. He was short and overweight and had a beard he had only been growing since he was seconded to Personnel. From the way he kept running his fingers through the sparse reddish whiskers, it was plain that the beard still itched. He did it now, letting his jaw drop open and squeezing his thick lips into a fish's mouth while he waited for me to speak.

Pulling myself into role, I said, "Why don't you just shave?"

Bernie shrugged. "The coach said it was good to have a hobby."

"I think he meant golf, Bernie. Or keeping bees."

The force had paid for two sessions of outplacement coaching, part of the package. To help us through the changes we were facing. To help us think about our futures. The coach asked me what my goals were. I said I'd always wanted to get out as early as I could and not have any kids myself. He didn't get it and I didn't feel like explaining. He talked about my options and gave me a couple of handouts plus the title of a book he said I might like to look at before we met again. I went home early, drank several large whiskies and re-watched an early series of *Homicide: Life on the Streets* on DVD. At least I'd managed not to have the kids.

If Eddie were alive, this wouldn't have been happening.

Bernie said, "My dad had this portrait of his grandfather. Great-grandfather, probably: the first one out of the shtetl. The man has this big white beard down to here" – he held his hand out flat, about level with his diaphragm – "that he'd trained into two points, like giant hairy tusks."

"Christ, Bernie. You'd look like ZZ Top."

"It'd be a disguise."

"Except it would be you."

When we first talked about what we'd do for money, it was Bernie who joked about robbing banks. But Sutton's Law – *go where the money is* – was part of my accountancy course. Alone among my fellow students, I took the time to read the book.

Karen returned with Bernie's coffee. She said, "There you go, Detective Inspector."

Bernie looked up at her. His wet eyes and scruffy red beard, and that pathetic upward gaze, made him look like the portrait of some unfortunate saint by a school-of painter no one had ever heard of. He said, "Please. I'm on secondment."

Karen smiled brightly. "Not for much longer."

A secondment implies a job to go back to.

When she left, Bernie said, "Does she do that on purpose?"

Karen had just been doing what employees do: judging power, and distancing herself from those without it; finding amusement where she could. I couldn't blame her. I said, "What was it with the bags, Bernie?"

Bernie shifted in his chair, spreading his chubby thighs. "I don't see the problem."

"They're cheap. Shoddy."

"It's not as if they have to take much weight."

I let that go: we'd get to the take later, when DC Moody arrived.

"I've always said we do this properly or we don't do it at all."

Bernie sighed. "You have."

"So?"

Bernie held his hands up. "So shoot me."

There was a moment where everything stopped and then Bernie dropped his hands again. I could see in his deep sad eyes he wished he hadn't said that just as much as I did.

"Next time I'll get better bags."

Mostly Bernie did what I told him, which wasn't always the case with Moody, though why either of them ever followed my orders wasn't obvious. Technically, I outranked them both – Moody was only a constable, even if she had made detective; Bernie a DI – but I'd never worn a uniform, and in the force that counted for a lot. They were cops, even if they were poor cops, and wouldn't be cops for much longer. I was an accountant.

Before Bernie was seconded to Human Resources, he'd run a serial rape-murder investigation with at least seven victims. I found that hard to believe. Bernie? Running a major incident room, a team of detectives hanging on his orders and working round the clock? I couldn't see it. He told me the investigation took the best part of three years before he managed to send a man to jail who would subsequently get off on appeal.

"Did you ever get the real killer?"

From the way Bernie looked at me, I knew I'd asked another civilian's question. He said, "He was the real killer."

It was always possible.

We'd met a couple of times before Bernie told me this. You can never tell what anyone is capable of; I can't, anyway, which perhaps explains why I'm an accountant, not a detective.

One June evening when I was sixteen, I stacked all my revision notes in a neat pile and walked out into the tiny garden behind our house. It had been a clear day and I could feel the early summer's heat radiating from the walls and the concrete slab outside the backdoor that served as a patio. My father was watering runner beans, holding the galvanised iron can in both hands. He was a small man, short and thin; at sixteen, I was already a head taller than him. He heard my footsteps on the concrete and set the can down. He straightened up, squinting against the evening sun, fingers pressing into the small of his back to ease the stiffness.

"Are you ready then?"

"As I'll ever be."

He nodded. "Then the best you can do is get a good night's sleep. That'll be better than any more reading."

"I know, Dad."

"And you know the best way to get some sleep?"

I did. "A bit of fresh air and honest toil?"

He nodded again. He pointed at a spade stuck upright in the thick clay soil. "Those spuds want banking up." He picked up his can and began watering again. After a moment, he put it down, pulled off the rose and stuck his finger into it, trying to remove a leaf that had been blocking the flow. He asked what I wanted to do, if I could do any job in the world. I had no idea.

My father was an engineer – a glorified grease monkey, he said – who kept the machines working in the University labs. He said, "At your age, I wanted to be an auctioneer."

I was surprised. Dad had always been an engineer; that's what he was. I said, "What, like at Sotheby's?"

He laughed. "Can you see me pontificating about antiques? No: the livestock markets. I used to help your granddad. There was a chap there, I thought he was the bee's knees. Talked faster than anyone could hear, I swear, but he really pushed the prices up. We always did well when he was there. And he had a suit, and shoes that shone like morning on a mountain lake, and a car. Leary, the man my father worked for, he had a tractor, of course. He even let me drive it. But nobody we knew had a car."

I had heard my father talk about the farm before, how

things were before the war, about granddad and granddad's pigs that weren't really his, they were Leary's. But this was the first I'd heard about a man with a suit and a car.

"So how come you're not an auctioneer?"

"Oh, you know. Your granddad didn't want me to have anything to do with animals. He said he'd spent his life covered in pig shit – pardon me – and I wasn't going to do the same. So I went to college, and spent my life covered in oil instead." He laughed, reaching up to put his hand on my shoulder as he spoke. "So come on. Who do you want to be like?"

I tried, but I couldn't think of anyone. After a while I said, "There's you, of course."

He pretended to cuff me round the ear. "You can do better than that."

I shook my head. He was trying, I knew; but, really: no. There was no one.

"Who do you want to *beat*, then? Who do you look at and think: *I could do better than that?*"

There was no one.

"Oh, well."

Dad picked up the watering can and pointed to the half-finished row of potatoes, as if to say they wouldn't bank themselves.

The office door opened again and DC Moody said, "Karen said to come straight in."

"Did she offer you a coffee?"

Moody turned the second uncomfortable chair around and straddled it, crossing her arms and leaning on the back. "I don't drink coffee."

Bernie said, "No wonder they're drumming you out of the force."

"It's bad for the reflexes."

Rachel Moody was taller than Bernie – which wasn't that

unusual, even for a woman – and about half as wide. When she walked, she swung her shoulders, not her hips. Her hair was black and cropped close to her head; even so, the strawberry blonde roots showed. She said, "Hey, Bern." And when he looked across at her she said, "It makes your trigger finger twitch."

She was looking at Bernie, but she was talking to me. I said, "So what have we got?"

She turned to face me. Her eyes were a metallic blue I always found disconcerting. She said, "Are we not going to talk about what just happened?"

"I am talking about it."

"We discharged our firearms, sir. You and me. One apiece."

"And I'm asking you what we got for it."

I forced myself to keep looking into those blue eyes until she said, "You're a harder bastard than I thought."

I wasn't, and she must have known it.

She said, "Twenty-two four hundred."

"That's it?"

"Plus Bernie got us a bracelet, three necklaces and four watches – a Tissot, two Seikos, one Swatch. None of it worth a thing. Plus seventy-four pounds eighty-six in change."

Bernie said, "Shit."

Moody said, "It's more than anyone else here's going to earn today."

"And a lot less than they'll earn over thirty years."

Thirty years was the kind of time we were looking at.

At the start, last September, there'd been forty-six members of the Outplacement Network. HR broke us up into sixes and sevens, and hired an outplacement coach to facilitate our first meeting. After that we were on our own. DC Moody sat right opposite the coach in the circle of chairs he'd laid out. I sat between the coach and a man from Payroll with two missing fingers and a stammer. Bernie was at nine o'clock, between a couple of uniforms. Apart from the Payroll guy, I hadn't met any of them; from the way they acted when they arrived, I guessed none of them knew each other either. Moody crossed her arms and put her right foot up on her left knee. She wore Doc Martens – not the shoes so many uniforms wore, but eighteen-hole cherry reds – and I noticed they were new, the patterned soles not yet worn smooth, the leather's shine lacking any real depth. When the coach asked us to introduce ourselves and say a word or two about what we hoped to get out of the network, she said, "This is such bullshit." The coach asked her to explain, and she said she wasn't supposed to be there. She'd made detective just last year and was already getting results. There had been some fuck-up in Personnel, because there was no way it was supposed to be her coming to this bullshit network. The coach stepped over to a flipchart in the corner of the room. He lifted a couple of sheets over the back and drew a diagram with a fat blue marker pen. He said, "Kubler-Ross' five stages of bereavement start with denial."

"No they don't," said Bernie.

I was the only one who laughed.

The next time, when it was obvious there'd been no clerical mistake and her name was definitely still on the list, Moody said it was because she was a woman. There was a short silence while the rest of us looked at each other, then one of the uniforms said, "But we're all men, detective."

"Yeah. And you're getting chopped because you're crap, or past it. No offence. For me it's because I'm too good – and a woman, and young. They can't handle it."

The man from Payroll said, "That's b-b-b-bollocks." It was the only thing he said throughout the morning; he didn't come to meetings after that.

Bernie said, "Suppose you're right – what difference would it make?"

By then Moody had already had her first individual session with the outplacement coach, a session that apparently lasted rather less than the allotted ninety minutes. She said, "Don't get all fucking coach-y with me."

"You're still out of a job."

"And you're still a wanker."

I found myself signalling for calm, raising my hands and lowering them together. Doing my best to imitate the coach's slight adenoidal hum, I said, "How does having DC Moody call you a "wanker" make you *feel*, DI Jenks?"

"Horny."

It wasn't the answer anyone expected, and that's what made us laugh. Moody said he was disgusting and just proved her point. The uniform who hadn't spoken before said even he thought Bernie was out of order, but after that the meeting went much better.

When I turned up for the third session, at the start of October, there were still six chairs in a circle, but it looked like Bernie and I would be the only ones attending. Bernie obviously hadn't shaved for a couple of days, and I wondered if the stress was getting to him after all. While we waited, he said he'd pulled DC Moody's personnel file. He waited for me to ask what was in it so he could answer:

"She's a mite over-enthusiastic, if you know what I mean. Watched a bit too much TV."

"Don't you all?"

"Maybe, but for some it's just a matter of time before they do something stupid. All in the name of justice, of course. Moody's one of them. Keen on martial arts and firearms training. Not too keen on record-keeping."

Bernie leaned back in his chair, locked his fingers and put

his hands on his head, palms up. Under his arms the seams of his shirt were yellow.

Then DC Moody turned up for the meeting after all and the three of us talked about what we might do when the axe fell. That was when Bernie made the joke about robbing banks. As far as I know, he never mentioned the file to Moody, because the conversation took a different turn. I said: *you can't rob a bank on charm and personality,* and Moody asked what I was on about. I explained it was what Willie Sutton said: when he was going to rob a bank he always took a pistol or a Tommy gun. "He never shot anyone, though. He robbed a hundred banks and never shot a soul. They say he never robbed a bank if a baby cried or a woman screamed."

Moody said, "That's just stupid."

It also wasn't true, I knew, if only because Sutton's MO was to take control of a bank half an hour before opening time. He'd be gone before the public ever turned up. It was just something people said because, for a while, Sutton was a hero.

Moody said if she was going to get the guns, she was going to get ammo, too. We didn't have to shoot anyone, but we had to know we could. And would. Otherwise, what was the point?

Willie Sutton died in 1980. When a journalist asked, "Why do you rob banks?" he was supposed to have said: "Because that's where the money is." But he never did. He never said it; the journalist made it up. In the end, though, it made no difference: when he wrote his autobiography, that's what he had to call it – *Where the money was*. He had no choice.

After that, we moved the meetings to my office, because I had an office, which was rare. Money is power, even when it isn't your money, and I'd inherited some of the trappings from the days when Likker did the job. Before he moved up; before he retired and died. When I leave they're going to take the office out, and squeeze in a few more open plan workstations.

Moody said it wouldn't be hard. It would just take cash. By now our conversations really had taken a different turn. I said I'd take care of that. I didn't want to know who Moody knew. It made me uneasy when I couldn't do everything myself, but I knew that if I wanted guns at all – and by then I knew I did – then Moody was my best bet. The kind of deal she would have done with the kind of people she shouldn't have been doing deals with – the very reason she was here in the Losers Support Group in the first place – was just exactly what we needed.

"So what do you want?"

What I really wanted was a Tommy gun. But I needed to frighten people, not make them think I was an actor.

Moody said, "MAC-10? TEC-9s? They're pretty popular these days. And cheap."

"We don't want cheap."

"No?"

I said, "If we're going to do this, DC Moody, we're going to do it properly, with style. We don't want to look like crack heads. We want class. When we're in a bank we need people to feel we're in control, that we know what we're doing. That way they'll do what they're told."

"You hope."

"Basic psychology."

I'd read it in Willie Sutton's book.

"Class costs."

"Of course. But the initial stake is mine."

She said she'd see what she could do. But, she said, if she was getting guns, she was getting ammo, no two ways about it. Anything else was just stupid.

Bernie said, "I can't shoot anyone."

"We're not shooting anyone."

"I can't."

"But we might want to put a bullet in the ceiling," Moody said. "Just to get their attention."

At the time, I could see the sense in that.

Now, in my office, Bernie had pushed back the heavy chair. He was up on his feet saying: "*Go where the money is*. That's what you said."

I stood up, too, putting one hand on the small of my back to help me straighten up. The main problem in robbing banks wasn't the alarms or the security guards or the strength of the vaults, it was that you can't do it alone. It takes at least two other people, and sooner or later, one of those two will let you down. Willie Sutton said that, too. *You involve yourself with a very low grade of person when you become a thief*. Out of my office window, a long way down, I could see the van we'd used, parked alongside a couple of others in a car park mostly full of ordinary, civilian cars. I turned back to Bernie. "That's right, I did."

"So where's the money?"

Moody said, "It's in the van."

"That's not what I meant."

Sutton never said banks were where the money was. He said he robbed banks because he enjoyed it. He loved it. So he kept doing it, even when it made no sense. He had no choice, but at least he knew it.

I said, "I know, Bernie. Willie Sutton said –"

"You know what? Fuck Willie Sutton. I read the book you gave me. Willie Sutton got 126 years."

"At least he was alive."

"Do you ever ask yourself why nobody else robs banks these days, Bill? Do you?"

I tried to answer, but Bernie didn't let me. "And don't give me that crap about how no one's got the dedication, or the skill, any more. How they're not prepared to work. And it's not because the security systems are better, either. Is it? Is it, Bill?"

This time I wasn't going to even try to answer. Bernie had to have his rant. It was what he did, the way he coped. Just as I planned the next job.

Bernie said, "Nobody else is stupid enough to rob banks, because Willie-bastard-Sutton was *wrong*. Maybe he was right once, but he's wrong now. There's no money in banks. No real money. Look at your payslip, Bill. It's all electronic transfers and direct debits. There is no fucking money."

We stared at each other, Moody the only one still sitting.

I said, "The thing is – it was *never* about the money anyway. *That's* what Willie Sutton really said. It's about the craft. About doing it right. He said, *The money was the chips, that's all.*"

Bernie shook his head. "Two women died for chips?"

I didn't answer.

Moody had been letting us get on with it. It was what men do. But now she looked up from her chair at the two of us, squaring off against each other.

She said, "What women? Who's dead?"

# 4

AT THAT POINT nobody in the public area of the bank, including even the remaining gunmen, knew whether there had been one person in the interview room who had been wounded and then put out of her misery by the second gunman, or two, one of whom had been traumatised by the sight of the other being shot and had screamed and then wailed/keened in horror and fear before being shot herself in an attempt by the second gunman to reduce the level of noise, and possibly the tension and stress being experienced by the people who could hear that noise. If anyone had asked me at the time, given my training and experience, I would have opted for the simpler scenario of there being one person – probably a woman, given the pitch of the screaming/wailing/keening – who had been hit and presumably horribly injured by the first, stray bullet, and that the screaming was in response to her extreme pain and possibly also shock and confusion, the woman having been shot in a room that contained nobody else and certainly nobody with a gun. An alternative, more complex, scenario was, however, certainly conceivable. In this scenario, the screaming was the equally understandable response of a bank customer to the shock of seeing someone who had, just a moment before, been advising the hypothetical screamer about the pros and cons of offsetting her mortgage debt against resources in her other accounts and convincing her that it was the right product for her, holding out a pen and waiting for her to sign, and mentally perhaps spending the commission she would receive as a result of that signature, and who was now, without any prior warning or threat or opportunity to lay down on the floor and avoid injury, quite suddenly flung sideways, with the right side of her face, as the screamer looked at it, intact while the left seemed to burst and flower and spread itself across the table, and across the carpet and walls of the small interview room, and possibly across the screamer herself, which would, in all likelihood, add to the fear and trauma involved, without actually increasing the pain or suffering of the already dead bank employee. Such a scenario should, I know, only be considered if and when the more straightforward option has been disproved or discounted. If, for example, there had actually been two distinct screams issuing from different screamers, however briefly, one in extreme pain, the other in fear and horror at the traumatic sight confronting her. Or if, later, after the gunmen had left but before the emergency services arrived, I had managed to look into the interview room for myself and see not one but two corpses with obvious and unmistakable head wounds, as perhaps I should have done. At the time, however, I was preoccupied with the continuing stand-off between the first gunman and the older, professor-type man who was still, at this point, standing, walking stick pressed between his arm and his body, tucking his still empty wallet – despite his unhurried calm he had not, in fact, withdrawn any actual cash from the cash machine – back into the inside pocket of his tweed jacket and looking at the gunman with an expression of mild interest or curiosity. Because of the helmet, I could not see the gunman's face, just his eyes and his mouth, which was narrow, as if he were pressing his lips together tightly.

I can see D leaning way back in his chair, sliding down until he is almost horizontal, then hauling himself up like a walrus at the water's edge, making sure, even while I read, that we all know he's here, and that he's bored. He fiddles with the memory stick, spinning it like a top until Theo catches his eye. D plonks his finger down heavily. The memory stick hits it and stops spinning and instead skids across the table towards Theo, who picks it up and passes it to me to pass back to D without a word, which I do.

The second gunman, the one who had fired the second shot, now came back into the public area of the bank, no longer wearing a balaclava. It was only at this point that I realised that the second gunman was in fact a woman – having previously been misled by her height and bulky, shapeless clothing, including heavy boots and the thick stab-proof Kevlar jacket; by the balaclava itself; and, of course, by years of cultural conditioning and straightforward factual reporting which led me to assume that an armed person who robbed banks and possibly shot another person simply to reduce the noise that person was making was in all probability a man; but I had been wrong. I saw then that the robber's gait, despite the heavy boots and a certain self-conscious swagger, was that of a woman. And her face – high, wide cheekbones, pale eyebrows and freckles that seemed at odds with her dark, cropped hair – was without doubt that of a woman, who said, It's OK. Let's get on with it. The hands on her sub-machine gun were red with blood; there was blood on her stab-jacket and blood on her face.

The first gunman seemed to be in charge and able to tell the other two what to do just with signals, as if they'd done this before, or practised, and he'd drilled it into them, what they had to do. I found it easy to imagine a disused warehouse somewhere near the river, the first gunman, the boss, saying, What are you going to do if? over and over until they'd worked out all the permutations and the others had all got it. One of them, probably not the woman with the sub-machine gun, more likely the short one with the beard and a weight problem, would be a bit thick and would take all afternoon, and would probably say, Can't I just shoot him? more than once and the boss would explain why they wouldn't always want to do that. I hoped their practice and routines, their professional protocols or whatever, would probably include the situation where someone, for whatever reason, didn't agree to get down on the floor. It wouldn't necessarily make them panic or do anything irrational and dangerous – more dangerous than was inherent, obviously, in entering a bank at lunchtime with guns and claiming to be policemen, however unconvincingly. I relaxed a little. The situation was not entirely out of control.

The first gunman, the gang leader, kept his eyes on the older, professorial man who was still standing up and signalled with his gun to his accomplices. I noticed then that they carried large, cheap-looking holdalls, the sort you see on market stalls or shops that appear in shopping centres and don't last very long – the shops, that is, although the bags often don't, either – and I thought that, if I were going to rob a bank and haul off large amounts of cash I might choose something more reliable to carry it in, not to mention something classier. The second gunman, the one who had shot the woman screaming in the room behind the partition wall and was in fact actually a woman, went back to the female bank employee she had forced to open the door for her when literally punching the key pad hadn't worked. She bent down and stuck the barrel of her sub-machine gun in the employee's ear and asked where the cash was, and the woman repeated the word *Cash* in a quiet, soft voice with a rising intonation, as if the gunwoman had asked about something of which she had never heard, or perhaps asked about something she had read about in old books, but which no one actually used any more, like spats or sealing wax or woad. The gunwoman pushed harder on the gun, which forced the female employee's head over to one side so that her other ear, the ear that did not have the barrel of a gun in it, almost touched her shoulder. The gunwoman, who still had blood on her face, told her to get up and stop fucking about. She was white and her voice was calm and evenly-modulated and, frankly, middle-class. It is probable that armed robbers tend not only to be men, but to be drawn from those strata of society with limited access to legitimate wealth. Why rob a bank when you can manage one, as my father used to say, although he never worked in a bank, or anywhere else, as far as I could tell. The female employee got up and led the gunwoman back through the door in the partition wall. I expected the third gunman to follow but instead he unzipped his large black holdall. The third gunman was the one with the straggly reddish beard which he would scratch from time to time, pushing one hand – the hand not holding his gun – up under his balaclava helmet; he had deep-set eyes that struck me as somehow melancholy and, as he moved, he hitched his trousers and adjusted his Kevlar jacket as if neither fit him well. He squatted down beside the nearest customer and told him to chuck his valuables in the bag. The customer – an Asian man in his twenties with spiky black hair and a white jacket with a number of superfluous zips – said, What? and the gunman told him: Valuables. He said it was best not to be a smart arse and said he wanted a wallet, watch, phone, jewellery. The young Asian man in the white jacket asked what this was, some chickenshit mugging? He called the gunman *boss*, although he did not appear to be the boss. He said he thought they was robbing the bank. The gunman said, We *are* robbing the bank, and called the younger man *dickhead*. He motioned again for the Asian man to give him his valuables, and the Asian man said that this was cheap, and called the gunman

*man*. The gunman straightened up; he pulled his leg back and it looked as though he was going to kick the Asian man, but he didn't.

The first gunman said to calm down and just get the stuff. He called the other man Perce. I wondered if this was short for Percy or Percival and whether it was in fact the gunman's real name or an alias. I wondered who adopted Percival as an alias. The gang leader's voice sounded cultured and authoritative, but a little disappointed, perhaps, like a teacher, or a patient father, who has explained something over and over to a child who just won't learn. The Asian man squeezed his left hand in between his chest and the floor where he was lying down. He reached inside his jacket. He pulled out his wallet and held it up. The gunman who had thought about kicking him, but hadn't, now said: Thank you. He took the wallet, then unstrapped the watch from the Asian man's wrist and dropped it into his holdall. He stepped over to another customer, a woman with an organic jute shopping bag stuffed with vegetables and things wrapped in plain brown paper that had spilled out onto the floor. The gunman bent down, picked up one of the packages and unwrapped it. He held it to his masked face and sniffed. He asked if it was Brie de Melun. The woman nodded. The man re-wrapped the cheese and slipped it into his pocket. He seemed not to realise that he had got cheese on his balaclava. He asked for the woman's purse and the necklace she was wearing.

The gunwoman and the female employee came back into the public area of the bank. The female employee sat down again and the gunwoman looked around the bank, examining the faces of the customers and staff, as if deciding which one to pick for her netball team. She chose a man sitting in the corner with his head resting on his knees whom I had not previously noticed. The gunwoman thanked the female employee and walked over to the man, who was wearing a suit that was not made of synthetic fibre and did not have piping in the red corporate colour of the bank. The gunwoman said something to him, and the man shook his head. She hit him, not hard, with the barrel of her gun; he shook his head again. The gunwoman called out, Looks like we've got us a hero.

The gang leader did not move, or take his eyes from the older, professorial man who had not got down on the floor, but said: Tell Mr Wenlock that we all admire his courage. His employers will be most grateful for his fortitude. Obviously, if it were just Mr Wenlock, there would be nothing we could do that would persuade him to give us the second half of the combination. Wild horses would not drag it from him. We know that. But do please remind Mr Wenlock that he has a duty of care to his employees and customers; their safety depends on him.

Mr Wenlock – whose reactions to hearing his own name coming from the mouth of the leader of a gang of armed robbers three times were, first, to look up in surprise, with his mouth slightly, and his eyes fully, open; second, to close his eyes but not his mouth and to sigh, heavily; and third, to close his mouth, pulling his lower lip between his teeth and biting down hard enough to leave visible marks when he subsequently released it from his dental grip. My reaction on hearing what I now took to be the name of the branch manager from the mouth of the first gunman was to assume that the gunwoman's recent examination of the people in the bank had been a charade, that she and her colleagues had known from the start that the manager was here amongst them in the public foyer area of the bank, probably as a result of their having extensively cased the joint in the days and weeks prior to attempting the robbery, as a result of which surveillance they had no doubt established that the manager, Mr Wenlock, could be relied upon to be in the public part of the bank at this time of day, rather than in his private office in some more secure part of the building, either because he was on his way to or from lunch or because of a regular commitment to working alongside his employees, showing his face and demonstrating that he was very much *one of the team*, perhaps in compliance with some corporate HR policy over which he, as a local branch manager, would have had little or no influence and with which he would have been compelled to comply, irrespective of his own personal attitude, management style or natural inclination vis-à-vis face-to-face interaction with his employees, colleagues or associates, and that it was this – i.e. the reliable presence of a branch manager in the public foyer area of the bank, together with his presumed importance in providing the second half of whatever entry code was required to reach the more attractive areas of the bank, robbery-wise – rather than any particular or especial recklessness on the part of the two gunmen and one gunwoman that had led them to attempt to rob the bank during what must surely be one of the busiest, if not *the* busiest, time of the day, with all of the increased risk and complication that having to control and intimidate a large number of customers and employees inevitably brought in its wake, as a result of which I revised upwards a notch or two my estimation of the credibility and professionalism of the gang and their leader, and correspondingly reduced my level of anxiety re. the risk or likelihood of further shooting or injury.

Mr Wenlock had evidently heard not just his own name but everything the leader had said and therefore did not need to be told anything by the gunwoman, which, obviously, the leader would have been aware of. His choice to address the gunwoman rather than speaking to the branch manager directly must therefore have been more a question of rhetorical effect than of any actual barrier to more direct communication, a judgement on the gang leader's part that his words would have greater impact if experienced by Mr Wenlock as it were at second hand. In this judgement it appeared that the leader was correct as, after opening his mouth and eyes, then closing his eyes, sighing and biting his lip, Mr Wenlock rose surprisingly quickly and led the gunwoman back into the private area of the bank.

During all of this, the older man had remained standing in front of me watching the first gunman, the gang leader, who was watching him. Neither man moved. Eventually the gunman said, Please don't be foolish. Get down on the floor. The older man did not reply, just watched the gunman, his eyes never leaving the other's masked face, his look inquiring rather than challenging. The gunman walked carefully forward, stepping right over me, as a result of which I noticed that he was wearing trainers with thick, curved soles that looked a bit like orthopaedic boots but are actually supposed to make you fitter, and I wondered if perhaps he had some history of spinal problems, my father had suffered terrible lumbar pain, and it occured to me that it was likely that the actual amount of time the man spent on his feet robbing banks was insignificant in comparison with the time spent sitting around planning the heist and exchanging brutal but witty irrelevant banter in dark rooms at the back of strip clubs or abandoned import-export warehouses, or wherever. The gunman, the gang leader, the man who had fired the first shot that missed the older man by millimetres and either killed or wounded a woman behind the partition wall that separated the interview room she was in from the open, public area of the bank, now lifted his gun again, lifted it up high, his wrist cocked so that the gun remained all the time pointing at the older man, then lowered it slowly and precisely until the muzzle rested against the older man's forehead. He said, Get down on the floor. The older man raised his hand, balled into a loose arthritic fist, and coughed gently into it, and said he would prefer not to. The gunman kept the short fat barrel of his gun pressed against the older man's forehead and said that, if he moved, he would shoot him. The man shrugged his shoulders and bent down towards where I was still lying on the floor along with everybody else except the older man, the gunmen and, presumably, the manager who had agreed to accompany the second gunman – actually a woman – into the private, secured area of the bank. As the older man bent down, the first gunman lowered his gun, keeping it pressed against the older man's head, but did not fire. The older man asked me politely if I would care to stand up. I looked at the gun – which I now noticed was the G-version DA/SA model with a de-cock only feature operated by ambidextrous levers on the slide, and no actual safety catch – and thought that, if I moved, it was the older man who would get shot, or get shot first, and then possibly me. I shook my head in so far as it was possible to do so with my face pressed against the linoleum, and stayed on the floor. The older man shrugged again and straightened up, the gunman's hand and the gun following his rise. He stepped slowly forwards, compelling the gunman to walk backwards to keep his gun in place, and then bent down again beside another customer, the man who had been behind me in the queue and whom I had heard voicing impatience about the older man's apparent other-worldly slowness before any of us became aware of the presence of three armed persons and the whole robbery/hostage situation began. The older man asked, in the same polite way that he had spoken to me, if the man would care to stand up, but the man said no, there was no way he was going to move. He said the older man should get down and shut the fuck up before he got everybody killed. The older man offered no response, but simply straightened up and walked – still attached to the gang leader at the forehead like some bizarre and improbable parody of conjoined twins – slowly over to another prostrate customer, and then another and another, repeating to each his simple enquiry as to whether they would care to stand up. None did. Eventually, after working his way clockwise around the open, public area of the bank, the older man, accompanied by his armed shadow, reached a male customer in a high-visibility jacket, hard hat and heavy boots with scuffed toes through which the steel cap reinforcements could be clearly seen, and who was also at that point the object of attention of the third gunman, the one with the beard and the ill-fitting clothes whom the leader had called Perce, although it would be premature and probably naïve to assume that this was his actual name, and who had been working his way anti-clockwise around the bank taking the personal effects and valuables of each of the customers and placing them in his large, cheap-looking black holdall. Craning my neck to observe while trying not to draw attention to myself, I could just make out the following tableau: the customer, presumably a builder from one of the many construction sites in the vicinity, lying face down on the floor with two men bent over him from either side, one pointing a gun at the back of his neck, the other leaning on a stick with a pistol pointed at his own head by a fourth man who stood above them all, possibly wondering how it had come to this. The older man asked the builder if he would care to stand up. The man with the beard and the gun and the black holdall half-filled with valuables said to the gang leader that following the old man around with a gun like that was making them all look stupid; the gang leader did not reply. The older man straightened up for the last time and said quietly, as if to himself, Then it appears that I shall have to leave alone. He walked slowly but steadily towards the doors, which made a whining electronic sound as the automatic mechanism strained against the stick or baton placed through the handles, but did not open. He pulled out the stick or baton and placed it carefully to one side, then pulled open the left-hand door and walked out into the street. The gang leader made no attempt to stop him.

At this point, the female gang member with the sub-machine gun who had taken off her balaclava and was covered in blood returned from the private, interior area of the bank carrying a holdall that, while not completely full, was nonetheless, judging from the way she carried it against her right hip whilst her upper body canted over to the left, obviously much heavier than it had been earlier. She nodded to the gang leader who said that it was time to go, and they left.

For a moment nobody moved, or spoke, or did anything but lie where they were on the thick red cool linoleum floor. Then the bank employees got up to raise the alarm. I was not technically on duty, but nonetheless accept that what I was about to do did not follow protocol and am, frankly, now at a loss to explain my actions. I got to my feet and walked rapidly out into the street where the air was thick and wet after the air-conditioned bank and saw the gunmen climbing into the back of a van that was mostly white but which had yellow and red chevrons painted on it and could have been a police van, and which drove off towards the river, blue lights flashing. The van slowed behind a car and gave a short, two-note siren blast. You know that this is not like me at all. I followed the van on foot for a few yards, but soon gave up, watching other traffic pull aside to let the van pass, and pedestrians hold back to allow it through a crossing although the lights were red. I heard more sirens in the distance. There is a hospital just around the corner from the bank, a police station down the road: there are always sirens here, always flashing blue lights. Turning back towards the bank, I saw the older professorial man turning the corner, heading towards the station, or perhaps the cathedral. Knowing that it was still possibly not too late to return to the bank and the scene of one or possibly two potential claims, I nonetheless instead walked quickly after the older man, sweat gathering already under my arms, and in the small of my back, the air was humid and thick, but by the time I reached the corner, he had disappeared.

There is a silence during which four in-bound and three out-bound trains pass before Theo says, Well?

D says, I'm sorry to say this, Sis, but you fucked up. He does not look at all sorry.

There is another silence, during which Theo neither defends me nor criticises D for swearing and Alex meets nobody's eye.

Eventually Theo says, I'm afraid it does rather look that way. And then he says, But let's not jump to conclusions.

I straighten the pile of paper in front of me and replace the paper clip. Theo glances at the clock and says that, in view of the time and the circumstances, we will postpone the rest of the agenda until our next meeting. He thanks us all for our participation, as he always does; he asks me to stay on for a moment after D and Alex leave.

# 5

AT THE BANK I have to wait fifteen minutes before I get to see the manager, which is no great surprise but still pisses me off. The PA parks me on a fake leather sofa with a cup of coffee even I can tell came from granules in a jar. She looks apologetic – which I like, because it makes her smile nervously at me – but she says Mr Wenlock is talking to the police right now. She doesn't know how long he'll be, but she does know he's already spoken to my colleague this morning. Am I sure a second interview is necessary?

It's also no surprise a real loss adjuster got here first – it happens – though this is a bit quick off the mark. The place was only robbed yesterday. I say there are a few details I need to check. She doesn't look convinced, but she gets on with her work, and I get on with watching the way her breasts move whenever she reaches up for a file on the shelf above her desk.

Wenlock's door opens, and there are two policemen in it. One's a uniform, the other's a DS I know to nod to. A few years back, I turned up early at a dubious family suicide/slaughter job that was obviously never suicide (or I wouldn't have been assigned it in the first place) and found the police still there. Mother in the bath with her wrists open and the bathwater an interesting shade of purple. Father and two kids in the car, the car in the lock-up, a garden hose jerry-rigged to the exhaust. What other, legitimate use they'd ever had for a hose living in a twelfth-floor flat wasn't obvious to anyone. I asked for the story and DS Proctorow said living in this shit hole was enough to make anyone kill themselves.

"Or each other?"

"Both. Don't quote me."

I said not to worry, I wasn't a reporter. Which was true, to an extent.

The kids got Limbo. Given their age and context, I thought that was pretty harsh. It wasn't what I recommended, and was the last time Theo let me near anything with self-harm in it. The mother went down. The father survived and got life. Which, when I told him, Alex said was pretty much proof of God's essential sarcasm. The kind of thing Alex says.

Proctorow shakes my hand. I say, "I thought they wouldn't let you anywhere near bodies these days?"

Since the murder/suicide thing there'd been a serial murder-rapist thing that hadn't gone right, and the story was that his career got caught up in the fall-out. He looks puzzled for a moment, then his face clears as if he's given up worrying about it. He shakes his head.

I say, "We should have that beer sometime."

The guy's an oaf, but it never hurts.

When I eventually get to see Wenlock, he's professionally polite, but I can see it's an effort. The corporate red that covers most of everything else is more muted in his office. There's a computer on the desk, but it isn't switched on. The desk itself gleams like some exotic beetle.

"How can I help you, Mr Pitt?"

He has taken my card, and that's the name on it.

I say, "I appreciate that you've already been over the systems issues with my assistant." I'm getting that in right away, to get off the defensive and flatter the guy with the idea he's dealing with the top dog now. *And* save having to talk about alarms and CCTV for half an hour. Pretty slick, I think, but Wenlock says, "Actually, she seemed more interested in one of the witnesses."

She? There are women loss adjusters, real ones, I know. I've met a few. I slept with one once. (Even I was surprised when the *beautiful without your glasses* thing worked.)

I was the one who called what we do loss adjusting. Alex has some crap about Ancient Egyptians, Rada goes straight theology; I prefer something a bit more up to date. Loss adjusting is a real profession in the insurance industry: they have exams and an institute and everything. We're not in the insurance business, exactly, but the term appealed to me. It's a kind of metaphor. Alex raised his eyebrows when I said that, like he was surprised I knew what a metaphor was, but Theo said he liked it. That was the first time I thought I might be there for the long term, not just waiting for something better to turn up. A loss adjuster. Who I am.

I smile chummily and say, "For the moment, I'm interested in the victims."

"Quite right, Mr Pitt. I don't have to remind you that the bank is the real victim here."

I suppose bank managers have to be heartless bastards – it goes with the job like a pension and a reserved parking space – but, even so. He looks young for the job, dressed up in his father's clothes.

"As a business, which is worth more to you, Mr Wenlock – an employee or a customer?"

"It depends . . ." He clamps his thin lips tight to cut himself off. "We like to think of our people as people . . ."

I can't help laughing at that, and Wenlock looks startled.

"OK. So when one of your employee-people and one of your customer-people both get shot in the head, which is the bigger loss?"

Wenlock presses a button underneath the desk.

He says, "I made quite clear to your colleague this morning that nobody here was shot in the head, or anywhere else. Shots were fired and a number of our *people*" – he underlines the word in a way that makes it almost visible – "are suffering from shock. One man is being treated for a possible broken rib. But nobody – *nobody* – was seriously injured. Nobody was shot."

"You're sure?"

"If someone had been shot in my bank, Mr Pitt, do you think I wouldn't know?"

I pretend to think about that.

"You might be lying."

He pauses long enough to show that he has registered the insult but isn't going to react.

"The police were just here, Mr Pitt. They are investigating a robbery. They are quite clear about that. It is only you and your colleague who seem to think otherwise. She was very insistent – and, I must say, quite offensive – on this point."

Now I know it can't be a coincidence.

"This colleague of mine? Tall girl? Pale? Short hair? Mid-thirties?"

Wenlock nods. But I didn't really need to ask. It wasn't the insurance company that had got here first.

The PA appears in the doorway and Wenlock says that Mr Pitt is leaving.

I stop off at the café between the bank and the office, and order an espresso. A girl with studs in her face says "Double?" and I nod without thinking about it.

There are no claims to adjust. Rada has already been in asking questions she shouldn't, so she must know already. Theo said the MI would decide if there was a disciplinary case to consider. Which in my opinion is a fucking stupid question because there isn't any question. She walked out on at least one and maybe two dead contenders, when either or both of them might've had claims we'd be interested in. Plus she waltzed off after some nutty old professor who by rights should've been dead but wasn't, and therefore wasn't any of our fucking business. Open and shut.

Basically, Rada's fucked up. And it couldn't have come at a better time.

So what's she up to now?

I pay for the coffee and take it over to a stool in the window. It pisses me off that she's beaten me to the bank. I don't care that she's getting herself into deeper shit: the deeper the better. Theo's retiring, but there's no way he'll let Riverside House stop him choosing his successor.

I should have got in first. I left first – Rada was still chewing her way through the horse food Gary calls breakfast. But she still got to work before me, even when she isn't supposed to be at work at all. I know how: she rides a bike and I drive. I park in the tiny, over-priced building site that passes for a car park around the corner from the office, and then walk up to the gym near the bridge. As Gary never tires of pointing out, my routine makes no sense. It's financially ruinous, environmentally disastrous and a massive waste of time. But what can I do? With a car like mine, it'd be a criminal offence not to drive it.

At least Alex won't be in yet. I'm pretty sure Alex will be rolling out of bed right about now, asking Gary if there's any coffee left. And Gary – who, let's face it, is a total pushover, even if he is a whiny, whale-hugging lefty-liberal git – is probably saying no, but he'll make some more. And he'll know what Guatemalan estate the beans came from and exactly how much the pickers got paid, because he bought it at the organic food co-operative where he's the biggest customer and that's the sort of bollocks they talk about. Alex doesn't give a shit about the coffee-pickers because Alex doesn't give a shit about anything, really, but he'd be getting a cup of coffee made, and by now Gary would probably be toasting him a slice of that bread he bakes that tastes like someone has been sick in the dough. Why my sister ever married Gary is beyond my comprehension.

God moves in mysterious ways, she says.

I finish my coffee. I'm wasting time. When I get to the office, I'll replay the conversation with Wenlock in my head. There's always stuff you can learn that way.

*We should make friends with our mistakes*. That's how we improve. I read that, I think. Or maybe it's one of those things Theo says? I'm pretty sure I read it.

I put down the empty cup. The thick porcelain clicks dully against the saucer, and I get a memory flash of putting down the cup Wenlock's PA gave me, putting it on the low glass table next to the gym bag I'd left on the table deliberately so I wouldn't forget it when it was time to leave. Great. Now I'll have to waste more time going back for it. I think about just leaving it there. Let them live with the reek of my sweaty shorts. I am definitely tempted. But there are expensive products in the bag, too. Things for my skin and my hair I don't want to be without. I'll pick it up at lunchtime.

When I get to the office, it turns out I was wrong about Alex, who's already there. If mistakes are my friends, I must be pretty popular today.

Alex seems to be trying to make himself as uncomfortable as possible – leaning back in his chair with his dirty trainers up on one arm of his L-shaped desk, twisting his body to type into the computer on the other, the phone cable curled around his back and under one armpit, the handset clamped all the while between his shoulder and his ear. On my way past to my own desk, I catch his attention and mouth: "R. S. I." Alex raises his eyes to the ceiling. He manages to shrug while keeping the phone in place. I slip my jacket onto my personal hanger, the one with the broad pads that keep the shape of the shoulders better. I sit down, hitching up my suit trousers slightly to preserve the crease, before I press the button on my computer.

When Alex hangs up he carries on typing for a moment. Then he says, "Mothers. Fuck'em."

"You said that yesterday."

"Did I?"

I say, "What's the case?"

Alex swings his feet off the desk. "Kid gets caught in the wrong postcode. Abdullah Hatim."

"Abdullah? Why are we even looking at him?"

"Because he was born Denis Spence and his mum never accepted his conversion."

"It's not her call."

"Not normally."

I wait.

"But Denis is fifteen . . ."

I whistle. I'm enjoying this now. I say, "Bad luck."

". . . and Denis' mum is Gina Spence."

I can see the name's supposed to mean something to me, but it doesn't.

Alex adopts his favourite tone. Like he's a professor and I'm a remedial student. "For your information, D, until her husband left and she couldn't cope with a six-year-old and the job, or didn't want to, Gina Spence sat right about where you're sitting now. She was one of the best. She has weight with Theo."

"Who always says we don't work for the living."

"Until the living turn out to be his old mates."

This gets better.

"Oh, you poor fuck," I say, shaking my head. "You poor, poor fuck."

Alex scowls. He picks an empty plastic water bottle off his desk and throws it at me.

I turn away, towards my PC, rolling my shoulders. I'm not ready yet to talk about the bank and, when I do, I won't be wasting it on Alex. I open my email. Nothing there that can't wait. A train rumbles past, level with the office window. I close my eyes. I breathe in deeply through my nose and out through my mouth five times.

Alex says, "Do you have to do that?"

I ignore him. Actually, I do better than that: I notice that Alex is talking, notice that it will irritate me if I let it, and I *choose not to*. I put both thoughts aside. I have read about this, too. I place myself back in the bank, back with Wenlock.

Wenlock said Rada pressed him about the dead woman – or women – which is how I knew it had been Rada. Because, if there weren't any dead women, then surely only somebody who'd been there at the time and heard the shots and the screams and really thought somebody was dead, would have done that. But what exactly had Wenlock said? I put the question aside and concentrate on my breathing. I feel the way my diaphragm rises and falls, feel the air pass over my nostrils. I count one – in; two – out, up to ten and start again. I can see Wenlock's desk reflecting the light from the window, Wenlock behind it – he hadn't stood up or offered to shake my hand. Wenlock's face was pale and round, his collar tight. He took the card I offered and called me Mr Pitt. He had watched me closely as I made my opening pitch and had interrupted me: *actually she seemed more interested in one of the witnesses.* Not victims: witnesses. I'd assumed she'd gone there about the dead women that weren't dead – just as I had – and that's what had offended Wenlock. But Rada had really been interested in the witness.

I feel a surge of energy that comes with knowing I've found something. I almost open my eyes – it is hard to stay in the chair but I force myself to concentrate on my breathing again. One – in; two – out; three – in . . . *Which witness?* Well, that's obvious: the professor, the old guy Rada said she followed and lost. It wouldn't be hard to track him down; not if the bank was willing to play ball. The ATM records would show immediately who had withdrawn money in the middle of the robbery, just before the first shot was fired. That would give them a name, an address, everything. But Wenlock wouldn't have given out that kind of information to Rada. So what has she got? And what is she looking for?

I put the questions aside, concentrate on my breathing again.

Alex says, "Ommmmmmm."

I throw the water bottle back.

Alex says, "Peace, man."

He's sitting there in holey jeans and dirty trainers saying this to me? I tell him, I'm not the fucking hippie.

Alex shakes his head slowly. "And yet you come in here with your meditation shit."

"I'm not meditating, dipstick. I'm focusing my mental energies. Something you might want to try, if you had any. I'm using visualisation to . . ."

"If it looks like a duck . . ."

"That's just stupid."

"And quacks like a duck . . ."

This is the sort of thing that pisses me off about Alex. He brings nothing to the party. Just sits there quacking. Quacking about quacking. I say, "It's a technique I read."

Alex laughs in a way that makes me want to seriously hurt him. It is not a laugh that means what I said was funny. It's a noise that's supposed to let me know I've just proved I'm a moron. But I'm smart enough to know that's what his little snigger was supposed to do, so I ignore it.

He says, "Was that in an actual book?"

I sit down again, make a point of opening an email.

Alex says, "No, but really? Did the author have a middle initial? And a PhD?"

I open another email; Alex waits. It seems like he has all the time in the world. Some of us have work to do. I delete the email unread, open another. Alex's breathing becomes gradually louder until I can no longer pretend not to hear it. I delete another email without even opening it and stand up suddenly, sending my chair skittering back across the office.

"Focusing your mental energies?" Alex asks placidly.

"Oh, fuck off."

Theo arrives just as the last 'f' dies on my lips.

How has that happened? Theo steps into the middle of the office, between my desk and Alex's. He carries a cane, with a silver handle in the shape of a dog's head. He is wearing the pale grey Prince of Wales check, and a hand-made shirt the colour of pus. His tie is lime green, though I imagine he calls it something else. He must have been very cheerful when he dressed this morning. Now my profanity causes him to shake his head sadly. He even taps the cane on the carpet.

"That's enough, boys."

I am twenty-nine. Alex must be thirty-six, the same as Rada. He latched on to her at university and hasn't let go since. We're a bit old to be 'boys', even if Theo himself came out of the Ark. I keep the thought to myself. Not much longer, now.

Theo looks each of us in the eye. He plants the cane between his feet and folds his hands over the dog's head.

"While Rada is, ah, absent, we will of course have to cover her workload. I will take two cases myself, but I have to ask you boys to share the rest out between you. It should not be for long."

I'm so surprised I can't stop myself. "You?"

Theo smiles. "Indeed. It is not too preposterous, I hope? I thought it might be quite fun to get back into the field again. Before I finally let go."

Fair enough, I suppose, if that's what he wants. But things have changed a bit since 1812, or whenever it was he last stepped outside. The internal combustion engine, manned flight, genocide, methamphetamine, the internet.

"I'm not that old," Theo says.

Alex says, "Of course you are, sir. That's the point of you."

And that, right there, is number three or four in the list of one hundred reasons why I'm going to step into the old man's shoes, and Alex isn't.

I find myself saying, "Rada was at the bank this morning."

Theo waits.

"OK. I was there, too. Afterwards. She got there first."

"And what did you discover?"

If Theo hadn't asked – if I hadn't walked myself into a place where he was bound to ask – I might not have had to tell him. Not until I'd had the chance to work out what it meant and what I could get out of it. But now if I don't tell Theo about the lack of bodies, I'll be in deep shit when the facts come out. Which they will, in the end. I have no choice.

"There aren't going to be any claims."

Alex sits upright for the first time since I arrived. Even Theo's arrival hadn't straightened him up more than a few degrees.

"Rada got it wrong. The manager says nobody was shot. Nobody was even seriously injured. No bodies: no claims."

Theo lifts one hand from his cane and strokes his short, trimmed beard.

"Do you believe him?"

"I said he might be lying, just to see if he reacted. But he was adamant. Got cross, which made me wonder. But, honestly, why would he lie?"

Alex says, "It's possible."

"But why? What's in it for him?"

"I mean it's possible no one got hit. All we know is a shot goes through the wall, Rada hears screaming, the gunwoman goes back into the room behind, fires a second shot and the screaming stops. Maybe there's a woman in there who got a bit hysterical when a bullet came through the wall, and maybe nearly hit her, but didn't; the gunwoman comes in, fires a shot through the ceiling to get her attention and she shuts up. It's possible."

Theo says, "Why did we assume that somebody was dead?"

I say, "Because Rada said so."

"Are you sure?"

I'm not, honestly.

Alex says, "If there were no claims to walk away from, Rada didn't do anything wrong. There's no point in a disciplinary." He swings his chair to look directly up at Theo. "You can let her back and call off the investigation."

"I admire your concern and your loyalty, Alex, but I'm afraid I cannot do that. It would not have been unreasonable for Rada to suppose that at least one death had occurred, if not two – just as we did when we heard her report. By her own testimony she did not investigate this possibility. We therefore need to establish exactly what she believed to have happened at the time before we can reach any conclusion."

"How are you going to do that?"

"I have already contacted Riverside House. Mr Lopez will be here tomorrow. He expects to remain until the end of the week. In the meantime, I will take on Moon and Brewster; I expect you two to divide Rada's remaining caseload between you. You only need do what's urgent for now, but please keep them ticking over."

Theo swings his cane in front of his feet precisely, as if sinking an easy putt, and strides into his office.

Alex whistles and says, "Lopez. Shit."

I don't ask.

Alex says, "The Grand Inquisitor."

I'm still not going to get into this. Alex is just winding me up. If he isn't, I'll find out soon enough.

At lunchtime I call into the bank to pick up my gym kit. I ask to see Wenlock again.

"I'm sorry, sir. Mr Wenlock is very busy. Normally he would be out on the floor at this time of day. But, today . . . you'll understand."

"Then perhaps you can help me?"

The PA looks uncomfortable, but asks what she can do. I can think of any number of answers to that, but this really isn't the moment. I say, "I need the ATM records for the morning of the robbery."

"Would that help?"

Of course it would help. It would help me, anyway. I say it would help establish precise timings, but the woman doesn't give up.

"We have everything on CCTV. We've already given it all to the police."

Of course they have. It looks like I'll be having that drink with Proctorow sooner than I thought.

I summon up my most endearing smile, the sort of smile

my father used to give my mother when she found the pair of us in the tree house with a bottle of vodka and a radio tuned to the World Service. I say, "Triangulation."

Her eyes cloud over and her bottom lip disappears between her teeth. It looks cute, even if it's just stupidity.

"I really can't say any more. But it *is* a matter of life and death. Well, more than that, really."

I can practically hear the cogs turning in her head. She sucks on her pen and says, "I couldn't authorise that."

"Are you sure?"

She giggles. With heroic effort, I keep my voice calm. I am patient, I am just enquiring; I am not threatening her.

"So who could?"

"Mr Wenlock."

I smile again. This is harder muscle work than the gym. "But Mr Wenlock is very busy. You can't disturb him."

She shakes her head.

"So . . . ?"

"I'll ask the deputy manager."

Bugger.

She makes a phone call. I watch the way her lips brush the handset. I have to get something out of this, after all.

"Mr Meersow will see you in Room 1 in fifteen minutes."

"Room 1?"

"It's one of the interview rooms downstairs. I'll show you the way."

I sling my gym bag over my shoulder. She leads me to the lift and presses the button for ground level. It's only a couple of floors, but still takes long enough for the silence to feel awkward. I say, "Have you worked here long?"

She shows me to the interview room, says Mr Meersow will be down soon, and leaves me at the door. She doesn't even offer me a coffee. Whatever the deputy manager is going to say, it's not going to be *of course, you can have the information you want. Anything to help.*

I look around the small room. It's about ten feet by eight. No windows. It smells of disinfectant. There is only one chair and that's trapped between a table and the wall too tightly for anyone to pull it out or sit on it. It looks as if the table has been pushed back from the centre of the room. Sure enough, I can make out four dents in the carpet where it must have stood. Like everything in the bank, the carpet here is mostly red, but I can make out darker patches, that might be coffee stains, just about where a person would have sat at the table, before it was moved. I close my eyes and breathe deeply. I begin to count: one – in; two – out. I visualise my movements coming from the lift to the room, ignoring the image of the PA's arse I had focused on at the time, working out my bearings. Right out of the lift, facing the street. Left, left, right into the room. The wall now on my right would be the one that separated this room from the foyer, the one the bullet must have come through. I look up and sure enough, at about head height, there is a coin of fresh plaster the size and shape of a fifty pence piece. On the wall opposite hangs a large poster in an aluminium frame, advertising a savings bond. The application deadline passed last week. By the time the deputy manager turns up, I've used a buckle on my gym bag to remove a couple of the screws – enough to lever the poster frame forward an inch or two and see the dark stains sprayed up the wall behind.

# 6

I KNOW OF LOPEZ.

We've heard stories, but no one admits to having met the man. Theo must have met him.

D says we should divvy up Rada's cases. He seems to be in some sort of hurry. He logs on, leaning back and grunting like a sow at the tardiness of his PC. He does this every day, as if it would make a difference. You would think he might learn.

He says, There's only five.

Five files is nothing. It is not nothing, but it is not many. I have a couple of dozen, myself, perhaps thirty.

D says, My sister always was a completer-finisher.

Is that something he read?

He says, Theo's taking Moon and Brewster. That only leaves three. And two of us.

I dig a silver coin out of my jeans pocket. Heads or tails?

What are we tossing for?

Loser takes all?

That's not fair.

He sounds like a toddler, and I tell him so.

He says, But it isn't.

I sigh and open the files on my own screen. I say, Sister Angelina's got to be a shoo-in?

OK. You take her and the traffic guy. I'll take Rodkin.

The traffic guy's a repeat drunk driver who ploughed into

a crocodile of primary-age kids on a pedestrian crossing. He only died because the airbags in his unnecessary SUV suffocated him. The case would take about ten minutes. I could write it up without leaving the office.

Are you sure?

It's OK.

Only Rodkin's a suicide.

Rada and D don't do suicides; I do. D always says he wouldn't mind. It's just that he never does.

D says, It's OK.

He's positioning himself, showing he can handle everything now. I don't much care. He's still not getting Theo's job. But Rodkin probably deserves better. Whoever he is.

I say, It's my field. Theo shouldn't have given it to Rada in the first place.

If D wants to push the point now, he'll have to acknowledge there's a problem that has to do with suicide, with his father, and I know he won't do that.

D says, I didn't know you cared enough to have a field.

I shrug and print the file.

D says he's going to lunch.

The thing about suicide is you never quite know where you stand. There's always a presumption against, but even God seems to recognise a degree of wriggle room. So much depends on context.

The God I can't quite believe in makes most things turn out all right in the end, but doesn't involve himself much in the details. When we were at university, Rada was the sort of student who went to the careers advisers and the recruitment fairs. It was a tutor who suggested she talk to Theo. Her God intervenes and takes sides; he has rules and punishes people.

It was Rada who suggested I talk to Theo, too.

I'd been at the Office six weeks when he handed me my first suicide claim: a woman with a devoted husband and grown up children, who also had a perforated liver from the bottle of wine or two she'd drunk each day of her adult life. Her note said she was sorry, she just couldn't bother with it all any more. The husband spent most of our interview pulling out photos of them both dressed in waterproofs on one hillside or another. She had always been so full of life, he said.

Back at the flat that evening, I rolled two cigarettes and tried to explain. Rada said, It always matters.

I mean to me.

I didn't know then. She hadn't told me.

She was dressing to go out. She smoothed a non-existent crease from her skirt and asked how she looked. She was meeting Gary, who worked in the library and had recommended her latest favourite author.

I said, Tall.

That's not very helpful.

You're not helping me.

Rada had always known stuff, had always helped. I said, The Book's not much use.

I expected her to sit down then, to ask me what it had to say. To which the answer would have been not much. What there was made no sense.

I said, There's Judas, I suppose.

Rada tugged at the sleeves of her blouse.

And Samson, sort of. Died a hero; buried beside his father.

She turned back towards the mirror, then, away from me. She began brushing her hair.

I said, Zimri.

I'd been looking this stuff up. It wasn't at the tip of my tongue.

Over her shoulder she said, Who?

First Book of Kings, chapter 16.

She turned back towards me. She put the brush down and ran her fingers through her short hair until it looked just as it had when she started.

He was only king for a week.

Rada stepped into a pair of shoes, took them off again.

Ahithophel. Hanged himself in a fit of pique. But he ends up buried in his father's sepulchre. No word on his soul. Being buried beside your father seems to be a major plus.

Rada closed her eyes for a moment, then grabbed a jacket from her wardrobe and said she was going out. I asked what I should do about my report and she said I'd have to work it out for myself.

In the end I argued that the woman's suicide was an act of contrition for a dissipated life: the severity of the transgression only demonstrated the sincerity of her repentance. She went down anyway, but Theo made a point of letting me know that Riverside House had been impressed by the quality of my report.

On the bus I read what notes there are in Rodkin's file. It is a life. The bus is crowded and hot. The man sitting next to me turns sideways to talk to a friend across the aisle. He pushes his backside into me and drops bits of fried chicken on the floor. I could have caught the train. I'd have been here in five minutes, but speed is not my goal. Goals are not my goal, either. I have always done my best to avoid them.

Rodkin was forty-nine; he would have been fifty in two months. He married late, and had two children, but divorced while they were still at primary school. Rented a flat just round the corner from the family so he could see plenty of the children. Ordinary, then: gross contribution negligible. D's average piece of shit. Maybe there'll be something more.

Rodkin was a solicitor – family law, which is ironic,

perhaps, but hardly cause for suicide. He made modest charitable donations every month.

Rada's notes show Rodkin visited his GP twice in the last year: once with persistent indigestion, once complaining of an intermittent loss of sensation in his left arm. He would wake from a disturbed night's sleep, the sinister limb completely numb, immobile. When he got up, sensation would gradually return, although muscle aches continued. The GP took his blood pressure – which was normal – and ordered tests, none of which had proved conclusive by the time he killed himself.

The bus shudders to a halt opposite a depot. A handful of passengers, including the man next to me, alight from the centre doors, which close behind them. The driver turns off the engine. He picks a clipboard from behind the steering wheel and scribbles something; he unhooks the metal box that holds his fares. He stands, and reaching up above the forward door, turns a lever; the door opens with a heavy pneumatic sigh. He steps off into the street. The door closes again. With no air coming through the stationary windows the temperature inside the bus rises rapidly. I can smell food and acidic, greasy sweat. After a while, two or three passengers stand, then bend down to look out of the windows. One of them punches the seat in front of him. The rest sit silently waiting for a new driver to come. I should have got off, too. I could – any of us could – turn the same lever that the driver turned and let myself out, but passengers are not supposed to do this, and none ever does.

The next stop is only a hundred metres away.

It isn't suicide itself – the act or the mechanics of it – that interests me. It is the motivation. I am constantly surprised so many people care enough about whatever it is they care about to kill themselves. Statistically, suicide is a major cause of death.

I told Rada that, just after the woman with the liver. I said she'd be surprised.

Rada had seen Gary a few more times by then; he'd been at the flat for dinner. He was still there the next morning, making coffee and toast, when I got up. Rada skipped around the kitchen in cycling gear, scooping keys and phone and diary into her pannier bag, getting ready for work, all without taking her eyes off Gary. I couldn't see the attraction.

If Rada was surprised, she didn't show it; she pretended not to hear what I'd said.

I picked a slice of toast off her plate. I said, Apart from natural causes, suicide is right up there: second only to traffic accidents. I still didn't know.

Gary said, Alex?

Two and a half thousand people every day. More than war and violent crime combined.

That's very sad.

Every thirty-six seconds someone somewhere decides all the monumental tedium isn't worth it.

Neither of them was looking at me.

I said, Tell me they're wrong.

In my defence, I didn't know about Rada's father then.

I'd known Rada almost three years at the time, and she had never mentioned it. We'd shared a student house. We'd been drunk and stoned and off our faces together. We'd been away on holiday after finals, six weeks in Spain and France and Italy, sharing rooms and even beds when we had to (although she kept her underwear on). I'd told her that I loved her, once. She'd told me not to, kissed me on the cheek and asked me where we were going next. When we got back we rented a flat together, started working, moved here, but she'd never told me about her father.

She said, I'm going to work. I'll see you there.

When she left, Gary said: Well done.

He didn't mean it.

She'd told Gary. She'd known Gary a fortnight and she'd told him.

And he told me.

Rodkin's flat, when I find it, is no surprise: a one-bed basement in a monstrous nineteenth-century terrace set back from the main road by six metres of cracked concrete and weeds. The weeds have wilted in the heat, but they'll be back. Three cars are parked at intersecting angles on the concrete; none is less than ten years old. As a rule, nothing is easier to break into than a basement flat, but this one is really only waist-deep below ground level, and constantly overlooked from the busy street. Worse still, there are wrought iron cages bolted over both the door and the big bay window. The bars look out of place – Mediterranean, like those on the Catalan castle Rada and I stayed in, before she went and married Gary. But they are strong enough.

I climb the steps up to the main door, half a floor above street level. A house like this would have been home to a solid bourgeois family and their servants. Now half a dozen buzzers are screwed raggedly to the wall beside the door. The one at the bottom has a label: *Basement flat*, but no name; the one above says: *Howard*. I press it, and nothing happens. I press it again, and step back to look up at the windows on the upper floors. The front door opens about ten centimetres and a woman says, Who are you? She is young and skinny and has nothing on her feet. She crosses her arms over a stained and dirty shift the colour of cold tea that might be a long shirt or a short nightdress.

Ms Howard?

I thought you was someone else.

Are you Ms Howard?

Only, I wouldn't've opened the door.

I hand her a card, according to which my name is Pitt and I am a chartered loss adjuster. She looks at it blankly, turns it over and looks there, too, as if expecting to find some further explanation. She stares at me, at my jacket that was once part of a suit, at my tee shirt and jeans, and hands back the card.

Perhaps I should have gone to the Spences' after all.

Ms Howard? I'm here about Mr Rodkin. The basement flat?

There ain't no Howards here. Do I look like a Howard?

I indicate the bells. The woman opens the door a little wider to see what I am pointing at.

She says, Just a name on a bell. Nothing to do with me.

And Rodkin?

He's dead.

I nod. There is no arguing with that.

Did you know him?

The woman looks me in the face for the first time. The corners of her eyes are dull yellow. Her hair had once been ironed straight but has started to curl in the humid weather. Who d'you say you work for?

I'm a loss adjuster. Mr Rodkin had insurance.

No good to him now.

He had family.

Yeah?

You never met them?

I never met *him*, to speak to. Man went off all suited and booted in the morning, came back late. Separate entrance.

She points over the steps to where the basement door sits locked behind its iron cage.

I heard music sometimes, through the floor.

I grab at that, the only personal detail she's offered.

What sort of music did he like?

What sort?

You know: pop? Jazz? Classical?

That shit with the violins and stuff. He played that. Fucking loud, sometimes.

Did you ever complain?

The look she gives me says: *you don't live here, do you?* She says, I shouted Shut the fuck up a couple of times. But I wasn't really bothered. He got worse from me and Kurt.

I say, Is there another way into the basement? From the hall, perhaps?

She tenses up again.

What d'you want to get in there for?

I'm a loss adjuster . . .

You said. Whatever that is.

. . . I'm trying to understand the circumstances of Mr Rodkin's death.

Her glance mixes greed and cynicism. So you can pay out the insurance?

I'm just trying to understand what happened.

She shakes her head and crosses her arms tightly underneath where her breasts should have been.

She says, The man slit his throat with a bread knife, bled to death. There was police all over the place. It was in the paper.

I want to know who he was. Why he did it.

I know this is thin. Life policies don't pay out on suicides. Who'd care why he did it?

Rodkin's neighbour seems to feel the same. She says, Why the fuck does anybody do anything?

A man comes up the steps behind me, speaks over my shoulder to the woman. He is taller than me, which doesn't happen often, and two or three times as wide. The woman says, Some creep wants to know about downstairs.

The big man reaches out and puts his hand on my shoulder. It's like being pawed by a bear.

Rodkin? You want to know about Rodkin?

Did you know him?

The man pauses. His head is like the round end of a huge brown egg, hairless and with no discernible neck. His ears are thick and fleshy and have been stuck on sideways, as if by a cartoonist. He smiles, and I can see a couple of gold teeth. He says, We met at church. Are you a reporter?

I shake my head.

I'm a loss adjuster.

The man smiles again and nods. If he knows what a loss adjuster is, he doesn't care; if he doesn't know, he isn't letting on. He says, You got a name?

I say, Pitt, and hand him the card the woman had given back. He studies it, then slips it into his pocket.

Well, Mr Pitt. I can get you in for fifty.

I agree. Fifty is steep but there's no point in arguing. It would just make an enemy out of someone who at least knew Rodkin; and it isn't my money. Theo never queries my expenses.

I hand over the cash, and the big man pushes the door open; the woman steps back to let us pass. He leads me through a broad hallway with cracked tiles on the floor and nothing on the walls except a few numbers scribbled in biro and a monstrous ejaculating penis boldly outlined in black marker. We go down half a flight of narrow steps; there is no banister rail, and the walls on either side are marked with broad bands of greasy finger marks. At the bottom of the steps, he unbolts a door that leads back outside. He says, There's no way in from the house. It got bricked up when they converted the place. But there's a back door.

The garden is a long thin strip with high fences on either

side and a brick wall at the bottom. The wall is topped with giant tinsel – six inch curling fronds of galvanized steel sharp enough to tear through clothes and flesh – that glints dully in the hazy sunshine. I guess the wall backs onto the bus garage. At its foot there is a solitary, faded gnome. Some sort of vigorous weed with thick, fleshy leaves and tiny, brilliant blue flowers like old-fashioned sweets has overrun the whole garden.

Have you lived here long?

I never said I lived here.

That doesn't mean he doesn't though.

I say, Are you Kurt?

At the back the basement flat is level with the ground. There is a half glass door into a small kitchen. The door is barred like those at the front, but the big man has a key. Perhaps this was worth fifty after all.

What kind of business did you do with Rodkin, Kurt?

The bars are hinged like a second door. The man swings them open, then unlocks the glass door and holds that back, too, ushering me inside. He says, Never said I was Kurt, either.

You didn't say you weren't, though.

The kitchen is empty. Almost empty. There are no pots and pans, no plates, no sign of any food. But there is a magnetic strip on the wall above a counter, stuck to which are half a dozen knives. I can see a carving knife, a cook's knife, a meat chopper and some smaller blades, including a boning knife. No breadknife.

The big man closes the door. He leans against the kitchen counter, putting his bulk between me and the knife rack. He says, Now, Mr Pitt. You're going to give me your wallet. And your watch. And your mobile phone.

I do as I am told.

# 7

ONCE I DIDN'T have to stop myself thinking about the dead woman, I found I was free to think about the old man who wouldn't get down on the floor, even when I'd put a gun against his head and told him to.

Mostly what I thought was: what makes anyone that sure of what he wants and does not want?

Karen opened the door without knocking. She asked if I was willing to see Gerald Pryor, who had no appointment but wanted a quick word. Gerald was the Head of IT and would be looking for money, hoping that my imminent departure would make me magnanimous. I agreed to see him.

Gerald didn't look like a Head of IT – he was round and jolly with a shiny bald head and a luxuriant moustache that he appeared to have borrowed from a raffish uncle. He was no more capable than any other IT Head I'd ever met of preventing computer projects running hideously over time and over budget. He asked how I was and I told him I was fine.

"Looking forward to retirement?"

"I'm fifty-six, Gerald. My father lived to ninety-three."

"Still . . . no kids, no wife, thirty years on the clock. You must be minted."

It wasn't the money – money was just the chips. I might have had another forty years.

"I won't starve."

Gerald laughed. He said, "So what are you going to do with yourself?"

"I thought I'd take up robbing banks."

That's what I'd been saying whenever people asked. That or drug-trafficking. Once I said I'd re-train as an assassin. Hiding in plain sight, I told myself. It seemed to work.

Gerald said, "You don't want to do that."

"No?"

"There's no money in banks these days. Internet fraud, that's where it's all at. Speaking of which . . ."

And there it was: the pitch. The digital security project that had spiralled out of control but which he could just bring to heel with another half a million. I told him to write it up and take it to the Programme Board.

"Oh, I will, Bill. Of course. But I just thought . . . the Board would take it a lot more calmly if I could say you're happy with the money side."

Of course they would. And I could do this, if I chose to, even then, when we were sacking people to make my budget add up; even when I had less than a week to go. I could have made a half million problem go away. If I'd wanted to.

"Sorry, Gerald."

Gerald didn't leave immediately, of course. He hung around making a bit more conversation about my future, but his heart wasn't in it.

At last he stood up and put out his hand. "All the best, Bill."

I shook his hand and decided there was nothing on earth that would make me turn up to my own leaving-do.

As Gerald waddled out, I told Karen I was not to be disturbed for the rest of the afternoon.

Yesterday afternoon, when Moody said "Who's dead?" I had

assumed that she was being deliberately obtuse, that she was trying to rub our noses in it. She'd straddled the uncomfortable office chair, her arms crossed over the back, her head resting on her arms. She looked like a truculent teenager. I said, "Come on."

She lifted her head, pushed herself up with her arms. "No. Who?"

It was intolerable. If I'd shot someone, it was an accident. The sort of accident that happens, perhaps, when you take loaded guns into crowded places and point them at strangers. But I hadn't intended to hurt anyone. DC Moody, on the other hand, had walked into a room, found an injured, traumatised woman, and shot her. Face-to-face.

I said, "The woman. In the bank. The woman we killed. You and I."

"I never killed anyone."

Not a teenager. More like a five year-old playing hide-and-seek, putting her hands over her eyes and saying: *you can't see me.*

"I'm not saying you didn't think you had to, but you *did*, Rachel. We heard it." I turned towards Bernie, trying to implicate him in my appeal to the brutal truth. "We both heard you."

Bernie looked at the floor, but Moody was having none of it. "Heard me what?"

I sighed and closed my eyes. I spoke slowly, deliberately, as if for the record. "I fired my pistol. Earlier than I meant to, I admit, but I was aiming to miss. I did miss. But the bullet passed through the wall and hit a woman on the other side. She was screaming. You went in, you fired a shot. And she stopped screaming."

I stopped. I opened my eyes. Moody was looking up at me with her mouth open. I had hoped for guilt, contrition, even fear, but had expected denial. I had not expected this: disgust.

"What? You think I shot someone *for screaming*? And just carried on? Jesus, Bill. Sir. You're sick."

"I . . ."

"Sick."

Bernie was just catching up. He said, "You didn't? You mean, nobody's dead?"

Moody said, "That's right, Sherlock."

He balled his fists and punched the air, like a boxer blocking blows to his face. He hopped from foot to foot. He almost ran over to Moody's chair and kissed her. "Oh, thank you. Thank fuck. Thank God. Thank you. Thank you, God."

Moody pushed him away, but gently, for her.

For three hours, ever since the screaming started and then, just as suddenly, stopped, I'd felt numb, anaesthetised. You can't rob a bank on charm and personality alone. But when I'd asked myself if – when push came to shove – if I could ever shoot someone, I'd always thought I never could; and now I had. But Moody hadn't. I said, "What happened?"

"You hit her, Bill. I'm sorry, but you did."

I sat down behind my desk. I steepled my fingers and leant my chin against them. "And?"

"There was blood all over the place. She was hysterical. I couldn't see where it was coming from. I put one through the ceiling just to get her attention."

Bernie interrupted. "Like you said you might?"

"Just like I said. And it worked. When she stopped fighting me off I saw she'd been hit in the arm, probably the brachial artery, from the blood she was pumping about."

Bernie said, "Yuck."

"So I used my balaclava as a tourniquet. She'll live."

As my anaesthesia faded, scepticism returned. "Your balaclava? Is that possible?"

Moody groaned, like a disappointed teacher. "You push the top through the mouth hole? It makes a loop you can tighten and tie off with a plasticuff."

I must have looked blank.

"Honestly. Civilians. Did you skip First Aid, or what?"

I said, "I did a lot of it when I worked at the hospital. We didn't have much call for balaclavas."

"In Accounts."

"I don't remember them much in A&E, either."

"Whatever."

Bernie said, "Who cares? The point is – she's not dead. Not. Dead."

Moody and I ignored him. Something was still bothering me. I said, "You left the balaclava behind?"

Moody nodded. "Would you rather I'd let her bleed to death?"

Now, when I got off the train I felt a few fat spots of rain. I sheltered briefly in a doorway, cigarette butts at my feet, but the rain wasn't coming to anything, so I headed across the river. The dog returns to his vomit, I knew, the detective to the scene of the crime. I wasn't a detective.

On the bridge, I paused and leaned on the parapet wall. Below me the river was dull and grey, the colour of the battleship moored downstream. I watched a sleek-necked bird fly downriver, skimming the water until it seemed to pause, then plunge and disappear. A cormorant. I watched, waiting, scanning the turbid water for its re-emergence. Just when I had given up, it broke the surface, a slim black curve like a geisha's eyebrow. It floated back upstream, effortlessly, because that's the way the river was flowing – inland, past the heart of the city. It was just the tide, I knew, but it still felt wrong, somehow out of joint. The river was almost full, lapping against the highest reaches of the embankment walls; soon the tide would ebb and the river would flow down to the sea again.

The old man had walked out but he did not raise the alarm. It was as if the robbery, the guns, the threats were simply nothing to do with him. I told myself he was the least dangerous witness in the whole affair: of all the people in the bank, he was the only one who never saw Moody's face.

And yet.

And yet, something told me I had more to fear from his mild indifference than from Moody's unmasking, from Bernie's instability, or from the investigative prowess of our colleagues.

Something told me I had to find the old man, to understand how he could have done what he did.

Something? Call it a hunch.

An accountant's instinct.

Willie Sutton wasn't really Willie at all. *Willie the Actor, Slick Willie* – they were just nicknames the FBI made up. Nobody called him that. He was Bill, like me. But Willie was what it had to say on the jacket of his book.

I straightened up, both hands pressing into the small of my back to ease the stiffness, and continued over the bridge towards the station.

At the bank I was greeted by the chubby blonde woman who had greeted me the day before. She smiled. Without my balaclava and black uniform she did not recognise me. She warned me that the bank was about to close. I thanked her and walked on into the middle of the foyer, which, at that hour was almost empty. Two or three customers were withdrawing money or bending awkwardly over the narrow ledges the bank provided for people to lean on to complete paying-in slips, and which were always at exactly the wrong height. There were no queues. I hesitated, uncertain what to do now that I was there. I had expected things to be different: crime scene tape, perhaps, cordoning off the cash machine the old man had used, the one above which my bullet had pierced the sign and passed through the partition wall into the room behind. But it appeared that nothing had changed since the moment I entered the bank the previous day. I checked my bearings: the machine directly in front of me must have been the one. Above it a laminated sign read *Cash Withdrawals*. The sign was undamaged and must, I thought, be new. I could not see the manager, Mr Wenlock – whom I knew from our surveillance would not normally have been in the public area of the bank at that time, anyway – or of the woman Moody had bullied into co-operating. I could see no evidence that the raid had taken place at all.

A young man emerged from the door into the private interior of the bank. He approached me and asked if he could help. He was tall and thin with blonde, almost colourless hair and a face both pitted and cadaverous, as if teenage acne had been followed by malnutrition; if he had been in the bank the day before he must have remained out of sight in the offices upstairs.

I said, "I would like to see Mr Wenlock, please."

The young man looked doubtful. "Do you have an account with the bank, sir?"

"I am with the police."

It was not strictly a lie. If ever I wound up in court, they would not have been able to add a charge of impersonating a police officer to those of aggravated robbery, possession of a firearm and whatever else I would have had to plead guilty to. I said, "My name is Pitt," which was a lie: Pitt was the first name that came to me, the name of my predecessor. The one after Eddie Likker, but before me. A harmless alias, but it seemed to mean something to the young man.

"Ah. Perhaps I can help. My name is Meersow; I am the Deputy Branch Manager. Please, follow me."

He led me through the locked door and into a small interview room in which the table had been pushed close up towards the rear wall. He indicated a chair, but warned me to be careful: the wall behind it had recently been painted: if I leaned too far back I might stain my clothes. He took a second chair and sat facing me, on the same side of the table. Our knees almost touched. On the wall behind him, I could see a large framed poster advertising a savings bond for which the application deadline had recently passed.

He smiled but said nothing, as if, now that we were settled, he was waiting for me to begin. He rubbed his hands along the tops of his thighs, then lifted the creases in his trousers and folded his hands in his lap, but still he said nothing. It occurred to me that he had not demanded any identification. You might think that a bank so recently robbed would have been more cautious.

I said, "Thank you for your help, but I would prefer to see Mr Wenlock, if I may."

"I am afraid that is not possible. You will understand that Mr Wenlock has experienced considerable stress within the past twenty-four hours. He went home shortly after lunch today; I believe the investigating detective was informed of his intention to do so."

This was a question, and an implied criticism; the young man was evidently sharper than I had supposed. I said something about messages not always being passed on in large organisations. I was sure a man such as he would understand?

Meersow nodded and smiled again, but did not commit himself either way.

I said, "I – we – need to trace all of the witnesses."

"Naturally."

I felt clumsy, like a child on new skates. It was hard to believe I was convincing the Deputy Manager that I was a real policeman. "Of course we have taken statements from the employees and customers who were present when our officers arrived . . ."

"Indeed."

". . . but we understand that . . . one customer . . . left? While the robbery was taking place?"

Meersow looked directly at me and raised his eyebrows. "That is our understanding, also."

"I understand he withdrew cash during the raid. Or attempted to. So you should be able to identify him from your records."

Meersow stroked his fingertips along his thighs again. "Of course. I cannot recall the name, but I know that we passed this information to your . . . colleagues earlier this afternoon."

That was all I needed to know to get what I had come for. In my excitement I failed to appreciate Meersow's slight hesitation before the word "colleagues", or what it might mean.

I muttered something more about poor communications and apologised for taking up his time. I stood and expected Meersow to do the same. But he remained in his chair. He looked up at me and said: "There was a second witness you may not be aware of. A young woman who left shortly after the gang, before the police arrived."

I was not much interested in the woman, but knew I should pretend to be. I sat back down. "Can you tell me what she looks like?" I should probably have pulled out a notebook and a stubby pencil, but I had neither.

"I can do better. I can tell you her name." He paused for effect. "It is Rada Kalenkova."

It meant nothing to me. "Russian?"

"Possibly."

We sat in silence for a moment before it occurred to me to ask: "How do you know?"

Meersow passed a hand airily in front of his face, as if shooing a lazy fly. "She is a regular customer."

I had come for the old man, and had him in my grasp. I did not understand what this young man was trying to give me now, and whether it mattered. I said, "And you did not pass this information to the . . . to my colleagues?"

Meersow said smoothly, "It has only just come to light."

And he winked – I was almost certain of it.

Outside on the pavement I was buffeted by home-bound crowds. I watched trains pass overhead, into the station or out towards the suburbs and the country. I wondered which way the old man had walked from here the day before. Towards the station? That was the way the bulk of the impatient crowd was heading now. But I suspected the old man would not have followed the herd. The cathedral, perhaps? Here since 606.

I wondered about the Russian woman. She must have been the one behind the old man in the queue, the one who had tried to warn him and had called out when he trod inadvertently on her fingers. The first customer he had asked to stand up with him. The first to refuse. But did she matter? If she had followed us out of the bank she would have seen us drive away. But that was of no importance. We had parked the van right outside the bank because we could afford to have it seen. The woman was irrelevant. It was the old man I needed and now I could find out who he was, and where he lived. His mother's maiden name. Digital security's the thing.

Meersow said the bank had passed the information to the police that morning. It would be easy to find out which detective was leading the investigation, but I couldn't ask him, of course. Not without prompting awkward questions. Luckily, I didn't need to. I pulled out my mobile phone, scrolled through my contacts, tapped one. A voice said: "Gerald Pryor."

"Gerald. Is this a good moment?"

# 8

BY THE TIME I turn my bike to the right and feel the stretch of the steep hill in my calves, I know I have wasted the first day of my suspension and am no further forward. I also know that this is not what I will say when I get in, a little early, and Gary asks how my day has been with no more than the usual care and concern and trepidation even in his eyes about the nature of the response he is about to receive. He is always wary because I have told him about my job and what it can present me with and he doesn't always want to know. I come through the door and carry my bike down to the cellar before Gary knows that I am home. It is humid outside, and the rain that should have happened hasn't happened and I am hot and sticky from the ride home, which has been longer than usual. I take off my helmet, which is round and black and devoid of those aerodynamic grooves and fins most helmets have, and which, Alex says, makes me look more like a riot cop than a cyclist. I run my fingers through my hair, which is wet; a bead of sweat trickles down into my left eye and I wipe it away with the back of my right hand. It is cool in the cellar and I lean my forehead against the bricks of a pillar where the paintwork has not flaked too badly. I breathe slowly and deeply, trying to reduce my heart rate and to think what answer I will give to Gary when I go up from the cellar into the kitchen and he hands me a glass of chilled water from the fridge. Gary will want to know what I have been doing and I am not keen to answer this question, because I have not yet told him that I have been suspended, even though it happened yesterday and I might reasonably have been expected to have mentioned such an important fact before now. A truthful and honest account of my day would therefore come as something of a surprise. I know he will be sympathetic and will do whatever he can to help me, but I sometimes feel that Gary does not respond altogether well to negativity and there is no upbeat or positive or even, let's face it, neutral way to explain that I was suspended yesterday and today has been a total washout in a particular way related to my complete and utter failure to find any trace of the old man in the bank who refused to lie down when an armed robber pointed a gun at his head and told him clearly to, that I have today achieved nothing and, in fact, simply by returning to the bank at all and asking questions I have no right or professional duty or locus to ask, I have made things measurably worse for myself, and thus for Gary and Matthew, whose welfare is entirely dependent on my gainful employment.

It is at least true that I have not spent the day in a funk of precipitously lowered self-esteem, at home in bed, perhaps, as I have once or twice been known to do at moments of extreme stress or crisis, allowing Gary to bring me nourishment and nameless green infusions I cannot actually drink and have to surreptitiously empty into the toilet, all day.

Today, by contrast, I rose at my usual hour and made tea for Gary and helped Matthew dress for school, remembering to sign the slip and to put it in the tiny envelope provided along with four coins, so that my son could visit a museum with his class and draw pictures of stuffed animals he will later show to me and explain are badgers or tapirs or possibly weasels. I left before he went to school, as I usually do; Gary would have made his packed lunch and walked him down the road. Matthew will be eight on Saturday and he will unwrap the biggest box of Lego bricks he or I have ever seen, and several other things besides, and will go with five friends from school, not all boys, to the cinema to see an animated film about a chameleon which, for all its knowing cynicism, will underline a genuinely unobjectionable moral truth such as the importance of friendship or the courage to be found within oneself at moments of extreme stress, and I will be glad of this and may even find a tear in the corner of my eye.

D was also up and dressed at his usual time and we had breakfast together: muesli for me and something you put straight from the freezer into the toaster for D. If I remember correctly (remembering being one of the things I did for a living every day, until today) D said that I should not take it too hard, it was not the end of the world. To my relief, neither Gary nor Matthew overheard this trite and possibly well-intentioned suggestion and therefore did not ask what it was that I should not take too hard, so I did not have either to explain or to lie.

D and I left together. I clipped a pannier to my bike and swung my leg over the saddle as I usually do and D, as he usually does, climbed into his car. He looked at me with a puzzled expression but then shook his head and did not ask why I was getting on my bike at all because, let's face it, I hadn't got a job to go to, had I? D's car is a rich subtle grey I'm surprised D likes; it makes a noise that reminds me of a holiday we had when our father was still alive and drove us up to the coast. It was not our father's car that D's car reminds me of, but, on the way, we passed a military airfield and pulled over onto a verge full of cow parsley and watched a huge silver aeroplane, bigger than an airliner, bigger than anything I have ever seen, come in to land. It flew so low over our heads that there was nothing we could do but watch, there was nothing else to see or hear and I thought my heart might stop from the sheer nameless overwhelming pressure, but it didn't. I remember that D's mother, my stepmother, was not with us, but I can't remember why.

D must source his processed breakfast supplies himself because they are not sold in the shops Gary uses and he would not buy them if they were, it would offend the very core of his being, he says, smiling and inviting D and Alex and I to take this as a joke, although it is entirely true. I am uncertain and perhaps conflicted about having my younger brother and my oldest friend living in the house that Gary and I bought to be our family house but have never lived in together on our own. Gary has not once complained or even shown that he thinks the situation undesirable or unusual, even. Alex is here because he always is, because that's who Alex is. D sometimes says he is a leech, a parasite, but at least he says it to Alex directly, and in a way that, although he means it, cannot be taken too seriously, either. Alex never takes offence. Alex is a little like a dog that attaches itself to you in the park or out on the street, for no obvious reason, but is friendly and insanely loyal even though its loyalty is wholly misplaced and every time you turn around it's there even though you tell it to stay or go back to whoever owns it, or go indoors and shut your door, but the next day there it is, sitting happily in your garden, just looking up at you with bright eyes and a wet nose and its head cocked on one side waiting for you to throw a stick or just walk or even just sit in your own doorway and scratch its head or whatever, it won't mind and will be happy: that's who Alex is. At university, even people who knew us assumed that we were lovers, but we weren't.

In the kitchen Gary has already poured a glass of water and is holding it out to me as I walk through the door. He is wearing a heavy cotton apron on which enlarged reproductions of two heads of artichoke, originally engraved in the eighteenth century, sit roughly where his breasts would be if he were a woman. He hands me the glass and says, How was your day? at the exact same time that I say, Where's Matthew? He explains that Matthew is still at his friend Ivo's house, where he went to play after school, and that he, Gary, will go and fetch him in a minute, but, really, first, he says, how was my day? I say, Oh, you know, and drink some of the water. I say, I need a shower, and carry the glass out of the kitchen and up the stairs before Gary can ask me any more.

In the bathroom I peel off my things and drop them into a basket separate from the basket where Gary and I place our ordinary dirty laundry because my cycling clothes are soaked with sweat and cannot be left mixed in with other dirty, but not actually disgusting, garments and I step into the shower. I know that it is not practicable to keep the fact of my suspension secret from Gary much longer, even if it were desirable and not likely to cause a breach of trust and perhaps undermine the strength of our relationship when it comes out in the end, which of course it will, if it has not already, because of Alex and D both living in the house and being certain to say something, if only to me, and not necessarily to Gary, not deliberately to expose me, but just something, expressing concern even, that would be bound to give the game away. The only reason they probably haven't already was that last night, Monday night, was Gary's Tai Chi class and Men's Group night which, as it happens, both fall on the same evening and so, unusually, keep him out of the house until after eleven o'clock, so he wasn't surprised when I came home a little early yesterday, it is what I always do on a Monday, to take over looking after Matthew while Gary goes out, and when he came home, Alex was already in his room, D was reading a book about delegation and I suggested that we get an early night and Gary, after shaping and setting two loaves of dough to prove overnight, agreed.

Before he came to live with us and to work at the Office of Assessment, D always said we lacked ambition, that there had to be more to life than worrying about what happens to people when they die.

I dry myself and push the wet hair out of my face. In the mirror I see a face that is still young: my father's face, mostly. I will tell Gary now, I think, before the others return and say something that will make it so much harder.

When I return to the kitchen, however, Gary is not there. I have put on a thin sleeveless cotton dress and sandals and, where I haven't properly dried myself from the shower, such as the small of my back just where the spine begins to curve outwards again, the material of my dress has soaked up the water and there are damp patches. The dress is pale blue, which I like and which Alex says goes well with my skin colour and my eyes, which are also blue, although darker than the dress, and the damp patches show up dark and clear like old bruises on pale skin. Gary has gone to collect Matthew and before he returns D comes in full of the exciting (to him, but for me difficult, potentially dangerous and hard to explain to Gary) news that somebody, at least one person – without blood-type and/or DNA tests it is not possible to say positively whether it is more than one, but it certainly looks that way to D – was definitely hit in the interview room at the bank; that a person or persons unknown to D were injured badly enough to bleed on the carpet and not only to bleed but to spray blood up the wall opposite that which the bullet initially penetrated. D has come straight into the kitchen and is still wearing his suit when he tells me this. He goes to the refrigerator and tries to tug a can of lager out of the plastic cuff that chains it to three others.

It would be easier to take all the cans out of the fridge to start with, but D does not do this. Trying to pull out just one of the cans is awkward and, in the effort, D knocks out a plastic tub of houmous, which lands sideways-on, popping off the lid and spilling a small amount of its contents, about a dessertspoonful, onto the hardwood kitchen floor. With the extra room to manoeuvre thus created D manages to extract a can of lager and puts it on the counter beside the fridge. He is tall, like our mothers, and when he bends down to pick up the houmous tub the jacket of his suit, which is cut slim and waisted in a way that Theo would not approve, rides up his back and he has to shrug his shoulders to free the jacket where it catches under his armpits. D picks up the tub with one hand and, with the forefinger of the other scoops the spilled houmous from the floor and puts it into his mouth. He straightens up and says, Who the fuck makes their own houmous, anyway? and I know that this is not actually a question and that the answer – Gary – is too obvious to both of us to need articulating, so I say nothing and D says, I prefer the stuff from the supermarket.

Because I know from experience that there is no point whatever in debating D's culinary preferences or notions of hygiene or civility, and because I need to know what D knows and want to get the conversation over with before Gary and Matthew return, I say, The bank manager told me nobody was shot.

D carries his lager over to the kitchen table. He takes off his jacket and hangs it on the back of a chair. He sits in another chair and puts his feet up on a third. He takes a swig and smiles up at me. He says, Is that right, Sis?

Nobody was seriously injured, the manager said.

D smiles again. That's right, he says. He did say that. But it isn't true.

D does not say how he knows this. Instead he says, How come you were there anyway?

I have thought about this. I have anticipated this question, which was bound to come up sooner or later, and to which, from the Office's point of view, it was always going to be hard to frame an answer that would not in some way make matters worse for me. When we were children, our mothers, first mine, then D's, often told us that lying to hide or disguise an offence was usually worse than the offence itself, that it destroyed trust and eventually love between people: they had no time, they said, for the little white lie. Often they looked at our father when they said this and I always assumed that they were seeking his endorsement, or his approbation, or at least his collusion. Now I say, I was looking for the old man.

D'uh. I know that. But you're suspended. Theo's getting Lopez in for the investigation.

I can't pretend that this isn't a surprise that distracts me from the primary surprise that D knew I was looking for the old man not following up the dead woman or women. I say, Lopez?

'Fraid so.

D does not look afraid.

So the chances are, Sis, you're toast.

I'm sitting at the kitchen table opposite my brother and I say, Lopez only does major cases.

Uh huh.

Something occurs to me, some kind of a lifeline or rationalisation and it doesn't seem altogether likely, but it is possible there could be more than one reason for Theo – whom I have every ground, including his own testimony, to assume both likes me and respects me professionally and who has been known in the past to allow me some limited latitude, procedure-wise – to get Lopez in to investigate my possible, or assumed, or alleged misconduct, and only one of those reasons is D's evident assumption that, given Lopez's reputation as a major hard-nose and total bloodhound when it comes to tracking down policy infringements, not to mention his intransigence in prosecuting such infringements as he uncovers, which he always does, Theo is throwing me to the lions because he might as well. It is also possible, albeit not highly probable and something of a high risk strategy on Theo's part if he were really on my side in this matter, that he has asked for Lopez, despite the fact that this was not a case on the scale Lopez usually operates at, because if Lopez – given his reputation, etc. – found there was no case to answer then no one else would be able to quibble or accuse him – Theo – of letting me get away with something I shouldn't have got away with, which, in the long run, when Theo is no longer around to look out for me, would be to my benefit. It is possible.

I say, Unless . . .

D looks up. He looks at me warily like he thinks I might be stringing him along and he doesn't want to get caught out, but if I have thought of something he ought to have thought of himself he doesn't want to miss out on it, either.

What?

Another, less palatable but probably more realistic possibility, is that Theo – who, for all his seniority and reputational capital and general kudos within the organisation is, after all, about to retire – is not the one dictating events here and that Riverside House has assigned Lopez to the case for reasons of their own, such as the need to find a replacement for Theo and the fact that Lopez, for all his fearsome reputation and unquestionable skills as an investigator is going to need some mainstream branch management experience on his CV if he is ever going to progress to the higher executive ranks. Which might be where Riverside House want him, and see him going in the long run.

I say, Maybe Lopez isn't coming for me at all, not really. Maybe he's just coming to get the feel of the place before they drop him into Theo's job?

They can't do that.

But of course they can, and D knows this, so after a pause, more quietly and without the relish he might have displayed earlier, he says: You're still going to get chewed up.

I know this, so I say, But it won't do you any good, D.

In the circumstances D does not even bother to deny the obvious implication that he had hoped to profit by my downfall, even though he is my little brother, and he only got the job because I put in a word for him with Theo. He says, Shit. Lopez . . . You don't really think . . . ?

I don't know, D. Perhaps you should ask Theo.

He empties his can of lager and he says, Yeah, right.

By the time Gary comes in with Matthew, D has pulled another couple of cans from the fridge and handed one of them to me, and I have popped it and drunk half the contents in a single, extended swallow, because, frankly, I need a drink and I don't know why I didn't think of it myself, earlier. Gary looks at the cans and the still-full water glass I left by the sink and he says, I didn't know it was a special Tuesday. What are we celebrating?

I stand and swoop up Matthew and ask him about his day and if he has had fun at school, at the museum, and with Ivo, his friend, and this is so self-evidently special bonding time for the busy working mother and her son that Gary cannot interrupt. And D says, Hi, Matthew, and Matthew says, Hello, Uncle D, then D looks up at Gary and shrugs and says, It's a work thing, and finishes his second can and Gary says he'd better get on with the dinner, then. And D, missing the point, or perhaps spotting the point but deliberately blundering right past it in a way that, for once, actually helps me, says: What is for dinner, Gary?

Cous-cous salad.

D groans audibly and Gary says, It's been so hot today.

He goes to the other end of the kitchen and fills the kettle and puts it on to boil; he weighs cous-cous into a bowl and measures olive oil in a jug. He bisects and squeezes several lemons. He slices a red onion and starts on the peppers before the kettle begins to whistle, which it does because, although it is electric and equipped with a simple bi-metallic strip to switch itself off when the water boils, Gary likes the faux-traditional design, which I knew he would when I bought it as a birthday present a couple of years ago. When he unwrapped it Gary did not, as D said he might have done, slap me and say he was going to the pub, and did not sulk, even, but was quite unreasonably pleased and kissed me and then immediately made a pot of some organic, flower-based infusion that smells like spinach that has been left at the back of the fridge too long.

While Gary cooks, Matthew tells me about the museum, which has a walrus, a real one, and he dashes back up the stairs up to the hall to get his book bag and brings it down and pulls out his sketchbook with the badger/tapir/weasel pictures and another one he makes me guess what it is and I say, It is obviously a spider, a great big, hairy spider and although he does not say anything except, It's a chimpanzee, I nonetheless see a moment's disappointment in his eyes, a moment where he has rubbed up against the inadequacy of real people like his mother, which is a moment I wish I could have spared him and protected him from, but I know I can't. It is gone as soon as I see it and Matthew is telling me how his friend Ivo put his hand in one of the fish tanks and had his fingers nibbled by a prawn but he – Matthew – didn't want to, but I saw it all the same, the disappointment, or disillusion or whatever. I think about what I have done, how I have allowed the old man in the bank somehow to fill my mind, pushing everything aside so that I followed him, yesterday, out of the bank, followed him and not the gang, which a concerned citizen might just have done, the sort of person who helps the police with their enquiries and it is not a euphemism, and anyway I walked away from one or possibly two potential claims and followed a man who was still alive and of no interest to my employers. It is my job that pays for this, for this house, this food Gary buys and cooks, the wine and bread and heat and light and water, the clothes we wear, the museum trips and toys and music lessons and the Lego sets and birthday parties, and my employers do not want me, or pay me, to follow the quick, however brave or stupid or desperate or indifferent they might be in the face of death: my employers do not care, and neither should I. I can see now that I made an error yesterday, a monumental error, and that today I have compounded my misjudgement. I have found nothing that might help and anyway there was nothing to find: the old man is of no concern to the Office and therefore of no concern to me. I look up from Matthew's sketchbook and see Gary tearing mint leaves from their stalks, D finishing his lager, Matthew watching me, his eyes alive again. It was foolish to risk all of this, to risk the protection of my son, the comfort of my husband, and even that of D, who is a bit of a slob and pretends to be a brute, but isn't really, and anyway is my brother, and I love him and I love them and it isn't until Gary brings the salad and some loaves of bread he baked this morning and a pat of butter over to the kitchen table and goes back for the plates that anybody, even me, stops and says:

Where's Alex?

Gary has warmed five plates because there are five of us, including Alex. He has laid places for five, as he always does, putting out five knives, five forks, five spoons and five glasses, but there are only four of us.

D says, He was going to see Gina Spence.

Gina? Why?

Her son, apparently.

Before I can think what that might mean, that it might mean a conversation I don't want now, with Matthew here, I say, Denis?

Abdullah. He converted, apparently.

Gary says, Reverted.

The point is, D says, cutting Gary off, whatever he was, he isn't any more.

I can see that Gary still hasn't got it, it's not his work, after all, and I can see that he's about to say something more, about Islam, probably, something sensitive and theologically correct, but nonetheless missing the point entirely, the point being that Gina's son is dead because why else would Alex be going there and I just hope that Gary doesn't say anything that's going to make D spell it out and then it's too late because Gary opens his mouth and D holds his right fist up by his ear as if tugging on a rope and lets his head flop on one side and his tongue loll out and Gary says, Oh, and shuts up and turns back towards the cooker, though there's nothing cooking, everything we're going to eat is already on the table and Matthew is watching D with a smile on his face, and then he's copying his uncle, his own small fist in the air his own head hanging loosely to one side and D does it again, and Matthew does it again and they both laugh and I say, Stop it! so loudly and so sharply that Matthew jumps and shrinks away and I notice that and know that I have failed to protect him, again. That I have made things worse. Shrinking is a metaphor, it is something people say, not what they actually do, but now the metaphor has come alive and I can understand and see why people say it because watching my son as I snap at D and, if I'm honest, at Matthew too, they were both doing it, it was a game they were both enjoying, and when I shouted I saw Matthew become actually physically *smaller* as well as more uncertain and concerned and I know that I have diminished him. I hug Matthew who is thin and bony and will be tall, like me, like his uncle, like his grandmother, but not his grandfather, when he grows up, and I think, Poor Gina. Poor, poor Gina.

I say it's not surprising Alex is late and we probably shouldn't wait, he might be hours yet, whatever the procedures say, this wasn't one for the procedures and D gives me a funny look and says he never thought he'd hear me say that and maybe breaking rules is getting to be a habit now I've done it once. I don't want anyone to ask or D to say what this means because right now I can't, I really can't get into what has happened and what I have been doing, or not doing, all day, we need to eat the salad Gary's made and get Matthew into bed with a story where nobody dies, a story about a chameleon, perhaps, and to keep pretending that the world is a safe place even though we all know that it isn't. Even Matthew. So I am almost glad when D says that maybe Alex won't get home at all tonight, that maybe he's got lucky, and I can tell him to grow up. He says you never know: a distraught, lonely, single mother, a few glasses of something to take the pain away, a comforting arm around the shoulder . . .

D? Grow up.

I'm only saying. Grief does funny things to people.

I say, How would you know? But of course he knows, and it is a stupid thing to say.

D shrugs. I'm only saying.

Gary sits down at last, and we eat, the four of us.

# 9

THIS MORNING IN the shower I get it. My bright idea. A fucking blinder, if I say so myself. I'm rubbing in conditioner when it comes. I'm in the shower stall, naked and in all my glory, but the water's not on yet. A hairdresser told me once I had fine, fly-away hair. He was definitely a hairdresser, not a barber. I laughed. But afterwards I had to admit he had a point. He said I should rub conditioner in my dry hair every day. My bright idea is not so much an idea as a question, or a question that follows an idea. An insight.

I can hear Rada out on the landing, knocking on the door, asking if it's me in here. I suppose because she can't hear water running, because, like I said, I'm still rubbing the conditioner in, and the water's not running yet. Give me time. Give me time. World enough and time.

Give me a lever and a place to stand. Who said that?

Give me a horse. That was some olden-type fucker. My kingdom for a horse. We read it at school. Out loud, line-by-line. No one wanted to read the women's parts.

Give me a boy under seven and I'll give you the man.

Gimme shelter. Bottom rung of Maslow's hierarchy of needs, along with food and heat and sex and sleep and all that basic biological shit. Including shit.

My point is, Rada's got no business chasing me out of the bathroom this fine Wednesday morning because Rada's got no business getting up at all and not spending the day in bed, sulking and crying and letting Gary rub pongy oils in her back or whatever it is he does, because Rada's got no business. No job. No chance. Nada. Rada has nada. Nada Rada. I chant that to myself for a while, in my head, not aloud, I'm not that stupid. Nada Rada. Rada nada. It's like one of those memory trick things I read about for remembering people's names. Except she's my sister and I don't need to remember. Nada Rada.

It didn't stop her yesterday, though did it? Didn't stop her getting up and eating that horse food she eats and getting on her bike and cycling off to work. Well, not to work, she's got no work. To the bank to poke her nose in where it shouldn't be. It's pretty obvious that's not what she told Gary. I reckon she's kept Gary blissfully unaware of just what's going on all through Monday night and yesterday. And, if she's up this morning, trying to chase me out of the bathroom, then I can only suppose she's planning to keep it up today as well. Which is a bit weird and I can see ending in tears. Boo-hoo. Not that I object to Gary having the wool pulled over his eyes – the dreary fucker has it coming – and I'm not above using my superior knowledge to twist Rada into knots of panic and embarrassment and shame and willingness to do pretty much anything her favourite brother wants. Her only brother, but still. I love my little sister, I really do. I mean, I'm happy she's fucked up, of course, but that's work. It's different. So this isn't any sort of moral qualm, but when I think about Rada and Gary, and Rada not letting Gary in on what's going on and carrying on like nothing's happened, I have to wonder just what exactly the point of that is?

Which wasn't it – my question. My killer question. But it kind of led me to it because it made me think – and this is it, this is the insight – that maybe sense isn't the point after all.

That what matters isn't the what, it's the why, if you follow my drift.

So the question *is*: Why do people do the shit they do? When most of it makes no sense to anyone?

And, more specifically: why did Wenlock pretend no one was killed, or even injured, in the robbery? And why did his deputy, Meersow, make it so easy for me to find out he was lying?

Follow the what and you get all tangled up in other people's stupidity – and, I don't know, maybe I've just been unlucky, but the other people I've come across in my twenty-nine years all seem pretty stupid, one way or another. But maybe if you stop pitying them long enough to get inside, like kind of *inhabit* their stupidity then you'll understand the stupid shit they do. And if you can do that, but still keep enough distance that the shit doesn't seem to start making any kind of sense (because if it does, that's it, you're lost, because there is no fucking sense) – if you can be inside but still also outside at the same time, understand the shit, but still see that it's shit – then, frankly, you're the king, you're the one-eyed man with a huge fuck-off telescope in the country of blind bastards, and they don't stand a chance.

By now Rada's banging on the bathroom door and the conditioner's like glue in my hair, so I turn on the shower and I think: Hold that thought. Come back to it at your leisure, Dmitry-boy, because that thought is going to make you a winner. I wash out the conditioner and I soap my chest and armpits and my crotch and I work up a real lather in the hair there and I think about giving myself a little squeeze, a tug, there, keep Rada waiting even longer while I do it. I think about the woman in the bank, about Rada waiting outside on the landing, but I don't do it because I'm genuinely excited and I want to get going, because this idea's actually bigger than sex.

Down in the kitchen Gary's poured out three bowls of horse food for himself and Rada and poor little Matt and is up to his armpits in a huge bowl of something floury that smells like a pub carpet. Same old, same old. I ruffle Matt's hair and tell him to keep his chin up, this too shall pass, as his granddad used to say, this too shall pass. Matt smiles and Gary gives me kind of a funny look and Matt says, "Hi, Uncle D" and I say, "Hi, and what's that you're having?" Like I don't know.

Matt says, "It's muesli." Only he says it *mooo-sli*, like a cow might, if a cow wandered into the supermarket to do its shopping, and had to ask for its favourite items, because it was unfamiliar with the layout of the various sections, and like I always say it to him. *Mooo-sli.* Chin up, I say again and go to the freezer for one of those pop tarts you put in the toaster and two minutes later you get a small flat grenade of transfats and super-heated sugar that tastes of ICI and early death and burns the skin off the roof of your mouth. When he sees or senses what it is I'm doing, Gary can't stop himself from actually tutting, the tip of his tongue up against the back of his teeth and pulling away with that wet, slappy disapproving sound, and there it is again, the power of my frankly blinding insight. As a culinary experience, eating pop tarts for breakfast is right up there with, say, chewing rats' entrails or gargling hamster piss. There is nothing at all to recommend it except this moment of involuntary disgust that shows just how *disappointed* Gary will be if I actually eat the fucking thing, which of course I will for just this very reason. Now, I can see how, in Gary's eyes, this is not just disgusting but literally incomprehensible. Why would a rational human being put himself through this horror when there are so many healthy and attractive and nutritious alternatives available? But that's because Gary has never for one moment stopped to think *why* I might be doing it in any terms other than the (risible) nutritional benefits involved. He has never once stopped to think that I might eat pop tarts in his kitchen every morning precisely and entirely in order to piss him off. That in a world of abundance and boredom, where a man like me is not going to starve for lack of a few rolled oats, the look on Gary's face and the wet slap of his tongue against his teeth might just be sustenance enough. Which is why Gary is Gary – one of the blind fuckers – and I, thank fuck, am not.

I have my telescope. I am the king.

I eat my pop tart and burn the roof of my mouth and I feel better than I have for days. I don't even think to ask if anyone's seen Alex yet because it's eight o'clock and Alex is never up at eight o'clock and it's not like I miss him.

In the car before I pull away I gun the revs a bit because Gary hates it and Rada's not out on her bike yet and the noise is like fifteen lions roaring in a room and will let her know that today she's lost. Then I tune to the classical station because I've got stuff to think about as I drive and I need to get Gary and Rada and all their petty shit out of my mind and concentrate on the power of my personal insight and what it means precisely, vis-à-vis Wenlock and Meersow and the games they're playing with the bank and the blood and the dead woman, or women. The traffic looks light and all's well, but after the news headlines the radio starts playing Shostakovich, which they've frankly got no right to do, not first thing in the morning. It is no aid to concentration whatsoever. When the book said classical it meant Mozart, basically. Dad used to play Shostakovich all the time, part of his tortured Russian soul act that everybody seemed to love so much. It was a pretty reliable guide to his mood. When he wanted to beat himself up he had a boxed set of string quartets that sounded like four cats in a sack. When he was feeling chipper he'd get out the symphonies, relive the siege of Leningrad or some such bloodcurdling catastrophe. He'd get a huge grin on his tiny Russian face and punch the air in time with the cymbals, and if I made the mistake of letting him spot me creeping past on my way to the door, he'd fling his arms around my shoulders and kiss my cheeks and yell, This music kills fascists! Which even when I was about five I knew it didn't. He would tell me the music was in my blood, that there was a reason he'd called me Dmitry, and this was it. Then he'd start in on my poor dear beautiful dead mother, even though it wasn't my mother who was dead, it was Rada's. I learned to retaliate by telling him Shostakovich was a bourgeois deviant aestheticist, or a self-serving Stalinist lickspittle, whichever I thought would goad him more at the time. All words, naturally, I'd gleaned from Papa himself, and not bad for a seven year-old.

I switch to the CD player while simultaneously changing gear, I am that at home with my machine, but the CD I left in there yesterday is a motivational selling skills thing about getting to yes that came with a book. It's meant to help you practise negotiation techniques by arguing with a cretinous pre-recorded customer who whines pathetic excuses not to buy your product or your services and leaves long gaps for you to persuade him otherwise. Yesterday this seemed like a good idea. When you get bored with actual negotiation, you can practise unfettered Tourette's-style abuse, yelling inventive, outlandish and increasingly obscene curses at the snivelling, turd-eating customer and his Neanderthal company, which is fun and good when you're in the car and the traffic's bad and nobody can hear you. You can threaten to disembowel the little runt and rape his wife and kill all his children right before his eyes and he will still ask if a discount is available, in that imperturbable voice that, now I think about it, sounds a bit like Old Man Theo. And then you really lose it and he's as calm as ever and suddenly you realise he's won. Bastard. You've been outwitted by a mindless recording, and it isn't fun any more. The come down's worse than any hangover, worse than drugs, and I don't need that this morning.

One of the things Dad told me about my poor dear beautiful dead mother, by which he meant Rada's poor dear dead beautiful mother, was that when she died – when her estate agent friend hit a tight bend too fast in his E-type and found a tractor on the other side – the last word on her pale, bloodless lips was: 'Dmitry'. He had a cello concerto on too loud when he told me this and it seemed pretty fucking unlikely to me. Not least because she wasn't my mother and I wasn't even born. I asked him how he knew. He said the estate agent survived the crash and came straight round to pass on the news himself. My father said he couldn't help but recognise the man's courage, the purity of his soul. And so, instead of stabbing the over-privileged moustachio'd nanny's boy on the spot, he had opened a bottle of vodka and together they'd toasted my poor dear dead beautiful mother, ending the long dark night the best of friends, united in their grief and mutual respect. "Oh yeah," I said (or wish I'd said) so where's your best friend now? My father's voice became flatter, business-like. He said, "He died, not long afterwards." I told him he was full of shit, which was wasn't original even if it was true but, even so, probably wouldn't have been the words I'd have chosen if I'd known they were going to be the last I'd ever say to him.

I turn the CD off. Some cunt cuts me up and I have to slam the brakes to avoid wasting my paintwork on the back end of his shoddy Mazda. I put my hand out of the window and give him a finger and the bastard slams his own brakes and actually gets out. I manage to cut out into the right lane and, to the sound of angry horns all over the shop, I accelerate and I'm pretty sure I run right over the guy's foot as I pass him. Maybe it was just a bump in the road, but I like to think it was his foot. I park in the scruffy, potholed building site that passes for the company car park – that's the first thing that's getting sorted when I take over; OK maybe not the *first* – and I realise that I've managed to get all the way in from the nineteenth-century suburbs to the fringes of the twenty-first-century city, not just five miles but two hundred years, without getting round to applying my blinding insight to the question of Wenlock and Meersow and just what the fuck is going on with the dead/undead women and I could have been listening to some decent music after all.

I make a mental note to ring DS Proctorow. It'll be worth a couple of pints or six to find out just how far up the wrong tree the cops are currently barking.

In the office I get up to the third floor and let myself in. I'm the only one here, which is no surprise. I hang up my jacket and boot up my PC and I make a cup of coffee. Then I think I might as well try and clear the decks a bit before I get stuck into the bank thing, because I'm looking forward to that but I'm actually also, if I'm completely honest, just the tiniest bit nervous about it. What if I train my telescope on Wenlock and Meersow and whatever shit it is they think they're up to and there's nothing there?

I'll start with Sister Angelina. I won't even bother reading the file, because, honestly, what am I going to do? The woman's a saint, and not just because she was a nun. The traffic accident guy ditto, though not the same result, naturally. You, my friend, are going down. I don't care how much you gave to disaster relief appeals, how much you loved your wife. I don't care that there was a little St Christopher hanging off the rear-view mirror of your piece-of-shit Mitsubishi 4×4. I find myself saying this aloud while I wait for the PC to do whatever it is that takes a computer so long to do to get going in the morning. I don't care how rich or powerful or fulfilled you were because nothing's going to save you now. Sometimes I love this job, despite all the associated aggravation. You thought your airbags would protect you? Your thought your God would save you? Well, newsflash sucker: God's got no time for wankers like you. Your wife's already shagging someone else and you, my friend, you're going to burn like you were soaked in kerosene.

I'm on a roll. I love it when the office is empty and I can pace around and talk aloud without Rada sniffing or Alex weighing in with some irrelevant hippie crap. Or even Old Man Theo, come to that, strolling through, giving us the benefit of his years of wisdom. I know things are going to change. I can feel it.

But I also know I'm cheating just a little bit. I'm creaming off the easy cases – Rada's cases – and they're the last ones in. The time management lecture I downloaded off TED a couple of weeks ago told me this is not the way. I can't let the caseload silt up while I just skim the surface. I have to take a crack at Likker. My ace in the hole, my get out of jail free card. Likker's the oldest case on my list, and the report will be long and complex. The guy wasn't exactly ancient – seventy-something – but he did a lot of stuff. Some of it was actually, genuinely heroic and totally selfless, most of it was miserable and ordinary, and then some was not even close to the line but way, way the fuck over, so this was never going to be an easy one to call. But I've been working on it. I've done the research and marshalled all my facts. I know where we're going here. The guy, if he only knew it, is my test case. I've assigned all the values and done the calculations for the presentation I was supposed to do on Monday. I have the answer. I've even tweaked it just a fraction, by way of thanks. He's doing me a favour, after all. Now it's just a matter of getting it down straight on paper.

I take a memory stick out of the inside pocket of my suit jacket, the pocket that's designed for a mobile phone, and I stick it in the port on the side of my monitor. Normally I put all my stuff on the server like we're supposed to and only use the stick for back up or when I need to carry things around, like for Monday's presentation. But I've been working on this at home, and, besides, I wasn't going to put Likker on the server because Likker's too important. I'm pretty sure Alex has spotted the fact that I've been up to something better than the usual pieces of shit. He's had that look in his eye, the one he gets when he's enjoying the contents of his own head, and frankly I don't trust the little fucker not to find his way into my files somehow and dick about with them.

The PC's finally brushed its teeth and swallowed its espresso or whatever the fuck it is it does, and it's asking me for a password. I type Al5x1saTwaT (a strong alpha-numeric mixed upper/lower case combination I can nonetheless remember) and it tells me the password is incorrect. I type it again carefully, checking the cases, and it tells me I'm wrong, even though I know I'm not. One more try and the bastard's going to lock me out for ever.

Could Alex have tampered with it? I don't think so. It's probably not beyond him, technically. Or morally. He comes over as a dozy parasite who couldn't organise a cheese sandwich, but he's sneaky and he's not actually stupid. It's just hard to see the point of him. But the fact is, I don't think he's had the chance: I was here when he went off to see Rodkin's flat and the Spence woman, and he wasn't planning on coming back to the office after that.

I take a deep breath and I try the password again. It tells me I'm still wrong and this time it throws in a cheery message to let me know my time's up and it's locked itself down for all eternity. I think this must be how some of my clients feel. Like the traffic guy. Except it's not my fault. I'm not a twat who drives a rubbish car into a line of school kids, and that makes all the difference.

I close my eyes and breathe deeply, five times, in through the nose, out through the mouth. This is not hippie bullshit. This works. When I am calm and focused I turn the PC off and turn it back on again. While it re-boots, I pick up the phone and leave a message telling Proctorow we should meet. When the PC's good and ready I sign in as Rada, whose offspring/birthdate-based passwords are criminally easy to predict. After three failed attempts I go through the whole switching off and on again routine and log on as Theo, who rarely uses a computer and whose password is written on a faded Post-it stuck to his screen. Miraculously, the machine lets me in. But, when I click on Sister Angelina it says: Access Denied. I switch to the traffic guy: Access Denied. Bridget Miller, a woman I'd written up a week ago who's husband persuaded her to stop taking her pills and jump off a bridge with him and both their children, and who I'd gone pretty easy on because (a) the kids survived, and (b) she'd had a shit time all her life, with a dad and a husband who both hit her, and who were both definitely going down, and (c) despite the depression and the drugs and the kids she was frankly gorgeous, there was something about her eyes and her mouth and, I don't know why, even her *ears* – which I know sounds insane, but is true, anyway – that made me think I could love this woman, that she could make me really happy, as well as fuck my brains out like a crazy person, if she weren't dead. Anyway, Bridget Miller: Access Denied. Henry Perowne (cancer, inoperable; tedious piece of shit): Access Denied. Pyotr Kalenkov (my father, who's definitely not in heaven): Access Denied.

Something, somebody – the *system*, as we say these days

when we mean computers, and not the whole military-industrial capitalist complex thing my dad would have meant – the *system* has locked everything down.

I try one last time.

Edward Likker: Access Fucking Denied.

I punch the screen and even as I do it I realise I'm expecting broken glass and maybe even a bit of blood, but that's not going to happen because the screen's a flexible, LCD job and all my punch does is send the pixels a bit screwy for a while. I'm wondering if I should just yank the cables out of the tower and chuck the fucking thing out onto the railway track, knowing I won't, because if I'm wondering about it, it's already too late – if I was going to do it I'd have done it – when a quiet voice behind me says: "Have you tried Password?"

I jump, and the hairs on the back of my neck do that thing they're supposed to do in ghost stories, but turns out to be literally true when you think you've seen, or at any rate, heard, a ghost. They stand up as a rush of pure adrenaline floods past in the wrong direction, out of my back and arms and shoulders and up through my neck into my brain.

"I'm sorry. Did I startle you?"

I turn and there's this little old guy standing over by Rada's desk. Not as old as Theo, obviously, not quite, but old enough. He's got a face like a disappointed Labrador and a suit that might have come from Theo's tailor. He's got a walking stick a bit like Theo's, too, except it's longer and has a silver eagle on top, where Theo's has a dog. The eagle's wings are spread and make the kind of V you can put your thumb in and push yourself up on when you're walking uphill. His hands are crossed on top of the stick and they're old man's hands: the skin sags around every bone, every vein, turning them into a relief map of the guy's life.

I say, "Who the fuck are you?"

He walks towards me, holding out one of those leathery paws.

"My name is Lopez."

His grip is firm and his eyes are clear and sharp and fixed on mine.

"You're Lopez?"

He nods, and there's a trace of a bow in the way he does it. I get a sense of old world – of the sort you mostly only get in the New World. Like Lopez isn't Spanish but maybe from Paraguay or Argentina or some gaucho/Nazi bolthole dump like that. His hair is white and there are lines in his face – not just the usual lines, but deep nearly vertical creases in his forehead where the bushy old guy eyebrows meet the top of his nose. There are more creases down beside his mouth. Creases you could abseil into.

I say, "Riverside House sent you?"

He shrugs and spreads his hands, one still holding the stick by the silver eagle.

"I am here."

"Or did Theo call you in?"

He sidesteps the question like I know he's going to. He says, "You were expecting someone younger?"

There's no point denying it, so I don't.

He smiles like one of those teachers who never get angry whatever stupid shit you do, but somehow manage to be *disappointed*.

"You understand why I am here?"

"Because Theo asked you to come?"

"Perhaps."

"Or because Riverside House sent you?"

"Perhaps."

"Only there's a difference."

He takes the time to show he's disappointed again, then says, "There may be."

There may be? There may be a chance I punch the fucker right here. I breathe and count. I say nothing, see how he likes it.

After a while he shrugs and says, "I am here, that is what matters."

"To bury my sister."

He doesn't deny it. "And naturally that troubles you?"

"Actually, no."

It's true, that's not what bothers me. What bothers me is that he's just so fucking *old*. I mean, I don't care what actual age he is, but it pisses me off that he's here, all suited up and talking that old man gnomic bollocks and won't answer a straight fucking question. He's basically Theo with bigger eyebrows and he's everything that's wrong with this place. Everything I'm going to change.

"Perhaps," he says again.

Perhaps, I think, I'll take that fucking walking stick and disembowel you with it, but I don't. Instead, I wait until he turns away and I pull the memory stick out of the port. My PC makes that sickening clunk/ping noise that tells me I've done something wrong, but I don't care. I slip the stick back into my jacket pocket and ask Lopez if he'd like a coffee.

# 10

It is a long time since I went to bed so early. Or woke so early, for that matter, if it is early. Usually, when I go to bed, I let the radio trickle war and crisis and calamity and weather into my ear, and I am thankful for the distraction. I resist bed, I resist sleep, I resist the end of the day and the little death that follows because at night, when I have at least the illusion of choice, life seems like something it might be worth clinging on to, I don't know why. It rarely appears that way in the morning. In the morning it is all up and at 'em, shake a leg, the sun's scorching your eyeballs out, shake a leg, shake a leg. It is Gary's homemade muesli and D's poptarts and little Matthew getting ready for school. I hear it all from my bed and I let them go. Rada means "hope". She told me that, once, I think. Or Gary did. Anyway, it is more than I can bear in the morning.

The light here is thin, grey, like water you have washed dishes in. Crepuscular, I believe the word is. It is not capable of scorching my eyeballs. It must be morning, though, unless it is evening. How might I tell the difference? When I came here it was day. It was afternoon. I know that much. I believe it was Tuesday. And now it is day again. Unless it is the same day? No, I am certain that it has been dark, and now it is light. On the first day God divided the light from the dark. It must have been the first day. How could it have been otherwise? He had no choice, once he'd thought of it. That was his first mistake. It's gone on much the same way ever since.

How do I know it's early? There are no clocks here, no radio or television. When Kurt left he took my watch, and my mobile phone. If his name is Kurt – he did not deny it, but he did not confirm it, either. It is light, however, and I believe it was the light that woke me, thin as it is. There are no curtains or blinds here to mislead the senses. The window above the bed is barred and half-submerged; it is also filthy. But from the rear glass door that Kurt led me through last night (you see how these certainties build, one upon another, standing on the shoulders of giants?) and, better still, through the kitchen window beside it, I can see the garden full of weeds, although I cannot see the blue flowers, which must have closed, or died. Outside, there are no shadows, or perhaps it is all shadow. I can see the gnome. The little sky that I can see has no colour. Dawn, then, or thereabouts. And when I came here it was June, very nearly July. The solstice was not long past. Druids had recently featured in the newspapers. Dawn must therefore be early, before five, I expect. Quod erat demonstrandum. Which was to be proved; or assumed.

It is still possible that it is late, that I have slept all day, and this is my second evening here. Or even, that I have not slept at all, or no more than fleetingly, and this is still the first evening. But I discount this possibility. As I say, I am certain that it has been dark, or as dark as it gets in a city of this size; and I am certain that I have slept. How can I be so sure? Because the first time I awoke I could not see. I could smell something fried in cheap and unclean oil, but that told me nothing. It was not a new odour, not current; it had seeped into the fabric of the building. I held my nose and opened my eyes. There was a faint sodium glow to indicate the whereabouts of the door to the kitchen, and the grime on the window above the bed pulsed pale orange, but it was not sufficient for me to make out detail. I could not, for example, tell myself how many fingers I was holding up on my right hand. The left hand was a different story. There was no possibility of holding up any fingers whatsoever of my left hand. It – the whole left arm, in fact – lay stretched above my head – a position in which I am not aware of ever having slept. "Stretched" might be the wrong word. It seems to suggest liveliness, a lithe vibrancy, albeit in abeyance: a cat might stretch before it curls and yawns or springs to its paws absolutely alive. A man might be stretched upon a rack, I suppose – or might once have been, the literature suggests the practice has fallen into disuse – but only so long as he is alive. If he fails to confess or to recant before the rack is tightened one notch beyond what he is capable of withstanding, his broken corpse is laid, not stretched, upon the bier. Even stretchers are generally reserved for the wounded, the quick, or at least the not yet dead. In any case the arm lay inert on the bed, beside and above my head, like a small, dense bolster. I should say *my* arm. There is no one else here to claim ownership. But it did not *feel* like my arm. When I touched it – gently at first, then frankly prodding – with the fingers of my right hand, it felt solid: cool and dense and rubbery like some primitive form of deep-sea life that has washed up on the shore. The sensation was all in the exploratory, dextrous fingertips. In the sinister arm itself – I use the term for its technical meaning – no sensation was triggered. At least, none reached my brain. I thought about moving it – it is not often one has to think about moving a limb, they generally seem to do it by themselves, although of course that is a cognitive illusion bred by over-familiarity – but it proved impossible. I could no more move my arm in the conventional manner – that of thinking idly that my knee, say, itched, and might usefully be scratched, only to witness my arm rise and the fingers of my hand curl; of willing locomotion and it being so; of the thought being the father of the deed, so to speak – than I could have moved the bed on which it lay without having to get up, put my weight behind it and heroically shove. So it was with the arm. With my right hand I reached up above my head, took firm hold of the lifeless wrist and hauled. The effort required was considerable. Life – in the form of a dull ache – returned slowly to my shoulder. With my right arm alone I levered myself into a sitting position. In time the pain spread from the shoulder down to the fingers of my left hand. When the pain receded and the power of analysis returned, I concluded that I had been asleep some while – hours seemed clearly indicated – and that the circulation of blood to my left arm had somehow been suspended for a significant portion of that time. I thought I might examine the recovered limb for signs of lasting damage, but it was still too dark to see. And quiet. Not silent, mind you, despite the cork. I was comforted to hear the faint thrum of distant traffic that never quite dies in a city of this size. Strange comfort. It means only that people are passing, possibly in both directions, no less unaware than ever of my situation, my predicament; that nothing much, in short, has changed. Which, after all, is the only comfort there is. I must have slept again, because I do not remember sitting in the dark until the light came, and yet it is light now. So there you have it. Time has passed; it has been dark; I have slept. We are into the second day, at least.

The possibility remains that it is now the evening of the second day – or even some subsequent day – but I do not believe it. For one thing it is cool, too cool for evening at this time of year. I recall that when I came here it was hot, and humid. Unpleasant. It was the day when outsized ants like ripe winged blackcurrants crawl fatly around the pavements. There is such a day each year, sometimes two or three. I presume the ants are capable of flight, given the existence of their wings, but they rarely seem to take to the air, preferring instead to congregate about the cracks of paving stones until they are trodden on by pedestrians at some point in the afternoon of their first and only day on earth. As a lifecycle it has much to recommend it. There is little opportunity for repetition, or boredom. It may have rained in the night, in the dark, or almost dark, but if it did, I did not hear it. It was not raining when I woke and wrestled with my lifeless arm, I am sure of that. That is to say, I did not hear – or did not notice – the sound of rain, whereas I did, you will recall, hear and notice the sound of traffic. It is not that I am deaf. But the weeds outside look wet, and it is cooler than it was. I suppose it could be dew.

Dew!

It is morning, there is no doubt about it. Or not much. I came here yesterday. Kurt charged me £50 and showed me in. The woman called him Kurt, didn't she? He stood between me and the knives on the kitchen wall and demanded my wallet, my watch and my mobile phone. I gave them to him, seeing no alternative. This was yesterday. I have spent the night here. It is Wednesday morning and I am up betimes and ready for my breakfast. I cannot remember when I was last up this early, although I have sometimes been up this late, which is a different matter altogether. I would like a cigarette and, to my surprise, I find the packet in my jacket pocket is not empty, that it is, in fact, half full. Or nearly so. But I have no lighter. I am sure I had a lighter yesterday, an old-fashioned steel contraption Rada gave me that burned petrol and had the words "Smoking Kills" engraved on either side. I have had that lighter for many years and now I seem to have mislaid it. I will ask Kurt whether he has seen it. If he has not, I will ask him for matches. I notice that I am assuming not only that he is called Kurt – the woman talked about a Kurt, but not when he was there, and I may have mistaken this man, my captor, for Kurt – but that

Kurt will come. There is no reason for me to assume this. As far as I recall, he said nothing about returning, but it seems to me implicit in the situation. To be honest, I am also assuming that he will bring breakfast, although he did not bring supper. I am hungry. The condemned man requires a hearty breakfast. Or should at least be offered one. I could eat bacon now, and eggs and black pudding and even kidneys. It is a long time since I ate kidneys for breakfast – a long time here implying years, possibly decades, rather than hours or days. Rada is not keen on offal, Gary even less so, though I can't think why, kidneys being both cheap and nutritious, and if they taste at all of urine, that's nothing to be scared of. I would have thought Gary would approve of kidneys, of liver and heart and possibly even brains and tripe. I would not know where to buy tripe. Kurt will not bring kidneys, I know that, but I imagine he may bring bread. He may have toasted it.

Is dew even possible in the city? In June? (Or July?)

I am hungry but I am not tired. I slept – apart from the incident with the lifeless limb which, in reality, was soon enough rectified – the sleep of the just, a fact which now, here, in a locked basement with the prospect of starvation or worse (if there is worse) looming, surprises me, but which seemed natural enough at the time.

When Kurt left with my few possessions – did he take my cigarette lighter? I do not recall him doing so – it did not take me long to explore my new environment. There was not much to see. The kitchen is small, not big enough for a table or chairs, just a sink, a fridge, a cooker and two rows of built-in cupboards of the sort where the drawers stick and the doors hang just off square. The fridge was empty of everything except ice. It smelled of wet towels left too long in a plastic holdall. The cupboards were empty, too. In the sink a block of white stone about fifteen centimetres long by six centimetres wide sat submerged in cold water. I tried to pick it up and found it heavier than I expected. I stood it on one end, still in the water. The underside was a dull pink-orange, a colour that, if it were paint, might be called terracotta. I had seen something like it before, I knew, years ago: I was a child. I trawled my vocabulary and dredged up: whetstone. I wondered if this could be right. It seemed too literal, simpleminded. It was a stone, and it was wet. But the 'h' made all the difference. It was the 'h' that told me I might be right. Not that it mattered. To 'whet' is to sharpen. Apart from stones, however, it seems only to be applied to appetites, (although knives can be put to other uses). As I am sure I mentioned, there was, there is, a magnetic rack of knives fixed to the wall – a carving knife, a boning knife, items of that sort, I am no expert – but no breadknife. I believe I mentioned that, too. The knives were clean and, when I tested the edge of one or two, sharp. There was nothing else to detain me in the kitchen. Whatever brought Rodkin here, he had left few traces. I decided to explore the rest of his domain. It was not really a decision. What else was there for me to do? Immediately adjacent to the kitchen I found a tiny shower room. When I pulled the cord to turn on the light a fan with a faulty bearing clattered into life. When I turned the light off the noise continued, like heavy-booted soldiers kicking through mounds of dry bones in the dark. I turned the light back on. In the shower I found an almost empty bottle of shampoo and a bar of soap that was dry and had a hair stuck to it. The hair was red, or at any rate not black, and too long to be pubic. I suppose these are the small mercies for which we must be thankful. The only other room is the one I currently occupy, the one with the bed. It is large: a mostly empty space inadequately illuminated by the semi-subterranean bay window I had observed from outside. There were, as I have said, no curtains or blinds, but the window itself is barred and caked in grime. The walls of this room are covered from skirting board to ceiling in cork tiles of about thirty centimetres square. I remember similar tiles on the floor and the side of the bath in the house my father left. My mother maintained they had been fashionable during the 1970s. The ones in our bathroom had not been properly sealed; water seeped into the cracks, causing some of them to swell differentially and become detached no matter how much adhesive my mother injected into the gaps between the now misshapen cork and the floor or bath panel beneath. I recall that the temptation to pick at the exposed edges was irresistible. No matter what sanction or retribution my mother threatened, I would lie in the bath detaching crumbs of cork as if unconsciously; I would float them in the water, setting up races, regattas and, once, recreating Nelson's daring manoeuvre at Trafalgar. The tiles in Rodkin's basement room are swollen only in the bay below the window where damp has penetrated from the wet clay and cancerous cement outside, but the remaining walls are pockmarked and cratered and studded with drawing pins. I envisage Rodkin – and Rodkin's predecessors; this is unlikely to have been the work of one man – lying in bed or standing by the wardrobe, picking idly at the tiles, flicking the crumbs of cork into ever-growing piles in the corners of the room. The dangers of imagination: there was no wardrobe in the room; at least, there is no wardrobe now. It is always possible that it was removed along with the cadaver and the rest of Rodkin's effects.

(I assume there were more belongings here when Rodkin was in residence; clothes, of course, but also newspapers, hairbrushes, correspondence, alarm clocks, books, quite possibly trinkets and ornaments, shelves or boxes or cases to put things on or in. However poor you are, it is hard to live without a certain quantity of stuff accumulating about the place. Without detritus.) In addition to the irregularities caused by picking and peeling fingers, there are several lighter patches on the cork walls. These are mostly oblong, and higher than they are wide. I presume they mark the places where pictures, or notices of some sort, have been pinned for long enough that even the weak light of this place could mark their presence, before they were removed, with one exception. By the door to (or from) the hallway a large sheet of poor quality off-white paper of the sort often found on office flipcharts remains fixed to the wall by a number of irregularly placed brass pins. Written on the paper in thick black marker pen are words I know well: *I am full of the burnt offerings of rams and the fat of fed beasts; and I delight not in the blood of bullocks, or of lambs, or of he-goats*. I am hungry. I am not full and would delight considerably in the fat of fed beasts. I have never to my knowledge eaten he-goat, but I'd be willing to try, if it were offered.

It was still light when I went to bed, having nothing else to do. That means little, of course. At this time of year it is light all evening and, indeed, well into the hours that, in other seasons, we would unthinkingly describe as 'night'. I say *I went to bed*, as if it were the most natural thing in the world, but here there were none of the usual preliminaries. I had no toothbrush, no flannel, no comb, and no pyjamas. There are no sheets or duvets or blankets, or even pillows, just a bare mattress on a plain metal frame. Bare? To be fair the mattress is elaborately decorated, a palimpsest of previous tenants' bodily secretions. It must have pre-dated Rodkin's relatively brief tenure. Like the intricately pecked cork I cannot believe this to be the work of one man. No single body could have secreted that much fluid without shrinking and curling, like a leaf in autumn. A novel form of suicide, perhaps, but not the one Rodkin chose. I lay down fully clothed – no, I remember now, I took off my jacket and trainers – the jacket is there, hanging on the only chair, the trainers beside it – and listened to the sounds drifting to me through the summer air. Traffic, mostly; sirens; occasional voices, speaking in languages or accents I could not understand at this remove. Later there was music from upstairs, and footsteps. The music was familiar without being recognisable. I imagined the woman who had answered the door now padding about above my ceiling – I recall I thought of it as my ceiling; how quickly we accommodate ourselves! – cooking, perhaps, washing up, trying to persuade Kurt to dance. Did Kurt live upstairs? As a child I would lie like this in summer, unable to sleep, with the sound of older children playing outside in the light warm liberated evenings, and of TV programmes I was too young to watch, drifting through my open window like exhaust fumes filling a car parked in the garage with the engine running. I imagined the woman and Kurt together, in a bed, above me. She was so small and scrawny, and he was so big, it was not an easy or a comfortable picture, but I managed it, mainly to give myself something to do. And because I thought I might want to masturbate. I didn't, though. In the end I must have gone to sleep early because what else could I have done?

Kurt has returned. I knew he would; or believed he would, at least. When we say *I knew* we are always right because we have the benefit of hindsight. He has brought me breakfast on a tray, like my mother used to do when I was ill. Or like hotel room service, to be less emotive. He does not take my temperature, or ask me how I slept. He places the tray on the small table in the middle of the room – did I mention that there is a table? – and stands back, allowing me to sit in the only chair. He waits, evidently intending to watch me eat. He has brought a bowl of cereal, some toast and a mug of tea. On the side of the mug are the words *World's Greatest Dad*. I wonder if the mug is his, or Rodkin's. The tea is sugared. I have not drunk tea with sugar since I was a child, but I am thirsty and I drink this tea. The toast is cold, the margarine is roughly spread and only partly melted – there is no beasts' fat offered. But I am grateful for the sustenance. I say, Thank you, Kurt. I ask if he has my cigarette lighter. And, if so, whether he would mind returning it to me, or at least lighting a cigarette. But Kurt does not reply, not even to confirm or deny that he is in fact Kurt. He stands by the door, obscuring the words of Isaiah, his arms crossed over his substantial belly, his head tipped back on its thick neck, leaning against the pockmarked cork behind. When I have eaten everything he has brought, he heaves himself away from the wall and steps forward to take the tray. He has not spoken a word and I cannot let him go without some intercourse. It seems unnatural. I am not a man who has always to be talking. Sometimes I have sat with Rada for hours while she read, or worked, and not felt the need to speak, I am comfortable in silence. But not now. Now I have to hear something from this man, if only a forecast of the weather. I say, What happens next? He pauses, the empty mug in his hand half way back to the tray. He puts the mug down and says, It all depends, Mr Lopez. Without thinking I say, My name's not Lopez.

It isn't Pitt, though, is it, Mr Loss Adjuster?

I have to admit he has me there, Pitt being the name I had given him, the name on the card, although of course, I don't admit it. Not aloud. Instead I say, How long does this take? And he says it is up to me. He picks up the tray and leaves. I stay sitting at the table, because there does not seem to be anything else to do.

I have never met Lopez, know nothing about him beyond his reputation. Kurt can't have met him, either, that much is obvious, or he couldn't have mistaken me for him. But that isn't the point. Kurt knows *about* Lopez. He connected Lopez to me, because I said I was Pitt, that I was a loss adjuster. Unless I simply look like Lopez? It is just possible. There are cases, I believe. Unrelated people who look uncannily alike. But surely someone would have mentioned it before now? Theo would have said something. Unless Theo has not met Lopez, either? Ridiculous. Theo has been around since long before the Ark. He and Lopez would have met at Riverside House. There are others, too. Old timers like Jackson and Rivers. I have never met Jackson, either. Or Rivers. It is a big company; I can't expect to meet everybody. Not even the bigwigs. Especially not the biggest wigs, the originators, the people whose idea the Office was and whose exploits form our founding myths. Jackson and Rivers – and Lopez – have no time for me. They have bigger fish to fry. Why does Kurt think I'm Lopez? Because I am a loss adjuster. Which means that he knows that Lopez is a loss adjuster, too, and that he was expecting him. But how has Kurt even *heard* of Lopez?

The answer must be Rodkin, but it is not much of an answer.

I stand up. The view doesn't improve, and I sit down again. The chair is hard, plain wood. Hanging from the back of the chair, the collar of my jacket is creased where I have leaned against it. It is easy to say I don't care, but I don't. Actually, it is not always easy. Not caring – about jackets, obviously, but about other, larger things, too – has been the closest I have come to aspiration. I crave disinterest. Is that a joke? An oxymoron? I hope not, but hope is one of the things I seek to do without. That and aspiration.

When I met Rada . . . what? What has that to do with anything?

If Rodkin slit his throat there must be blood somewhere here, however thoroughly it has been cleaned. Some stain in the carpet or on the cork tiles to mark his passage. I stand up. I lift the small table and carry it across the room. I place it upside down on the bed, and then put the chair on top of it. I have cleared as much of the floor as I can. I walk to the corner furthest from the door, the corner to the right of the bay window, and I get down on my knees. I begin to examine the carpet, one square at a time, moving right to left across the room. I find several stains, some of which may be blood, but they are old and dark: ingrained – almost part of the fabric of the carpet. When I reach the bed, I turn, and work my way back from left to right. If I move the bed now I will only have to move it back again. And if I keep moving things backwards and forwards every time I cross the room, there is always the chance that I will make a mistake, and miss a patch. Even if I don't, there will have been that chance, and I will never know whether I have looked everywhere. No, my plan is to examine everywhere else, and then to move the bed. That way I can be sure. Back by the wall to the right of the window – if you are facing the window – I find a small hole in the skirting. Actually, it is more of a gap. For ten centimetres there is no skirting, just rough lime plaster painted the same shade of tangerine as the woodwork to either side. Perhaps it had been cut out to accommodate some piping, or box work around piping, long since removed? The hole is in the centre of the gap, at the lower edge where the wall meets the floor. The edges of the hole are coarse-grained and irregular. It is just big enough to put two fingers through together, if one wanted, but no more. I decide not to. It is probably some rodent's home. If Kurt brings me an apple for my lunch – I am sure Kurt will return with lunch – I will leave the core by the hole, and observe what happens. I may make a companion in my incarceration. Kurt may even bring cheese. Hope springs eternal – the bastard. I return to my scrutiny of the carpet, but I am not much more than two-thirds through – not even counting the area under the bed – before

I give in. I stand up, feeling suddenly giddy from the change in altitude. There is no doubt that Rodkin's blood was spilled; finding it will make no difference. I am a loss adjuster, not a forensic scientist. The fact of Rodkin's death is not in dispute; the manner of it may have some bearing on my recommendation, but the position or the pattern of the stains is irrelevant. I lift the chair from the bed and put it back where it was, then do the same with the table. Then I sit down.

## 11

THE TROUBLE WITH corruption is that you have to corrupt someone, and then they know. From the moment the envelope crosses the table, the moment the promotion goes to the man who doesn't deserve it, from the first scratch on the back that comes with a promissory note, from that first moment you and he are in this thing together, bound closer than any marriage. You might appear to hold the power. You might have the money or the patronage he seeks, but, from the moment you grant his wish, he knows what you have done. He has seen who you are, and that is never comfortable.

I was about to use half a million pounds of other people's money to buy a name. Put that way it sounds ridiculous: extravagant, exorbitant. But perhaps Gerald was right. Perhaps we really did need to complete the digital security project, given all the time and money we had sunk in it already. Given that it might stop people doing what I'd just had Gerald do. Perhaps. It would mean cuts elsewhere, more redundancies down the line, but perhaps it would be money well spent anyway. Who knows? The fact is, when it is all over, when a career is done, nobody looks back and adds these things up for you.

When I asked, Gerald didn't bat an eyelid. At least, I don't imagine he did: on the telephone it was hard to be sure. Certainly, he did not hesitate, or make the mistake of asking why

I wanted to know. We both knew that was not a question I would have answered.

Now, on Wednesday morning, I stood by the window, looking at the view I was going to lose the following day. Karen stuck her head around the door to say that Gerald's PA said he was working on it and would two this pm be OK? I was disappointed but it would have to do. There was no real urgency.

"Oh, and DI Jenks is outside."

"Bernie?"

"I know. It's not a network meeting. Shall I get rid of him?"

Bernie, Moody and I had agreed from the start that we would only meet for scheduled Losers' Groups. It wasn't as if we were friends, or even colleagues. As far as the rest of the force was concerned, we were simply people thrown together by the casual brutality of Human Resources. But I was leaving the next day: nobody was watching what I did now. Nobody was interested.

"Send him in."

Karen was surprised, but she wasn't going to let it worry her. She showed Bernie in without using his rank again, without a word, in fact, just a nod of the head.

Bernie looked worse than usual. Even when he laughed – even when he was celebrating our first haul, throwing fistfuls of tens and twenties at Moody, even when he was bitching about her to me afterwards, about how she was actually a bit scary – he always had something of the depressed and elderly Basset hound about him. That's just the way Bernie was, and I never thought it meant too much. But now he looked worse, as if since yesterday he'd had far too much whisky and too little sleep, and what sleep he'd had was on a park bench. His beard was more matted than ever in the places where it grew thickly; more ragged where it didn't. Yesterday he'd been chortling in his joy because we hadn't killed anybody after all, and now he wasn't.

I said, "What is it, Bernie?"

He crossed the room and planted himself wordlessly in a chair in front of my desk. He sank his face in his hands. I turned from the window to sit in my own chair, bringing myself down to Bernie's level.

Bernie lowered his hands and raised his face. The rims of his eyes were red, the pouches beneath them dark and heavy. He said, "She was lying."

"Who was?"

"Moody. Detective Constable Rachel Moody. She lied to us. When she said nobody was dead."

He meant in the bank, of course. There were dead people everywhere, all the time. People die. He meant the woman in the bank.

"How do you know this?"

"Proctorow told me."

There was no reason I should know the name, but I felt a faint tug of recognition. The force employed fifty thousand people, one way or another. But the name Proctorow meant something.

Bernie said, "He was my DS on the thing that went all tits-up and got me shoved into HR. I picked him for that job. He could have been a good detective."

I remembered the case. There'd been a lot of talk about it at the time. Bernie had taken the fall. Proctorow had been pushed off murders, but the consensus was he was lucky to have a job at all.

Bernie said, "Bob Proctorow did most of the work, got us onto the guy in the first place."

"The one who got off on appeal?"

Bernie gave me the look again, the one that said I wouldn't understand. "The one with friends."

I managed not to laugh. "In high places?"

Bernie nodded. He wasn't laughing.

"How high?"

"Guess."

Bernie was never going to accept that he might have caught the wrong man. I decided I might as well call his bluff. "The Commissioner?"

"Higher."

I shook my head. There was no one higher than the commissioner.

Bernie said, "Your boss."

This time I did laugh. I couldn't help it. "*Angela?*"

Bernie was still serious. "It was before her time."

I thought about that for a moment. "You mean Eddie?"

Bernie said nothing.

Eddie Likker wasn't a policeman. He was an accountant. Like me. Only better, obviously. It was Likker who gave me a job, Likker who promoted me. I might say he was like a father to me, but it was better than that: I liked Eddie. My father wanted me to find a job I loved. Eddie would have laughed at that. He said you did what you had to: love didn't come into it. He'd retired three years ago; he died last month. At his funeral there was no room to stand, let alone sit down.

I said, "What's Eddie got to do with Moody?"

"He had a lot of friends."

"He was a good man. A lot of people liked him."

"I don't know about good. And nobody liked him. They owed him. There's a difference."

I couldn't agree, but I didn't want to argue the point.

"Proctorow owed him. After we arrested our man, Likker turned up in our incident room. Some bollocks about seeing how the latest efficiency measures were playing out on the ground. He took Proctorow aside, and by the time he left,

Proctorow wasn't so sure our man was the one. But the pressure was on from the Commissioner, so we charged him anyway."

"I still can't see what this has to do with Moody and the woman at the bank."

"I'm getting there. When the guy gets convicted, the Commissioner himself comes down, pats me on the back, tells Proctorow he's heard good things. But when the appeal goes through, the Commissioner's nowhere to be seen. There's an internal investigation and they announce they want someone who knows the force but isn't a serving police officer to chair it. And guess who that might be? Likker. Proctorow's moved sideways, off murders; I get canned. I knew I'd take most of the blame, but I still expected to be a detective."

"Bernie . . ."

"I'd rather they'd just sacked me."

"Well now you've got your wish."

He looked startled for a moment, as if I'd slapped him. He said, "When I left here yesterday I went for a drink. You know, to celebrate? The woman not being dead and everything?"

I nodded, but said nothing. Wherever Bernie was going with all this, I didn't want to distract him from getting there.

"Proctorow was in the pub. He comes over all full of himself and top of the world and won't I let him buy me a drink? And when I ask why, he says he's finally back with the stiffs. I ask how come, and he says Monday afternoon he turned up to a minor bank robbery – a piece of shit, he says; who bothers to rob banks these days? – only to find blood all over the walls and the bodies all piled up next door."

"Bodies?"

"That's what he said."

"Not 'body'?"

"He definitely said bodies. Two."

"Two's not a pile."

"He was rubbing it in. They're letting him keep the case and he couldn't be happier."

I thought for a moment. "He didn't say women?"

Bernie scratched his beard. "He said bodies."

"Then . . ."

"I didn't get too inquisitive, Bill. He'd come to gloat. He's made it back to the Promised Land. It wouldn't have looked right."

"But you're sure it's our bank?"

Bernie looked up, giving me that stare again. "How many banks in this city do you think get robbed in a day?"

I actually had no idea. We didn't keep the statistics that way – bank robberies were lost amongst all the other business crimes.

Bernie said, "Bugger all, that's how many."

The FBI are better at this. There's about fifteen bank robberies a day in the US. It's a bigger country, of course, with more banks and more guns. They break the stats down all ways, including by the total loot they took. They actually use the word *loot*; I find this obscurely reassuring, but the statistic itself is less than encouraging. In all the bank robberies in all the states of the union in the Year of Our Lord 2013, the average haul was less than $8,000. Hardly worth the bother. It made our twenty grand sterling look like the riches of Croesus. Then again, as Willie Sutton said, it never was about the money.

Bernie said, "Two bodies."

"But we heard the woman screaming, and then Moody's shot . . ." And then nothing.

"I've been thinking about this," Bernie said. "All night. Most of the night. When I wasn't thinking about strangling Moody. She must have found one woman dead, the other screaming. And then shot her."

"For screaming?"

I thought: just like she said.

I thought: never trust a rhetorical question.

If I'd been a detective, they'd have taught me that.

Bernie pressed both hands down flat on the top of the desk, thumbs and forefingers forming a diamond. "So she lied."

It looked like he was right.

"And now we'll be done for murder."

"Only if they catch us, Bernie."

He pushed himself up, out of the chair. "Proctorow's going to work this case to death. It's his ticket back."

I tried to reassure him. I said Proctorow would get somebody, but there was no reason to suppose it would be us.

"He thinks you're a Loser, Bernie, not a bank robber."

"Thanks."

He stopped thinking about getting caught, and started thinking more about what we'd done. He sat down again.

"Two women. We killed them, Bill. You said we never would, but we did. We shot them dead."

"You didn't shoot anybody, Bernie."

He made a sound somewhere between a laugh and a cough. "That's right. You did."

I closed my eyes. I saw the interview room at the bank, the fresh paint on the wall, the Deputy Manager's face smiling and winking.

Bernie said, "And Moody did."

I nodded.

"And she left her balaclava there."

He was right.

"And then she lied to us. What are we going to do about her, Bill?"

I had no idea.

"What, Bill?"

I told him I didn't know. I said I'd think about it, but not now. I said I had a meeting, and I had to go. It wasn't true, and Bernie knew it, but he said OK anyway, and he got up and left. He just wanted to be told what to do.

I checked my diary, pointlessly. There was nothing in it before 2.00pm, when I was meeting Gerald Pryor to give him half a million pounds in return for the name of the man who watched it all and wouldn't lie down. I wondered if I still wanted to know, how much difference it would make. It was only half-past ten.

When I'd given Bernie long enough to get back to his own floor, I stepped out of my office and told Karen I was going out.

"If anyone rings, I'll be back before two. Or you can get me on the mobile."

Tomorrow I'd leave for good: no one was going to ring.

Karen said, "Have fun."

I took the lift to the ground floor. When the doors opened Peter Thomson was standing there, waiting to get in. He had papers in one hand and held the doors open awkwardly and said, "If I don't see you . . ." If he finished the sentence I didn't hear it, I was already out of the building and heading east, then south, towards the river. It was still muggy, the air wet with the rain that hadn't come. I loosened my tie and undid the top button of my shirt. I shrugged off my jacket and flipped it over my shoulder, dangling it from one finger. I looked casual, like any summer office worker, but I was a murderer. I had killed one woman and been an accessory to the murder of a second. Last week I was not a murderer; when I went to Eddie Likker's funeral service I was not a murderer. Yesterday I was not a murderer. In between – on Monday afternoon – I had been a murderer, but only for a couple of hours; only until Moody said I wasn't. Yesterday I was an accountant who robbed banks because it was fun. Because, in fifty-six years, nothing I had ever done had been as much fun as robbing banks. That was the simple truth. Have fun, Karen had said. Now I was a killer. I looked into the faces of the people walking towards me in the street; a few of them looked back.

For the first time, I wondered about the woman I'd shot, about who she was, if she had a lover, a husband, children, if her parents were alive. I had no idea what she looked like, no idea how old she was: I'd never seen her. I didn't know if she was tall or short, thin or fat, old or young, black or white or none or neither, and it didn't matter, because she was dead and I'd killed her and she didn't deserve to die. No one deserves to die, but we all die anyway. That was no excuse. I'd killed her.

I'd always known it was a possibility, whatever Moody said. If you take loaded guns into crowded places and wave them around and shout, and everybody gets very tense and nervous, or excited, it's probably only a matter of time before somebody gets shot. I'd told myself that didn't mean they'd die, but that was always sophistry. I hadn't meant to kill anyone, but I hadn't stopped it happening. Moody, on the other hand . . . Moody had put a gun up to a woman's head and pulled the trigger.

I called her mobile, left a message. I said it was urgent and told her to call, but I had no idea what I would say when she did.

I was walking too fast. Sweat began to gather in my armpits and the small of my back. I slowed down. I had reached the river again, and it seemed appropriate to lean on the parapet wall and watch the turbid water. The tide was low and below me there was nothing but grey sticky mud. I thought it was just as well I hadn't come to jump in.

I'd thought about it often enough – about what I'd do if we ever, if *I* ever, shot anyone. Killed anyone. Because it was always a possibility. I'd never planned to, never meant to, never *wanted* to kill anybody – but that didn't mean it wouldn't happen.

I'd always thought I'd want to stop. The guilt would crush me; I'd fall down on my knees and vomit until the bile burned holes in the pavement and then I'd call the cops myself. They wouldn't have had far to come. But it didn't happen, and now I knew it never would. I thought about the gun, the Beretta, the weight of it in my hand, and I wondered what Moody had done with it. I thought about standing in the foyer of a bank, a new gun in my hand, watching cashiers filling holdalls with money. I thought about *not* standing in the foyer of a bank, about not telling the customers they had nothing to fear if they would just lie down and do what they were told, about never again walking out with the cash, the *loot*, and it was then that I felt sick. It was then that I felt crushed and I knew that I'd do it again. It was what I loved, what I wanted, there was nothing better in this life.

My mobile made the doorbell sound it makes when it receives a text. I nearly deleted it unread – I'm fifty-six, I have no children; the only texts I ever get are from the telephone company telling me how many texts I have left to use. But this one was from Moody. She was at a scene-of-crime, probably her last, but would try to get away at lunchtime. She'd meet me in a pub no one drank in. She meant no one on the force. I was pleased to see that, young as she was, she did not resort to abbreviation and the substitution of numerals for syllables. There was no real reason this should please me, but it did. There is a correct way to do things.

She was right about the pub. I'd never heard of it. But her message included a hyperlink that – to my surprise – took me to a map and brought up a photo: big bay windows and gargantuan flower baskets. When I arrived – an hour earlier than anyone would call lunchtime – I found stripped floorboards and burgers made of lamb, not beef. Salads were also available. I bought a pint and a packet of crisps and watched the place fill up. The other customers were mostly young, but looked prematurely middle-aged, the kind who read Art History before being given jobs in galleries or private banks. People for whom 'weekend' was a verb. I wondered where they all came from. I wondered how on earth Moody knew this place.

When she turned up I asked her, not because I really wanted to know, but because the alternative was to plunge straight into the bank, the dead woman, the dead women, and the fact that Moody had lied and I needed to know what had really happened, and I didn't want to know – not yet. She shrugged the question off at first, but then she said a boyfriend used to take her there. Which left me still wondering how – and why – she'd found a boyfriend who would drink in a place like this, or could afford to, so I asked if she'd met him in the line of duty. She actually blushed as she said, "No, school." There was something about the way she said it that suggested the school concerned was not a local sink; that fees may have been involved. Her face turned roughly the colour of her boots. I thought of the Moody I'd met in the first Losers Group, sprawled in a chair with her knees apart, arguing with the guy from HR; I thought of her saying there was no way she'd go into a bank with a gun that wasn't loaded, that was just stupid; I thought of her out in the woods the day she'd taught Bernie and me to shoot without killing ourselves or each other, and I thought she was a tourist. A rich girl slumming it. I asked why she'd shot the woman.

"What woman?"

I tried to give her the look Bernie gave me. "The woman

in the bank."

"You mean the woman you shot, sir?" She said 'sir' as if it were an insult.

"All right. The woman I shot. I didn't mean to, but I did. But then you went back there, didn't you? What did you find, Rachel?"

She started slightly at the sound of her own first name, but didn't answer.

"Rachel?"

She said, "I told you. I found the woman screaming and bleeding. I saved her life."

"That isn't true, though, is it?"

She took a long sip of her drink and said, "I was there. You weren't."

"I heard you fire a shot . . ."

"Into the ceiling."

"And now the investigating officer has told Bernie there were two bodies."

"Two?"

I couldn't tell if she was surprised or not. I decided that, in whatever future life we had, I would not play poker with ex-DC Moody.

She said, "Who is the investigating officer?"

I told her and watched all the tension drain out of her at once. She smiled as if a minor misunderstanding had just been cleared up.

She said, "Proctorow's a pillock. Plus he hates Bernie. I wouldn't believe a word he says."

It was possible, I supposed. "But why would he make it up? He didn't know Bernie had any interest in the case."

"He was just showing off."

"But Rachel, if you're telling the truth, there was nothing for him to show off about."

The blank face returned. She said, “It’s possible the paramedics made a bollocks of it. I mean, I tied the tourniquet. She should have been all right. I know she should. But maybe, when they took her to hospital . . .”

“Proctorow said ‘bodies’.”

The certainty returned to her voice: “Proctorow’s an idiot.”

It was possible. It was unlikely, but it was not impossible.

Moody said, “Have you seen the news in the last couple of days?”

I didn’t think I had. I couldn’t recall.

She said, “I have. National; local. Pretty much every bulletin. If we’d killed two people – one person – don’t you think it would be all over the TV?”

I pictured the bank again, the interview room where, apart from a fresh coat of paint, I’d seen no sign of a crime – no sign of one murder, let alone two. I tried to remember if there’d been a bullet hole in the ceiling, but it was no use. I hadn’t looked. I remembered Meersow, the Deputy Manager, whose pitted, cadaverous face seemed to float before me, saying nothing at all about murder, but being keen to talk about the second witness, the woman who had apparently followed the old man out of the bank. Kalenkova, he had said. Rada Kalenkova.

I began to tell Moody.

She interrupted me. “You went back to the bank? Are you out of your fucking mind?”

It was after two when I got back and Gerald Pryor was sitting outside my office. Karen had made him a cup of coffee – which meant Angela liked him and her PA had passed the message on. He was sitting with his knees together, the report to the Programme Board he must have cobbled together since I’d rung him the night before balanced on his lap. The report he wanted me to sign off.

I checked with Karen that there had been no messages – there hadn't – and ushered Gerald in to my office, to the chair where Bernie had sat that morning and cried.

We discussed the weather for a while – we agreed it really was unbearably humid – and Gerald asked what plans I had for when I left. Then he pushed the report across the desk. I picked it up and scanned it. It was fine. It wasn't my money. It might even have been the right way to spend it. I signed the cover sheet but before I passed it back I said, "So?"

"The investigating detective is DS Proctorow."

I nodded slowly, as if the name meant nothing to me.

And then Gerald said, "And the name of the customer who withdrew cash during the robbery was . . ." – he paused to do a little drum roll with his hands on the top of my desk – ". . . was . . ." – he pretended to consult his notes – ". . . Edward Likker."

I found I couldn't speak.

Gerald said, "Wasn't there a Likker who did Angela's job? Before my time. But it could have been him."

I almost said: *Do you think I don't know Likker?* Instead, I said: "It wasn't Likker."

Gerald wasn't much bothered; it wasn't his business. He said, "That's what the bank's data shows. Oh, and he didn't actually get any cash: request denied, it says. Insufficient funds."

I said, "Likker's dead. I went to his funeral."

Gerald shrugged: it wasn't his problem. He reached out and picked the report up off the desk.

## 12

THIS MORNING ALEX isn't here, still, at home, in his bed as he would normally probably be at this time on a Wednesday morning, or the morning of any working day, and I wonder if D was possibly in fact right and Alex, however unlikely, not to say inappropriate and unprofessional it might seem, has in fact stayed over with Gina, albeit possibly in some company/comfort-offering rather than specifically sexual scenario. It is not possible for me to picture Gina Spence and Alex in any kind of sexual scenario. I know that Alex is not at home in bed because I checked. His bedclothes were rumpled and creased in a way that suggested they had been slept in, but they were cold, suggesting that they had been slept in at some earlier point, and possibly for several days, or rather nights, or weeks, even, without subsequently being pulled tight or straightened or made up in any way. This does not concern me – the frequency with which Alex makes his bed, or launders his bedclothes being in a sense none of my business. Alex is an adult not related to me and for whom I am not in any meaningful way responsible. But the fact of the sheets' coldness does bother me to some extent.

I ring his mobile from the bathroom, and after six or seven rings it diverts to voicemail, which tells me nothing. I consider leaving a message but am uncertain what to say and so leave a few seconds of silence instead before I manage to hang up. If he is OK and has his phone he will know that it was me who rang in any case.

I dress in cycling gear and put my work clothes in my bag. I eat muesli with Gary and Matthew and ask Matthew if he slept well and what he dreamed about because the alternative is to tell Gary what is going on vis-à-vis work and my suspension and the frankly troubling arrival of Lopez in the situation and the impossibility, given my suspension, of even asking Theo what the hell is going on and if it's going to be all right. I am not up to telling Gary this. I am aware that not telling Gary carries a risk that the inevitable disappointment of finding himself married to a fuck-up no longer capable financially of supporting him and his – our – almost eight year-old son as I had hitherto done and had in reality, albeit implicitly, committed myself to doing for the foreseeable future but now would not be able to do, and that while it is theoretically possible that Gary himself could return to work, as a librarian, or a baker, perhaps, and therefore that the outcome of the situation, even if the worst came to the worst with the investigation and any subsequent disciplinary action, which the involvement of Lopez suggests has to be at least a serious possibility, would not necessarily be destitution, homelessness and scraping the bottom of skips for food and clothing, I nonetheless have to acknowledge that he – Gary – would be disappointed and concerned, and also that my not having told him for several days, would, in the event that this becomes clear to him, add considerably to that natural disappointment and anxiety a deep and wounding sense of very real betrayal. Gary may feel that my inability to tell him what is happening demonstrates a lack of trust that will itself make it harder for us to weather the storm and to survive as a family unit. I am aware of this risk. And yet I cannot bear to tell Gary what is going on. There will be some way around this, I am sure.

Gary reminds me that Matthew is going away on a school trip and will not be back until the weekend. He does this by talking to Matthew, not me, prompting Matthew to tell his mummy what he will be doing today. Matthew says it's going to be great. There are zip-wires and tree-walks where you go up twice as high as the house, at least, but I am not to worry because his teacher says that nobody has died there recently. I remember the teacher said the same thing at the meeting for parents about the trip, and some of us laughed. Gary has bought Matthew new wellington boots and new pyjamas; Matthew has announced that he will not be taking Gonzo, the cuddly toy gorilla that has accompanied him every time he has gone to bed since he was three months old. I hug Matthew and tell him that I love him and will miss him but he's going to have a fantastic time. I tell Gary that I love him too, because I do, and then I get my bike out of the basement and ride away without telling either of them what is happening to me, or where I am going, because even though it looks as if I am going to work, even though it looks exactly as it must look every other day when I go to work at this time on a weekday, I am certainly not going to work and do not in fact know where I am going at all, but I am going anyway, because I love them both.

When I get out onto the road D is already in his car, revving the engine in soft thrusts. It occurs to me that I could visit Gina Spence. It then further occurs to me that if I were to do so at this hour – that is, at 8.30 in the morning – it might, if Alex is in fact there, appear less as if I have come to offer condolences to an old albeit not particularly close friend and former colleague on the tragic death of her son, and more as if I am checking up on the whereabouts of my closer friend and current colleague, which of course I would be, but which would seem in any circumstances inappropriate and might, in these circumstances – if these *are* the circumstances – make the situation considerably worse, in that I imagine, if Gina *has* consoled herself and sought to assuage or at least distract herself from grief through casual not to say destructive and ill-considered sex with Alex, then there is at least a distinct possibility that by this time – that is, by 8.30am of the morning after the fact – she will be feeling guilty and disgusted with herself and regretting whatever it was she did, and not wanting to think too much about it, but will not yet have managed to get rid of Alex, much as she must want to, Alex not being physically capable, in my experience, of leaving anywhere or doing anything much this early in the day. A car passes within centimetres of my right thigh. It becomes necessary to stop cycling and pull my bike into the gutter and rest one foot on the kerb while I consider the quandary: (1) it would be desirable at some level, and certainly well-mannered and appropriate, to visit Gina and offer her my condolences, but I cannot pretend to myself that my prompt and motive for doing so at this particular moment is actually a matter of concern or etiquette rather than a desire to see if Alex is there, and therefore all right, and not in any physical danger; but (2) while my principal concern at this moment is to establish the safety, well-being and, if possible, whereabouts of Alex, finding him at Gina's house in, as it were, flagrante delicto, would create a situation that would render any condolences I might offer worthless, whilst quite possibly failing to convince Alex that his welfare is, in fact, my primary concern; I reluctantly conclude therefore that (3) I must delay my visit to Gina's house to find out if Alex is there long enough to ensure that he is not in fact there any more, if he ever was. I will then have to offer sympathy whilst subtly questioning Gina as to whether or not she has seen Alex recently and, if so, whether her "recent" is as recent as last night, not to mention this morning, rather than, say, a year or two ago, which will be skating on very thin ice indeed, offence-wise. Or, (4) it occurs to me now, I could cycle to Gina's street and wait, preferably inconspicuously, outside her house until Alex comes out, or does not come out. This is the option I select.

Gina's home address is in my phone contacts, assuming that she has not moved. I discover that it takes only fifteen minutes of steady cycling to reach her street, which is broad and nineteenth-century in layout, with fat mottle-trunked trees and uneven pavements. The houses are tall and thin and lean on each other as they climb the hill. I wonder why it is that I have not visited before. She has not visited me. It occurs to me that I may have been wrong to consider myself her friend.

Gina's house is number 56. I chain my bicycle to a lamp-post outside number 67 – five doors up and across the street. I estimate that the next tree must be more or less opposite her house, and that its trunk is large enough for me to lean against, as if nonchalantly, with one foot up against the bark and a cigarette, perhaps, in my hand, if I smoked, which I haven't since I met Gary, I could lean against the tree whilst remaining invisible to a casual glance from inside Gina's property.

I walk down the hill to the tree. I lean. I imagine a cigarette. I consult my watch.

To my left a woman in a straw hat and trousers the colour of death is clipping a hedge that is not holly or privet or any shrub that I can name and which even now, at the end of June, has dark green leaves and bright red berries I assume must be left over from last year and which must, therefore, be wholly unpalatable and possibly even poisonous to garden birds. As she clips, the leaves and clumps of berries fall like spattered blood around her feet. It is early in the day to be gardening, it occurs to me. After a few minutes of this the flaw in my strategy becomes impossible to ignore: whilst I may be invisible to Gina, or to Alex, if Alex is indeed in Gina's house, I remain nonetheless entirely visible to anybody walking down or worse still living on this side of the street, such as the woman with the hat and the shears, who regards me with evident distaste. I nod and smile the sort of half-smile one offers to strangers to reassure them that one's intentions are not hostile but which, in practice, makes one look less like a cheerful, harmless suburbanite than a troubled psychotic who will, at some later point in the proceedings, rampage through the neighbourhood with an axe. The woman does not look reassured. She returns to clipping her hedge for a moment, and then abruptly swivels on her heel and walks into her house. I imagine that she is ringing the police, but that the police will not, absent the axe, be especially interested. Nevertheless, I now consider the time that I can reasonably spend leaning against the tree consulting my watch to be limited, and decide, instead, to saunter, to walk as if purposefully but without undue haste from my present location to the end of the street.

As I pass opposite number 56 I glance casually across the road in the statistically almost certain confidence that the probability of Gina and/or Alex glancing *out* of the house at the precise moment that I pass, glancing *in*, is incalculably small, and can, therefore, be disregarded. What I see, when I do glance, whilst continuing to walk, or saunter, down the opposite pavement, is that the curtains of Gina's house (if it is, in fact, Gina's house, and she has not moved without informing me since I recorded her address and other contact details, which must, on reflection, have been several years ago, that is, since she left the Office of Assessment) are drawn. Having recently consulted my watch I know it to be some time shortly after nine, perhaps five minutes after, and I consider it unusual and noteworthy, albeit I am unfamiliar with Gina's daily routine, that all the curtains of her house remain drawn at such an hour, although whether they remain drawn as a result, or perhaps as an expression, of the grief of bereavement or of post-coital guilt, or even of some weird, distasteful combination of the two I cannot say with any certainty. Parked on the street outside the house is a small red car which does not belong to Alex, who does not drive and almost always travels by bus, and may not belong to Gina, given that there are cars parked bumper-to-bumper along both sides of the street and their owners must evidently park wherever they can find a space, not necessarily outside their own houses, even assuming that they live on this street, and have not driven from further away and parked here, in Gina's street, at the end of which, perhaps a quarter of a mile away, is a train station. The small red car tells me nothing.

I turn my head back in order to preserve the casual nature of my glance at Gina's house and continue walking. I reach a corner. At this point I have a choice: I can continue down the hill towards the station, as if intending to catch a train, or perhaps to meet someone getting off a train, albeit one that is not due any time soon, given the relaxed nature of my walking/sauntering up to this point; or, alternatively, I can turn and, by turning three times more, bring myself up, round and back to where I left my bicycle, the downside of which is that I will be out of sight of the house for the time it takes me to complete three sides of the square or (more likely) rectangular block. I can also, of course, simply turn around and walk back up the way I have come, but this would appear odd at best and, glancing back, I notice that the woman with the hat and the shears has returned to the pavement in front of her hedge and that she now has a dog at her feet. The dog is small but quite possibly noisy. If I continue to the station I will of course have to return at some point, without having either caught a train or met a disembarking passenger, and will simply be delaying the moment when I pass the woman and her dog, both of whom I judge now to be settled in for a full morning's gardening/neighbourhood observation. I decide to turn. Once out of sight of Gina's house I hasten my steps considerably, although not so much as to attract curiosity. By the time I make the fourth and final turn and descend towards my bicycle, which is still chained to the lamppost, I can see that the curtains in the upstairs room of Gina's house are open and the small red car has gone.

It is possible that the car's departure is coincidental, that Gina and/or Alex have risen, drawn the bedroom curtains and are, even now, descending to the kitchen for a solitary/romantic/awkward breakfast whilst a neighbour with no connection to either of them drives to work or to the shops or to visit an elderly relative in his or her small red car; it is possible, but somehow I also know that this is not what has happened. I have missed Gina leaving the house, and have no way of knowing now whether Alex left with her. Ignoring the woman with the shears, I cross the road and approach Gina's door. I pause momentarily – it is still theoretically possible that Alex will answer the door – and ring the bell. A muffled electronic chirrup sounds from deep inside the house. There is no answer.

I re-cross the street and approach the woman with the shears, who pretends to ignore me. The dog snaps half-heartedly from behind her legs. I beg her pardon. I hold out a card – another infraction for Lopez to add to the list – and tell her my name is Pitt and that I am a loss adjuster. She lets her shears dangle in one hand as she takes the card and reads it. She does not ask me what a loss adjuster is. She tells me she knew I was up to something. I concede the point and tell her that I am investigating a claim. I ask whether she knows Ms Spence at number 56; she says she might. I ask if she saw Ms Spence leave home a few minutes ago and she tells me that she minds her own business, unlike some. I ask if the small red car that isn't there any more belongs to Ms Spence and she says she couldn't say because, after all, it isn't there. She seems quite pleased with this answer. I ask if her dog is a daschund and she concedes that there may be some daschund in him. I ask if Ms Spence has a dog and she says she wouldn't know. I accept defeat and wish her a good morning. She does not reply.

I trudge back up towards my bike, ringing Alex again as I go. In one ear I hear my phone buzz to tell me his mobile is ringing; in the other I hear, faintly, a telephone ring. When his voicemail message starts I hang up. There is silence. I ring again, but this time it cuts straight to voicemail. I say: It's me, Rada. I say: Where are you? I ask him to call me; I say Love you and hang up. I wonder why I said that now, because it is not a phrase I use much and almost never in respect of Alex although I do, obviously, love him, in a way. Not romantically, and not exactly like a brother, either, but all the same. He told me that he loved me, once, when we were students on holiday and had to share a room because we couldn't afford two. He didn't say he loved me romantically, of course, that's not something anyone would say, and he didn't even say it that romantically, in the sense of candles or firelight or taking me in his arms or any of that, he just said it, but that is what he meant. He didn't mean he loved me like a brother, or a father, or even like a friend. What he actually meant was that he wanted to have sex with me.

I unlock my bike and wrap the chain around the saddle stem. The woman with the hat and shears has gone but the dog is still there. I begin to freewheel down the hill and, being a dog, the dog rushes up to meet me, barking energetically. I swerve past and my foot catches its belly with a soft and satisfying thump, which I tell myself is accidental.

Later, after I have spent some hours cycling nowhere in particular and can no longer think of anything else to do, I ring work, hoping to speak to D, and for a long time nobody answers. There is no voicemail because the Office does not exist and we consequently do not get a lot of incoming calls. Then a voice I don't know says Good morning. The voice is calm. In a manner that is calculated not to cause alarm, it asks who I am. Alarmed, I hang up, and ring D's mobile. When he answers I ask where he is and he says he's at work. I tell him I know he's lying and ask why he isn't there. He says, Why aren't you at home? The answer to which he knows, really, and is only asking for effect. I say I know he's lying because I just rang work.

Shit, Sis. That wasn't clever.

I say, Someone answered.

He would.

Who?

Lopez. Who else? Tell me you didn't speak to him.

Why aren't you there?

He's locked me out of all the systems. He says it's standard procedure for an investigation of this magnitude.

He said that?

D says nothing.

I say, D? Did Lopez actually say, 'of this magnitude'?

I'm sorry, Sis.

What does Theo have to say?

I haven't seen Theo since yesterday. I think he's keeping his head down.

I tell D to meet me in the café we sometimes go to on a Sunday when Gary hasn't baked his own croissants.

When I get there D's car is parked outside: inside D is eating something large and messy and drinking hot chocolate with whipped cream and marshmallows. He has his laptop out and there are sandwich crumbs on the keyboard. I tell him he is a pig and a child and order an espresso. He says he has been to the gym today, and work, and he has earned this, and what have I done? I say grown men do not eat whipped cream and marshmallows even if they have run a marathon.

Grown women don't lie to their husbands.

Yes they do.

OK, they do. But you don't.

I shrug. I don't really see what else I can do because he's right, and of course he's also wrong in ways that he probably hasn't even thought about, being a man and single and living with his sister at the age of twenty-nine. I ask D if he has heard from Alex although I know he won't have because if Alex was in some sort of trouble or thought we might think he was in some sort of trouble on account of his not having come home all night, and he had access to a phone, I know and D knows that it is me that Alex would call, not D, and I and probably D also both know that if he, Alex, were not in any kind of trouble and had simply stayed out because he had in fact, as D suggested, spent the night with someone, Gina Spence or anybody else, he would not call either of us and would just go to work and would have answered the telephone when I rang.

D says, Don't you want to know about Lopez?

I don't. I mean, I do, obviously, because it's important and he has my job and my future in his hands, and I'm not sure I now accept my own explanation that Theo asked for Lopez just so that when he cleared me I would be above reproach, that seems far-fetched now and like grasping at straws, but the fact is that at this moment I actually don't care about that as much as I want to know where Alex has got to and whether he's OK. I realise this and am actually quite proud of myself in a way that immediately undermines the selfless value of the feeling and so undermines the pride. So I say that I want to know that Alex is OK, and D says he told me: Alex got his end away and that's all there is to it. I don't believe this, or think it at all likely, but there's no point in arguing the point, so I ask D if he knows what else Alex was doing yesterday, apart from visiting Gina Spence, but D ignores my question and instead answers his own. He says, Lopez is like Theo: ancient. I see I'm not going to get an answer straightaway, so I say: What did you tell him about me?

Nothing.

I find this barely credible. D is my brother and is at some level fond of me and would probably not wish me any actual harm other than in a professional sense where that professional-type harm could in some way benefit him and his prospects, but I am aware that this *is* a professional situation in which, with Theo on the verge of retirement and D regarding himself as his natural if not only acceptable successor, an opinion we all know Theo does not actively share, D regards my alleged fuck-up as a helpful step in the right direction, and while he might not actually go so far as gratuitously to volunteer damaging information or opinions or speculations about my performance he is unlikely to have resisted giving them if asked. I say, Nothing?

D runs a finger round the edge of his mug and scoops the last of the whipped cream into his mouth, and says, He hasn't asked.

Don't you think that's odd?

No.

He's supposed to be investigating me.

He didn't ask anything, Sis. He was just showing off.

I nod because I think it's possible, probable even, although I don't know the man; there was something about his voice. I ask D again if he knows what else Alex was doing yesterday. D thinks for a moment during which he picks up his plate, tipping and shaking it so that most of the toast crumbs fall into the palm of his hand, while some fall on the table and the floor. He throws the crumbs into his mouth while I wait. He says, Bodkin . . .

I say, Rodkin?

D nods and says, Suicide. Two kids. Slit his own throat with a breadknife.

He enjoys saying this, as if he's proving that he can think about this now, about fathers who kill themselves with knives, that it doesn't bother him.

I say, It was my case. It should have been Alex's anyway.

It should. I have thought about this and I can only assume that Theo thought it was time, that he knew he was going to leave and couldn't protect me forever.

I point to D's laptop and say, You could get the address from the files.

I told you, Sis. Lopez locked down all the systems.

What if the file's on your hard drive? Or on that?

I point to the memory stick beside his laptop, but D says there's no way because it's not his case, remember?, it was mine and now it's Alex's, and there's no way Rodkin is going to be there. He says Theo should never have given me the case, and then he catches himself. He says the memory stick is just for Likker, nothing else, and he starts telling me about Lifetime Value and the presentation he would have given on Monday if I hadn't spent so long boring on about the old professor-type guy in the bank who wasn't even dead, and I ask him to check because you never know, maybe Alex had used the stick or the laptop before D, or when D wasn't around or by mistake and somehow there might be something; and D says you do know, it isn't going to be there, but in the end he has to prove it to me because I make a point of saying it could happen, and D (being D) can't let himself be wrong or even not demonstrably right. He searches the hard drive and there's nothing. He plugs the stick in and searches that and I don't believe there will be anything there, either, it isn't really possible, but there is. Not the Rodkin file, of course, but Rodkin's name in Likker's file. Because Likker, it turns out, made an appointment to see Rodkin a week before he died. There is a note of Rodkin's address in Likker's diary, which it turns out Alex had been right about, there being no reason why he shouldn't, and was very close indeed to Gina Spence's house. A short walk, in fact. It was the main road from which Gina's quieter street was a turning. I had probably passed it this morning.

Sis, there's something else.

D is pointing at the screen. The day before the appointment with Rodkin, Likker had made an appointment with a "Mr Pitt". The quotation marks are there, in the diary.

That wasn't you?

How could it be me? He wasn't even dead then.

There's a number for this Mr Pitt which I ring, from right there at the café table, with my own mobile, despite D telling me not to. He says I'm in enough trouble already, and he doesn't want me dragging him into to it, too, and even though he's saying this I can hear something in the way he's saying it that tells me that he's actually concerned about me, about my trouble, and I look up at him, surprised, as the phone rings and a calm voice, a voice I have heard before this morning, on the telephone, says: Good morning.

I hang up.

A moment later my phone rings and the number I just called lights up the screen. I switch it off without answering, and I'm saying, Shit, D, shit, while I switch it off, and he's saying, What is it, Rada? and not calling me Sis, I notice that even while I'm taking the back off the phone and pulling out the sim card and bending it, which turns out to be harder than I thought it would be, as it's small and I can't get much leverage, but in the end it snaps, and I feel like I'm about to cry but instead I pull myself together and I say, Who *was* Likker?

# 13

I'M FEELING LIKE I'm maybe one of the blind after all.

I thought I knew everything there was to know about Likker, I thought I'd got it all worked out. I'd got my formula and I'd plugged in all the variables and I'd come up with an answer. Like I said, I'd even tweaked it a bit by way of a little thank you to the guy, and now it looks like I know the square root of fuck all.

I tell Rada that she's not under any circumstances whatsoever to go near Rodkin's place until I've had a chance to do a bit of digging. I make her promise me she won't. I tell her she should go back to the Spence woman's, not because I think Alex will be there, but because if Alex hasn't seen her, she'll be wondering where the fuck we are. I don't really believe this or even much care one way or the other, but I say it because it might just persuade Rada to do what she's told. It's worth a shot. Then I get in my car and ring Proctorow again, who names a pub he wants to meet at, even though it's past lunch, and not yet knocking off time, really. I turn the radio on and this time it's Mozart, but it's an opera and I really can't be doing with that. All those speaky-singy bits, there's no chance to think at all. I switch to the CD and swear fluently at Negotiation Tony for twenty minutes without once actually losing my grip and I feel all the better for it.

The pub Proctorow chose is up in town, and when I find

it there's nowhere to park within half a mile of the place, so I pull up on to the pavement outside. I'll tell him if I get a ticket he's paying. Serve the fucker right. He should find a better pub.

It's dark inside, which is no surprise. It's dark inside every pub every policeman I ever met drinks in – I guess that's why they like them. But there's no chance of me missing Proctorow. He'll be sat with his back to the wall right beside the door, so he can slip out if anyone he doesn't like the look of should happen to come in. I pretend I haven't seen him and walk straight up to the bar. The barmaid smiles and I offer to buy her a drink. She says it's a bit early for her, but she says it like I should try again later and she might not say no. I tell her to keep the change from a twenty, which should help her remember, and carry two pints over to Proctorow's table. I tell him he should find a pub with a car park.

"I'm a policeman. I don't drink and drive."

He takes a long swig at the pint I'd put in front of him. Then he picks up the glass of whisky he'd bought himself and tips it into the beer.

I say, "How's that going, then? The policeman thing?"

He takes another drink, then smiles and says, "Same old, same old. How's . . . what is it you say you do again?"

"Loss adjusting."

He leaves a beat before he says, "Loss adjusting. Right."

I have a go at my pint and he has another go at his and neither of us says a thing for maybe a couple of minutes. Then I say the barmaid isn't bad, and he says she's a lesbian, and I say, Is that so? He says it is, and we have another go at our drinks.

"So," says Proctorow after another couple of minutes. "It's been pretty warm lately."

I go up to the bar and order new pints. I ferry them back to the table and before Proctorow can say anything else, I say:

"OK, now we're all caught up and shit, what I want to know is: one body or two?"

Proctorow manages to look genuinely puzzled.

I say, "Monday? Bank?"

Proctorow still looks blank. His eyebrows squeeze together and his mouth pulls up towards his nose as if he's concentrating very hard. Or inflicting pain somewhere I can't see.

"Screaming women? Blood all over the walls? You are investigating this one, right?"

Suddenly Proctorow's face clears. The brows unravel and the mouth settles into a flat smug smile. He leans back in his chair and takes another swig. All this surprises me. He surely can't have just remembered that he's investigating a murder? He says, "You've been talking to Jenks." Which surprises me even more.

"Who the fuck is Jenks?"

"DI Bernie Jenks." He puts on a voice an octave or so below normal and says, "A cop in a million . . . on special assignment to . . . Human Resources."

He seems to find this hilarious. I don't share his opinion. I put on a stony face and keep it stony long enough that even Proctorow has to notice.

"Come on – you must know Bernie?"

The stony face thing seems to be working, so I keep it up.

"Little fat Jewish guy? Used to be my boss. Up until, you know . . ."

I think I do know, but I still don't know what it's got to do with Monday. I say, "Until the serial murder-rapist screw-up thing?"

Proctorow nods. "They moved him to HR, and now they're moving him out. He's leaving tomorrow."

"Retiring?"

"Redundant."

I make a stab at a concerned sympathetic give-a-shit kind of face. I even whistle quietly. "It's a brave new world," I say.

He drains his beer. "Too right."

I'm back to stony face, then: "But what the fuck's it got to do with me?"

He looks up from his empty glass. "I was just winding Bernie up. I saw him in the pub looking a bit too full of himself, so I told him about the bank and I . . . *embellished* it a bit. Like I said, he's leaving tomorrow."

Unbelievable. I point to his empty glass. Just before he can say yes, I say: "It's your round."

While Proctorow creeps unwillingly to the bar I take a look around. It's a pub. If you've been in a pub, you'll know what it's like. I try to make some sense of the last few minutes. Proctorow seems to think I asked him about the murders because I've been talking to some fat loser I've never even heard of, who Proctorow has tricked for some sad fucked-up reason of his own. Which means either that Proctorow is lying – and lying better than I think he can – or that he's an idiot. When he gets back with our drinks I say, as if I've just thought of it, "How come you were kept on?"

"I was demoted. I haven't touched a corpse since."

"But still. You're not in HR. You're not redundant."

"I had a friend. He's dead now."

That would explain it, I think. He was an idiot. But a useful idiot, as Dad would say.

I say, "A friend? You must have needed one."

"It always helps."

"Because you're so obviously a shit detective."

Which he doesn't much like. Fair enough, I suppose: I hadn't meant him to. But when I tell him about the carpet stains and the poster on the wall opposite the bullet hole he doesn't have much choice but to look a bit abashed. Well, crushed, really. Like a man who's seeing the job he's been demoted to, the demeaning job he thought he was going to get promoted back out of one day soon, but which, in the meantime, is a whole lot better than nothing, and certainly better than getting axed like poor old Bernie Whatsisname, he looks exactly like such a man watching that very job burn and fade and crumble into ash before his eyes. I enjoy watching this for a bit – the way his mouth opens and closes soundlessly is not something you see for real every day – but in the end I take pity on him, after a fashion.

"You spoke to Wenlock?"

He nods.

"But not Meersow?"

He looks up, supplicant, defeated.

"Oh dear, oh dear," I say. Then I tell him how Wenlock had spun me the same crock of shit he'd obviously sold Proctorow but how, when I went back, I met the deputy manager – a lanky pallid cadaverous streak of piss – who hadn't exactly contradicted his boss but had arranged to meet me in the interview room where the signs were pretty bloody obvious, if he'd pardon the pun. During this Proctorow seems to recover a little spirit.

"So somebody got winged?" he says, when I give him the chance. "Bled a bit. That doesn't make it murder."

"Even so," I say, putting him back where he belongs, "it kind of ups the ante, don't you think? Shouldn't the investigating officer know about something like that?"

It's a point so obvious only desperation can have made him overlook it. He collapses again.

"But why would they cover it up?"

I've asked myself the same question, naturally, more than once. I've tried to exploit the forensic potential of my blinding insight vis-à-vis motive and sense and all and . . . and what?

*The mountain laboured like a bleedin' navvy and brought forth an effin' mouse, my son.* Sometimes when he drove a cab, Dad used to fake a Cockney accent and spout crap like that.

"Maybe Wenlock likes a quiet life? Maybe he's creeping up on retirement and doesn't want the boat rocked?"

It's the best I've managed to come up with. Proctorow looks appropriately dubious. I plough on. "And maybe Meersow wants the old man shoved aside so he can get the job?"

Proctorow doesn't buy it, and I can't say I blame him: "So why didn't he tell me? I'm the policeman."

Also obvious, and requiring desperation – this time on my part – to ignore. We both look at our drinks for a while. Proctorow lifts his up and looks at the wet ring on the beer mat beneath it. Then he puts the glass down again. I say, "What is it, Sherlock?"

He opens his mouth, then closes it again and shakes his head. In the end he says, "Why are you interested?"

It's a reasonable question, and one he really should by rights have asked before now, but hadn't, which may be why he's in the hole he's in, professionally. I say, "Just curious. My . . . colleague was there. In the bank. She says the first shot went through the wall and there was a lot of female-type screaming from the room next door. She says one of the gunmen – actually a woman – went next door and there was a second shot and the screaming stopped."

Proctorow tries to look bored. "That's what the witnesses all say. I've probably read your colleague's statement."

"Fifty says you haven't."

Now he looks annoyed. "How come?"

"Because she left before you got there. She left right after the robbers, but followed the old guy who wouldn't lie down. You do know about the old guy, right?"

"The bank gave us a name, but we haven't traced it yet."

"Too much to do?"

Proctorow nods, and I think: he really must have had a friend. I say, "Do you remember the name?"

Proctorow flaps a hand across his face as if it were of no interest. "Why do you want to know?" I wonder if he's quite as dumb as he seems.

I say, "It's professional. My colleague is in a bit of trouble. I'm trying to help her."

My words take me by surprise, and I wonder for a moment if they might even be true.

"And why should I tell you?"

"Because you need all the friends you can get."

Proctorow seems to think a show of strength, or at least of stubbornness, is necessary. "You think?"

I sigh. "You say all your witnesses confirm the story about the woman screaming and then another shot and it stopping?"

He nods, warily.

"And you probably go with the story that says the woman was scared and hysterical, what with a gun going off in the bank and a bullet flying through the wall at her? And then the second gunman – woman – goes in and fires a shot into the ceiling to get her attention and calms her down? And maybe, even, bandages her up where an essentially harmless flesh wound has spouted a surprising but non-lethal quantity of blood, which would explain all the stains?"

He's nodding, still, less wary, almost relieved. It makes sense.

"And the bank has covered up the mess for no more sinister reason than that it's an interview room and, let's face it, you go into the bank to talk about savings or a mortgage, or whatever, you don't want to find yourself sitting in what looks like a torture chamber, do you?"

He nods again, then shakes – agreeing. He can't wait for the punchline.

"So where's the injured woman?"

His head finally stops moving. The muscles in his face go slack and I swear to God I can hear the cogs grinding in his brain. After a couple of days he says, "Shit."

"Shit? Is that it?"

"Shit."

"Like I say, you need all the friends you can get."

Proctorow reaches down under the table and pulls up one of those bags with a strap that goes over your shoulder and a big flap over the front. He opens it up and slides out a laptop. He says it's all in there. While it's booting up he tries to make some excuses but I'm not interested; after a bit he drums his fingers on the table to let me know he's as impatient as I am, but he isn't. He's nowhere fucking close. If this laptop takes much longer I'm going to . . . I'm not. I think of Negotiation Tony and I am calm. I close my eyes and count lung contractions. I am cool enough to chill lager. I'm Zen. I'm the fucking Buddha. When I get to ten the third time round, Proctorow is saying, "Here we go." He's scrolling through a list of files saying, "Monday, Monday . . . Wenlock." Which is all very well but is not actually what I'm looking for. He opens up a file and it's a witness statement, and we both scan through it, skipping the formalities and the stuff we know until there it is: the name we're looking for. Except it isn't. There is no way on God's green earth this is the name I was looking for.

To be fair, Proctorow gets there first. He says, "That can't be right."

I nod but I don't think he sees me because he's still staring at the screen.

He says, "He used to . . . It can't . . ."

I finish the sentence for him: "It can't have been Likker. Because Likker's dead."

Proctorow looks at me now and I think he's scared – confused, OK, but actually more scared than confused – and he says, "How do you know that?"

I give him a look, like: What are you, stupid? And after it's sunk in, or at least after I'm beginning to feel a bit self-conscious sitting here with my eyebrows raised and my mouth all squeezed up, I say, "It isn't a secret." Then I say, "He was your "friend" right?" And I say it like that, so he can hear the quote marks, and he nods. He says, "He was like a father to me." Which, for all that Proctorow is about as sharp as a chocolate breadknife, I wouldn't have expected even him to say. Not out loud and to another actual person.

I say, "Probably not as bad as that."

Proctorow looks more confused – it's getting the edge on scared – and I think maybe what I just said wouldn't make too much sense if your Dad wasn't a lying cheating scumbag who offed himself when you were still a kid, but I don't say that, of course, or anything like it. I say, "Does the name Rodkin mean anything to you?"

Proctorow make a show of thinking about it, but in the end he shakes his head.

"How about Pitt?"

He says, "You're Pitt."

Of course I am.

The pub is pretty much empty now. Just us and the barmaid I wouldn't mind buying a drink and an old guy in the corner with the Wednesday off-peak meal deal. I point at the laptop, at the document where the manager of a bank that'd just been robbed and which might or might not have been the scene of a murder, or two murders, claims a dead man for a missing witness, and if I'm honest, I've got no fucking idea what's going on here. But I'm not honest, not really, so I say, "Have you got anything else?" Expecting the answer no, because there must be limits to just how useless even Proctorow can be, but he has, bless him. He's got the CCTV footage of the whole damn thing, only he hasn't thought to mention this till now and my faith in the whole limits to stupidity thing is shattered, but, on the other hand, he's got the CCTV footage. He clicks on the file icon and there's an awkward moment or two while it tells him he's got to download some software if he actually wants to watch it, and I can't bear to see him sucking his lip and prodding the keyboard with the end of one thick finger, so I send him to the bar for another round and sort it out.

And there it is: grainy, black and white, the colour of all the best crime scenes. The camera's somewhere over the street door, looking down at the queues, looking over their shoulders, and I recognise Rada. From behind, OK, the back of her head, but there's no mistaking my sister. The man in front of her is bent forward, away from the camera, and I can't see much of him. White hair. Carrying a stick.

Proctorow makes it back from the bar just as, on the screen, three figures in black waving what could be guns, or might just as well, at this resolution, be toys or even two fingers with a thumb cocked back. Except the one with the big fuck-off machine gun. There's no mistaking that. The people in the bank all get down on the floor, almost as if they've practised this. Which some of them have, of course, the ones who work there. Rada lies down, and even now, when I know that this is just a film and I know how it ends, I find my stomach does this thing where it seems to be in my mouth, or at least at the top of my throat. And I see the man in front of Rada, who hasn't got down on the floor, standing at the cash machine as if there's nothing out of the ordinary going on. Or maybe as if he knows just what's going on and he's got to show he's just too fucking cool to care. Except he does care, doesn't he? Because if he didn't, he'd just get down on the floor like everyone else and not make such a humungous fucking show of himself. He's not the only one who could get shot. The way the man with the gun nearest to him is holding the thing it's obvious he doesn't know what he's doing with it, and that's my sister right there on the floor behind the show-off, right between him and the knob-end with the gun. So, even though I know what happens, I'm still a little nervous, at this point. Mr Look-at-me-I'm-cool-as-fuck has still got his back to the camera, to the man with the gun that's pointing at his head, but I can see he's definitely an older man, with old-man white hair and an old-fucker cane, and a slight stoop where his large, professor-type head tilts forward under the weight of his own brains. But despite that, the stoop, his suit jacket fits him to a T, you can see that from here, from the CCTV camera, from Proctorow's laptop, from two days after the event. The suit is so obviously not off the peg, and you can see he's polished his shoes for years, or had them polished, maybe, and then it hits me and I know they'll have that deep, deep gloss that Theo's shoes always have. But it isn't Theo. It isn't Likker, either, or Likker's ghost, or anyone in any way related to Likker. Because even though I know Likker inside out, know him better than I knew my own father; even though I've been through his life in more detail than he could have thought anyone ever would or could; even though I know what he called his mother when he was five and what he found in his father's wallet when he was eight, searching through the bedside cabinet in his parents' bedroom when he was supposed to be tucked up in his own bed with scarlet fever; though I know the name of his first girlfriend – and the names of both her first and second husbands, neither of which was Likker, and what she liked to wear and do in bed; even though I know that Likker's one and only son died in a neighbour's car at the age of twelve and that Likker, a year or so later, was unsurprised to hear of a subsequent accident in which the neighbour, the neighbour's wife and both their Labradors died a slow and panic-filled death after their vehicle stalled and would not restart on a causeway where the tide seemed to come from nowhere, when it came, and turned a landscape of low, flat mud and oyster shells into what was certainly and unmistakably *sea* in moments that must nonetheless have felt, to Likker's neighbours, like a lifetime; even though I know the name of the first officer to offer Likker a *taste*, and the name of the second, more senior, officer to whom Likker threatened to report the first until the taste became a substantial meal; and even though I know the names of the officers and their widows and orphans Likker genuinely, honestly and anonymously, helped out with advice and opportunities and cold, hard cash over thirty, forty years or more; even though I know all this and have weighed it in the balance and calculated the score, I have never actually met the man, any more than I have met any of my clients. Whereas the man on Proctorow's laptop screen, the man turning now – turning two days ago – and gazing mildly up at the camera as if he knows it's there, as if he knows that pretty much every fucker in the bank is looking at him right now, this man, his face too pale on the CCTV record, his eyes large and dark beneath those bushy old-man eyebrows, his features immobile as if there's nothing going on here, while a second man points a gun at him, *this* man I have met. Just once; this morning; in the Office of Assessment.

I'm not likely to forget him.

# 14

IF IT WASN'T Likker trying to take money out of Likker's bank account on Monday – and I was certain that it wasn't: I had seen the man's body rouged and waxed and laid out in the padded box before the box slid through the velvet curtains and the organ doodled portentously – then who exactly was it? And why?

Well, why was obvious enough – follow the money. What I really meant was: why was someone trying to access Eddie's bank account now, when Eddie had been dead a month? Why did the bank not mention this to Proctorow? And apparently there was no money, anyway. *Insufficient funds,* Gerald had said, but surely the account should have been frozen? Knowing Eddie, his financial affairs would have been in excellent shape. Everything would have been prepared: it is extremely unlikely that the bank would not have been informed of his death. Yet, according to Gerald, the bank simply said there was no money in the account: which certainly does not sound like Eddie, either. Could the bank have been aware of the fraud? Or attempted fraud? Or whatever it was? Could they have been trying to cover something up? I thought about the interview room, about the poster on the wall, about the man I met with the pale skin and the acne, Meersow. Why had he been so keen to let me know about the second witness, the woman? He hadn't told Proctorow about her.

I called Bernie, asked him to come back up to my office. He wasn't keen, but I told him I needed to pick his brains. When he arrived, Karen let him walk right in without bothering to check, or even knock. He looked worse than ever; his face was pale and sweaty, the edges of his eyes were red. He looked at the carpet.

I told him to sit down and I asked him if the name Rada Kalenkova meant anything to him.

He looked up, his eyes met mine, and I got to see a faint light die right there in front of me. He looked away again. I remembered, then, and said, "I spoke to Moody. Don't worry."

"Don't worry?"

"She says Proctorow's an idiot."

Bernie had his elbows on his knees. He curled forward and puts his head in his hands. He mumbled something I couldn't hear.

"Moody says he's just winding you up. Showing off. She says if we'd killed two people it would have been all over the news."

Bernie didn't move. I could see the scalp through the hair on the top of his head.

"Bernie?"

He sat up. When he spoke, he looked past me, out of the window, perhaps, but his eyes were unfocussed. His voice was flat. "If we robbed a bank and accidentally shot a woman, and one of us saved her life with a balaclava tourniquet, wouldn't that be all over the news, too?"

He had a point. It seemed that I had not been paying sufficient attention. I said, "Moody didn't shoot anyone." I was almost certain I believed it.

"If you say so."

I nodded, acknowledging his sarcasm. "There's something else going on at that bank. Something that's nothing to do with us. The manager showed me into the interview room I must have fired into. There were stains on the floor and fresh paint on the wall. But . . ."

"Whoa. Whoa!" Bernie sat up straight. "You went back to the bank? You must be out of your mind."

I said, "At least you and Moody agree about that."

"You stupid, stupid bastard. Sir."

He said 'sir' the same way Moody had.

"According to the information they passed to your erstwhile colleagues, the man who wouldn't get down on the floor was Eddie Likker."

"But . . ."

"Quite."

Bernie shook his head. "Mind you," he said, "it's the sort of thing Likker would do."

"If he weren't dead?"

"Obviously." Bernie paused. "You're sure?"

I nodded. "I saw him with my own eyes."

"So . . . ?"

"The bank manager either doesn't know Eddie's dead – which I don't believe – or he was lying. I just don't know why. But he was very keen to tell me about the woman who followed the man who wasn't Eddie."

"That was Rada Kalenkova?"

So Bernie had been listening after all. "You know her?"

"I probably came across her dad. Pyotr Kalenkov. Aka Peter Caller; aka Pete the Pontiff. Because he could persuade you he was the Pope, if he had the mind. A conman who married well, by all accounts. And a mate of Likker's."

That took me by surprise.

"Eddie's?"

Bernie laughed, relaxing now. "I know. Shocking, isn't it? For an accountant your friend Mr Likker associated with a pretty low class of person. As well as with the high and mighty, of course . . ."

"So there could be a connection?"

"Who knows? Kalenkov's been dead for years. His son found the body in the woods behind their house. That's how I know the name. It was my case until the Chief called me in and told me it was suicide."

"But it wasn't?"

Bernie gave me that look again. "The coroner said it was."

"So it was?"

"If you say so. Me, I've never come across another middle-aged man who got pissed and tranq'ed and slit his wrists successfully; certainly not a right-handed man who slit his right wrist first . . ."

I found myself looking at my wrists, imagining a knife. I wasn't sure I wouldn't start with the right wrist. Once you'd cut the left it wouldn't be much use. But what did I know? I wasn't a coroner; I wasn't even a detective. Debits by the window; credits by the door.

Bernie said, "When the Chief told me, guess who was in the room?"

After a moment, it came to me. "Eddie?"

Bernie says, "You'd make a detective yet."

"If I weren't being sacked?"

"You want me to find her?"

"Could you?"

There was that look again. He said, "Of course I can. I work in HR."

An hour later Bernie and I approached a terraced house in a late nineteenth-century suburb. There were trees and wide pavements and speed humps in the road. There were wooden shutters in the big bay windows. Ms Kalenkova must have been comfortable enough for a conman's daughter. The door was answered by a man in an apron; his hands were covered in flour. Bernie said we were with the police – it was the same mis-truth I had used myself – and could we come in? The man in the apron looked uncertain, and didn't step aside. Bernie said we were looking for Rada Kalenkova and it was obvious from his reaction that the man knew the name. Bernie said not to worry, she wasn't in any trouble. She just had some information that we needed. The man said Rada wasn't at home.

"And you are?"

"Gary Kalenkov." He held up his hands to show he couldn't shake because they were covered in flour; he looked as if he were surrendering.

I said, "Her brother?"

"Her husband. I took her name."

Bernie tried not to laugh. I wondered whether it was just sexism or the fact that the woman's name was fake anyway that had amused him. He said, "Can you tell us where your wife is, Mr Kalenkov?"

"It's the middle of the afternoon. She's at work."

"And what does she do?"

"She's a loss adjuster. Why do you want to talk to her?"

"Ah . . . One of her clients has died . . . We need a little background information, that's all."

I was admiring Bernie's quick-wittedness until I thought: if we were interested in her because of her client, why would we ask what she does? And why wouldn't we have rung her office? But the young man was laughing now. Bernie stopped and the silence demanded an explanation. Kalenkov wiped his hands on his apron and said, "Her clients are *all* dead, officer. That's what she does."

~

"No. No way."

"Bernie . . ."

"There is no fucking way I'm going back to that bank. And neither are you."

It was four-thirty. We were on the broad pavement outside Rada Kalenkova's house. It was still hot and we had retreated to the shade of a plane tree. Fat black ants with wings crawled around our shoes. I could see sweat moistening Bernie's beard; above the hairline his cheeks had lost their pallor. I took this as a good sign.

I said, "If we're quick we can get there before it closes."

Gary Kalenkov had clammed up after his joke about his wife's dead clients. He claimed not to know the name of the company his wife worked for, or where its offices were. He told us he had to go and collect his son from school. It was only when we made it clear that we were quite prepared to keep him there as long as it took, that he gave us Rada's mobile number. As soon as he left, I called it: I told her voicemail that I was "with the police", that I understood she had witnessed a bank robbery on Monday morning, and that I would very much like to talk to her. I said my name was Pitt.

Bernie asked why Pitt, and I said that was the name of my predecessor, the name I'd used at the bank. Then I thought about the deputy manager again, Meersow, and the way he'd winked at me. I said we had to go back and talk to him again, and Bernie said we shouldn't.

At the bank I asked the cheerful-looking blonde woman if we could speak to Mr Meersow. After a moment's hesitation and confusion, she showed us into an interview room. It was not the room I'd been in before, the one with the fresh paint and the poster, the one I accidentally fired into. Meersow's thin frame entered the room sideways as if he was checking behind the door for a surprise attacker. I invited him to sit down as if this were not in fact his bank, but mine. I introduced Bernie as Detective Inspector Jenks. It was not untrue; as Karen had been so keen to remind him, Bernie retains his rank despite his transfer to HR. But it was not exactly true, either. I watched Meersow as I said it, and I felt rather than saw Bernie wince. Meersow may have noticed it too, because he seemed to relax a little. He nodded towards Bernie and then turned back to me. He said, "Forgive me, Mr Pitt, but I cannot recall your rank." Which was because I had not given one, as I am sure he was aware. I am not a policeman, but as a department head I did in fact have an equivalent rank. I doubted that telling Meersow I was an Assistant Chief Constable would help – no real Assistant Chief Constable would be seen dead at a crime scene without cameras present.

Bernie rescued me. "Mr Meersow, the information you passed to my colleague indicated that the account from which the witness attempted to withdraw money was that of one Edward Likker."

Meersow stroked his moustache, but said nothing.

"But the witness could not have been Edward Likker."

Meersow nodded again. "Indeed."

So the bank knew their customer was dead. I said, "Why was the account still open?"

"Because Mr Likker left specific instructions that it was to remain open until we received further notification from his solicitor."

"Why?"

"He did not share his intentions with the bank, Mr Pitt."

Bernie said, "So why was the account empty?"

Meersow turned his colourless eyes to Bernie. "Because, Detective Inspector, all of the funds had been withdrawn on Friday of last week."

"By?"

"Matthew Rodkin, I would imagine."

We waited.

"Mr Likker's solicitor. Mr Likker had given him power of attorney."

I said, "How much was in the account?"

"Four hundred and fifty thousand pounds. Plus interest."

Bernie whistled through his teeth. All cops watch watch too much TV. He said, "Do you have an address for this Rodkin?"

Meersow smiled, thin lips curling back over surprisingly large front teeth. "Rodkin died at the weekend. Apparently he slit his own throat with a breadknife. Do you not read the papers? I understand your . . . *colleagues* . . . do not consider the circumstances to be suspicious."

I didn't like the way he said 'colleagues'. I said, "You didn't mention any of this to DS Proctorow?"

"He didn't ask."

Bernie said, "This four-fifty. Did Rodkin take a banker's draft?"

Meersow interlaced his long fingers and rested his chin upon them.

"The money was withdrawn in cash, Detective Inspector. I arranged the withdrawal myself. We don't usually carry that much currency, you know."

And there it was again, that twitch, the faintest muscular spasm just below his right eye that could have been a wink.

Outside on the pavement Bernie whistled again and said, "You want to check out Rodkin's place?"

"I think we'd better."

"I was afraid you'd say that."

I waited for him to make a call, to find out where we had to go.

"Bill?"

"What?"

"You know we picked the wrong day to knock this place off."

"Four hundred and fifty thousand pounds?"

"And change."

"It's just the chips, Bernie."

Bernie pulled out his mobile and made a couple of calls. A few minutes later, we were heading back to the suburbs. We'd pick up Moody on the way.

# 15

WHEN HE LEAVES the café D tells me not under any circumstances whatsoever to go to Rodkin's place or anywhere near it, or in the same postcode, even, and I won't. But despite there being nowhere that I actually have to go, and the fact that the two places other than Rodkin's flat I might choose to go – *viz* work and home – are both at least temporarily off-limits for different, albeit related, reasons, I can't just sit here, in the café, all day. I have no book, no phone, or at least I have only a dead phone, a phone I've killed, and no work, on account of not actually being supposed to be working, I have nothing to do at all, so I cannot stay here, in the café, without experiencing considerable boredom, which I am not good at, and without attracting, after a while, the attention of the staff who might reasonably expect me to buy something to justify occupying a table no one else will use while I am here. They will not say anything, at first – they know me here, or at least they recognise me; I've been here before with D, and with Gary, who engages the owner in detailed conversations regarding the provenance of her coffee beans, the treatment of the soil and the employment practices on the various estates, which conversations the owner seems more than happy to engage in, although, after a while, I notice that she finds other tasks increasingly absorbing and distracting and eventually urgent. Now I think of it, I've been here with Matthew, too, and even Alex; it is the café we sometimes come to on a Sunday when Gary has not actually for whatever reason baked croissants or brioche or Danish, in view of all which, the staff will probably hold back for a while, in recognition of our previous acquaintance, and the regularity of my custom, and of the fact that it is not, now, in the early afternoon, the busiest time of day. But eventually one of them – the short woman, perhaps, with the pig-tails and the metal spike through her eyebrow and two more spikes through her lower lip and the Doctor Marten boots; Lauren, I think, or Laura, or Lara, I've never actually used her name, or been introduced, but I've overheard her talking with the owner – Lara will stroll past my table and ask – politely, not hassling me or anything, but letting me know all the same that she's noticed how long I've been sitting here, not buying coffee, or cake or a herbal infusion – whether there is anything she can get me? And once, maybe twice, I could say I'm fine, thanks, and smile, and she would have to go away because, after all, it is a café and people sit in cafes and she wouldn't be able to make a fuss or say what she and her colleague – Ray? Rory? – would actually be thinking because it wouldn't be polite and might cause a scene they wouldn't want. As time drags on, though, and teatime approaches and the café begins to fill up again, it will be harder, if not impossible, for me to say I'm fine and not buy anything, which is the problem. Because the fact is that when I went to the bank on Monday it was to pay in the cheque Gary's mother sent for Matthew's birthday and also to withdraw cash from my own account, which I was waiting to do when the gunmen – actually two gunmen and one gunwoman – entered the bank and began to shout and wave their guns about and tell us all to get down on the floor, which I did, as a result of which I never actually got around to withdrawing any cash or depositing the cheque and now, sitting in the café where I have already ordered and drunk a cappuccino and D has left without paying for his hot chocolate w/marshmallows and sandwich, or panini, or whatever, I realise that I have no money. Not exactly no money – nobody has *no* money; or almost nobody – but in this case what I have is £7.36 and I'm not sure that will even cover what D and I already owe, let alone allow me to order anything more, and the longer I sit here, not ordering, not responding to Lara's obvious invitations to order *something*, the more embarrassing it will be both in general and in the specific circumstances that £7.36 proves insufficient to meet my existing obligations. Which, it turns out, it is, but it's close enough for Rory, or Ray, who happens to be nearest to the till when I finally get up to leave, to make a bit of a joke about and tell me I can give him the rest the next time I'm in. Which, if I had known he was likely or able to do I might have been tempted to order another coffee after all, but now of course it is too late.

Outside the café it is hot, the pavement is sticky in the sunshine and the air is beginning to thicken. Across the street the guy from the deli in his heavy cotton apron with a picture of two artichoke heads where his breasts would be, if he were a woman, the same apron Gary has, or at least the same design, has come out to wind down his awning to keep the sun off the cheeses and the charcuterie in his window. The awning is a shade of deep dark green, like an old-fashioned racing car, and has the same picture of artichoke heads on it. Plus it has the words 'artisan' and 'traiteur' picked out in a clean un-cluttered white font against the dark green of the awning that makes me think of racing cars. When D was a child – and I was a child, too, although older – he had a model of a racing car he had painted and assembled from individual plastic parts pressed into the shapes of a steering wheel or an axle or a bonnet, and he had painted the parts of the car that would have been painted green – that is, not the chrome or glass or rubber or whatever – green, and he told me it was called British Racing Green. I remember our father holding up the model to the light when D had finished it and pointing out a tiny patch of grey plastic where D had failed to paint right to the edge, perhaps where he'd pinched it between his fingers to hold it still, and he hadn't noticed the missing paint, but our father had, so he, D, could not have been older than seven, because after that our father wouldn't have been there and D's mother would not have noticed a thing like that.

To the right of the deli is a nail bar-cum-tanning salon that used to be a post office; to the left a newsagent that used to be a different newsagent. But there is no bank in this little parade, the building that had once been a bank, and still has the word 'Bank' inscribed in stone letters above the double entry doors, is now a pizza restaurant, it has a phalanx of battered mopeds parked outside with large, corrugated plastic boxes on their back seats held in place by stretchy elastic cables. So I have no money and also nothing specific to do and nowhere to be, except, possibly, those places I can't or shouldn't go to.

I unlock my bicycle and coil the chain around the saddle stem and lock it again and put the D-lock in its cradle and lock that. I hook my bag to the metal carrier and secure it with the velcro strap and wheel the bike to the kerb and lift it into the gutter and don't know whether to follow the street down, that is, south, or to turn back up and head the other way, towards the city and in the end I decide to do that, to turn back the other way because I have to do something, and it might as well be that as anything else. I have no money and nothing to do. When he left, D told me he was going to see a man about a dog, it's the sort of thing our father might have said and D has inherited or absorbed or consciously affected, I don't know which, but he said it and when I asked him what he meant he said the man was a policeman, he told me Likker was dead and Rodkin was dead, and he didn't say anything more, other than that I shouldn't go to Rodkin's flat or anywhere near Rodkin's flat until he, D, returned. He said that. He must have thought, or assumed, that I was going to stay in the café all afternoon, he didn't know I had no money, or not enough money. He probably had not even thought about it, he left without paying for his lunch, let alone mine. But I can't stay, and not just because of my lack of money. I push off from the kerb and feel the muscles in my legs and the pedals through the sole of my shoes, first one then the other and I think about Alex and the telephone I heard ringing when I called him, or tried to call him, when I left Gina's house, before I came to the cafe and called work and heard that voice, Lopez's voice, and destroyed my phone. I wish I hadn't done that now. At the corner I turn and begin to loop back the way I'd come earlier this morning and, at the next junction, I turn again and begin to head up towards the city.

When I get to the railway bridge where normally, most days, I turn left and then left again for work I carry straight on, past the cathedral and over the bridge into the mediaeval heart of the city where there are plenty of banks, though most of them are not the sort of bank you can walk into and withdraw cash from, either from a machine or over the counter, they probably don't even have counters and are not the sort of banks you can rob, either, not by going in with guns and balaclavas and telling everyone to get down on the floor, and telling the cashiers to put the cash in the bag, there probably isn't even any cash there. I keep going, my legs pushing and rising, taking turns, the left and then the right. There isn't much traffic, but the streets are narrow and I have to watch out for people stepping off the pavements, stepping into the roadway without warning or precaution, it seems, without thought or awareness even of what they are doing, I have to swerve more than once, to risk falling off or being run down by taxis coming up behind me. Gradually, however, the streets broaden out again and there are more cars, but also more space for cars to pass and fewer pedestrians, certainly in the road, but also on the pavements, which seem to be mostly empty here, north of the city centre, I keep going, without really meaning to, without, as far as I am aware, thinking about it, keep going in as straight a line as possible in a mediaeval city, or at least a city with a mediaeval street plan, the buildings aren't all that old.

I pass the dissenters' cemetery almost before I realise I am looking for it. I dismount and chain my bicycle to the wrought ironwork fence, and pass through the gate, and look at the graves and find a bench to sit down on. The cemetery is tiny, set back from the road behind its gate and high, black-painted iron railings, squeezed between a steel-and-glass insurance company building and the grey blank old stone side wall of an eighteenth-century building that had once been a furrier's. The cemetery itself is older than either, the headstones uprooted and dragooned into ranks, eroded by centuries of weather and smoke and exhaust fumes, their inscriptions blunted as if disguising the dead, making them anonymous, the names and dedications and encomia blurred by age and lichen. Somewhere amongst these ranks, I know, are the gravestones of poets and political reformers, martyrs to causes, monuments to preachers and trade unionists and deportees. Our father brought us here, D and me, more than once, the last time not long before he died, I would have been fourteen, D would have been seven, before he died, before he killed himself. He was happy that time, I remember, his tie loose, the buttons on his tweed waistcoat open, his short thick hand on my shoulder as he pointed out headstone after headstone, people I had never heard of, people who had been dead a hundred years, two hundred years. D hung back saying nothing, even when our father spoke to him directly, which he mostly didn't do, because mostly he spoke to me in a voice he knew D could overhear, he would say: Your brother is a boy, Rada, he can't help it. Your brother has to fight me, to beat me, to trample me into the ground. That is the law. But he cannot do it. He is too weak, he is too like a girl. You are stronger than he is Rada, although you are a girl. You are strong, you know who you are, but D is weak, D is unable to challenge his father, even though he wants to challenge his father, even though he knows he has to, he cannot because he is weak, a weakling, a mother's boy. Mother's boy. Those were the words that did it, finally, that dragged D out of his sullen lethargy that made him put his head down and charge our father and bowl him over, both of them falling onto a grave, D's arms around his chest. D was tall, even then, but he was a boy, his muscles a boy's muscles and our father threw him off easily and, laughing, jumped to his feet and put up his fists and said, still laughing, Come on, then, Mitya, come on. D stayed on the ground, rubbing his elbows. Our father dropped his fists, he put them on his hips, he stood there like a gnome, like a troll, his face red above his beard, and said, more gently, Come on, Mitya. D did not move, did not look up at our father, and when at last he put out a hand to pull D to his feet, D turned without getting up, and scrambled away. By the time he got to his feet he was already running and he did not stop when he reached the cemetery gate, he kept going through and across the street, a bus missed him by what looked like millimetres, he kept going turning right towards the centre of the city. Our father did not move. I said we should follow him, catch up with him, but our father said no, D would be all right.

It is hot, even here, where the height of the buildings and

the narrowness of the streets keep the sun from reaching the headstones and the paths and the grass between them, where there is grass. It is not unusual, not exceptional, it is almost to be expected, a woman sitting on a bench, resting, taking a break in the middle of the afternoon in the quiet and calm of the graveyard, the only surprising feature of the scene is that I appear to have the place to myself, there are no office workers – no other office workers – smoking cigarettes or talking on mobile phones, no homeless men waving lager cans to punctuate their discourse with their demons. I am alone.

I was scared. Our father said, He'll be all right, he'll come back, and if he doesn't, he'll find his own way home. We waited but D didn't come back and by then it wasn't just D I was scared for. When we got home D was sitting on the doorstep, the house was empty, I don't know where his mother was, my stepmother. I don't remember. I remember our father called out when he saw D as if nothing had happened, he put his hand on D's shoulder and D shrugged it off. When he opened the door D went straight up to his room, and our father said to me, let's have tea, shall we, and I said, no, I wasn't hungry, I wasn't thirsty and I went to my own room and shut the door and when D found him in the woods behind our house, it was only a few months later, he was still seven and I was fourteen, the first thing he did when he had checked our father's pulse and found no pulse was to kick his corpse repeatedly in the stomach and the chest. I know this because D told me that is what he did and I have no reason not to believe him, plus the coroner recorded the presence of bruises, which he could not explain, but which he said must have been caused at or around the time of death but about which he could not be sufficiently certain to undermine or change or invalidate his overall conclusion that our father's death was the result of asphyxiation prompted by a combination of alcohol and painkillers and was not the result of foul play. Which means that our father must have been alive or very nearly alive when D found him. D only told me this – about kicking our father's body – years later, only after his business collapsed and he came to stay with me because he had no money and very large debts and nowhere to stay and I suggested that he might talk to Theo about a job and he said he didn't want a job and I said: What else are you going to do? When he told me, I asked him why he had kicked our father and he said it was obvious, wasn't it, it was because he hated him. We were in the kitchen sitting at the table, Gary in the background washing up and D had drunk five or six cans of lager at this point and was homeless, in a way, not hardcore homeless, not sleeping on the streets and urinating in his trousers, but without a home of his own and sleeping in his sister's second spare room, Alex already having taken the room we called the spare room.

It is after four-thirty p.m. when I leave the cemetery. I am surprised how late it is. I have been here more than two hours and I haven't eaten or drunk anything or seen anyone in all that time, and still have no money. I climb onto my bike and shuffle it round and point it back the way I came, back through the mediaeval streets of modern buildings, back across the bridge over the river and turn right towards work, towards the office but I'm not going to work. At the traffic lights I dismount and wheel my bike across the road towards the bank.

There are two men outside the bank, standing on the pavement, not going in or going out. One is short and fat and has a beard, although it is not much of a beard, but will perhaps be a beard when he's grown it for a few more days, or weeks, or however long it is these things take. He also has a mobile phone he's talking into while the other man, who is neither short nor fat, but is not especially tall, either, or thin, plus is clean shaven and, if he has a mobile phone – as in all probability he does – he is not, at this moment, using it, but is looking past his friend, or acquaintance, or colleague or whatever the shorter, fatter and more hirsute man is, looking over his shoulder directly and unmistakably at me. He holds his gaze for longer than one usually might, longer than is conventional or polite, or socially acceptable, and even though he does not nod or smile or speak or make any gesture that might suggest that he recognises me, or believes that he recognises me, or acknowledges that the way in which he has been looking at me is in any way unusual or impolite or socially unacceptable, there is nonetheless something in the way he keeps looking at me and then, eventually, stops looking at me, that indicates, without me being able to quite say why, that he knows me, or recognises me, or has at least seen me before somewhere. He says nothing, however, but turns to his companion, or colleague, who says something I cannot hear. They both turn away, towards the cathedral and the station, the way the older professor-type guy had gone, the way I had followed, although without ever catching up with him, and now, at this moment, I know that he, the taller man, *has* seen me before, even though he does not say so, or indicate in any conscious way that he recognises me, and I have seen him before and I know precisely where and when.

I have come here, to the bank, for a reason, to withdraw the cash I intended to withdraw on Monday, two days ago, but then failed, or had no real opportunity, to withdraw on account of the bank being robbed before I reached the front of the queue for the cash dispensing machine, as a result of which I still have no money, I have even less money than I had then, have exactly no money, in fact.

And yet:

I am certain that the two men, one tall, one not so tall, who were standing on the pavement in front of the bank when

I arrived and dismounted and began to lock my bicycle, are the same two men who, with one woman, entered the bank on Monday and waved guns around and ordered us all to get down on the floor. Strictly speaking, of course, the gunmen are no concern of mine because, not being dead, they are no concern of the Office and because – have I forgotten? – I am not working, am not allowed to work, I have been instructed, in no uncertain terms by Theo, a man I admire and respect, and usually obey without qualm, to go home, and not to work, not to even think about working, pending Lopez's investigations into the events of Monday morning.

I follow the two men, wheeling my bicycle along the pavement, until I see them get into a car, a police car, or at least a car with bright blue and yellow stripes and a large black number on the roof, and the word 'Police' painted or decaled or somehow inscribed on the door I can see and probably also on the other door, which seems enough to suggest, taken together with Monday's van, that the men – and possibly the woman, although the woman is not here – are in some way connected to the police, if not actual police officers, or possibly that they are actors or producers, or assistants to assistant producers, for a film or television company of some sort, a possibility that has not previously occurred to me. Could Monday's robbery have been some sort of stunt staged for the benefit of unseen cameras, or for the bank's own cameras which undoubtedly filmed it all anyway whether the robbers were real or actors and the guns real or fake? The guns were real. The screaming was real.

I lift my bike into the gutter and straddle it. I push off and pass the police/fake police car just as the taller of the two men starts the engine. The car pulls out behind me. The taller of the two men, the one who had looked at me as if he knew me, or had seen me before, and may therefore have realised that he has in fact seen me before, and where, and may have concluded that I am a witness to the robbery and possible murder, or double murder, is now driving the car which pulls past me; the road is very narrow and it passes very close to me.

At a junction, where the lights are red, I overtake the police/fake police car again, plus two or three other cars and a small van. I can turn left or right. Right will take me south, back the way I came, back towards home, towards Gina's home, towards Rodkin's home. I cross the junction just before the lights turn green, something I never usually do, and pedal rapidly. After a couple of hundred yards the small van passes me, and then the police car. The shorter, bearded man, the passenger, has wound down his window and has his elbow resting on the door, his fingers tapping the roof. It does not look as though he is watching me. As the traffic backs up for the next junction I pull into the middle of the road and pass the police car again. I jump the lights, carry straight on and, soon enough, the police car passes me again. At the next lights, I guess a left and then straight across a roundabout and I'm right both times and when the traffic thins and the traffic lights get more spread out I lose the police car but I know it doesn't matter, I know where they're going and I go there too.

# 16

I AM STILL SITTING at the table when Kurt returns. As I had imagined, he brings lunch, including cheese, of a sort. From the quality of the light and of my hunger, however, it must be much later than lunchtime. He places a tray – the same tray as at breakfast – on the table before me, takes a step back and says, Well?

I don't know what to say to this, and say nothing. He says, Have you decided yet, Mr Lopez?

I'm not Lopez.

So you say.

It is clear we have an impasse. Kurt has crossed his arms again. They rest on his substantial belly. I say, How do you know Lopez?

How do you?

It is a fair question. I say, I know *of* him. We've never met.

Is that right?

I say that it is.

I have given something. Surely he must now reciprocate? Isn't that the way these things work? He lifts one meaty hand to his face and rubs his jaw, which looks abrasive. He has not shaved for a day or two.

He says, And you've never met Likker, either?

He says it in a way that shows he knows what I am going to say, and I needn't think he's going to believe it. It isn't true, but I say it anyway: I've never even *heard* of Likker. Kurt snorts. He genuinely snorts. He leaves and I examine the food he has brought. The bread is white – the unnatural white of the teeth of young people in rich countries. I know that when I put it in my mouth it will offer no resistance, but will dissolve into a sticky gum against my teeth. Gary has explained to me why this is, and why it is so bad for me. The cheese is yellow and evidently sliced – or possibly extruded – by a machine. It has the glossy surface of expensive cars, but is not, I know expensive. I sniff it but both the cheese and the bread are odourless. They remind me nonetheless of lost times: the bread of sitting in my mother's car while she was elsewhere, in conversation with a neighbour, perhaps, and digging a tunnel through a whole loaf; the cheese of burgers eaten at three in the morning in the careless invincibility of drunken youth. I have finished the sandwich before I remember that I was going to give some cheese to my rodent companion. I'm sorry, I say towards the gap in the skirting. Next time, I promise. A few minutes later Kurt returns. He takes the tray away, but says nothing. Kurt? I say, as he leaves, but he does not even pause. I hear the kitchen door click to and the sound of the lock turning. He still has my cigarette lighter, if it was he who took it. I need a cigarette.

Later I take a walk as far as the kitchen. Exercise is good. It can release endorphins and lighten the mood. I am told it can reduce the craving for nicotine, although it does not seem to do so now. From the kitchen I can see the garden out of the window. The little blue weed flowers have opened again. There are two or three flies on the glass, on the outside. I tap on the window and they disappear, but soon return. I open each of the drawers and cupboards. There is nothing there that wasn't there yesterday, which was nothing. The knives are still stuck to the magnetic strip on the wall. Every thirty-six seconds somebody, somewhere, kills himself. Or herself. More probably a he. Four times as many men kill themselves as women, at least in countries where we have data. Of course, for every suicide who dies, nine or ten survive, and, amongst those who try, twice as many are women as men. Which tells us what? That women aren't really trying? Or just don't own as many guns? Men shoot themselves. Or drive their cars into oncoming traffic. They don't care. Women prefer poison, which is slow and inefficient and has a high failure and/or intervention rate built in, but is more considerate of those who will discover the corpse, or at any rate it is less messy. And a knife? A knife is somewhere in the middle. Most people who slit their wrists don't die. (I know, they all die, but not of that). Taking a breadknife to one's own throat is different again. It is very hard; few people are capable of even trying it. But if you can hang on past the initial pain and shock and terror, and you're not troubled by the mess you're making and the likely trauma for whomever it is you think is going to find your bloodied corpse, then it is going to work. No interfering doctor will sew your carotid artery back together unless they happen to be there in the room with you at the time, which seems unlikely, and even then the serrated edge and the inevitably jerky, tugging, hacking motions you would need to get through your own throat would make the severed edges too irregular, too fibrous and rough-hewn for reconstructive surgery to stand much chance of success. It is the choice of someone who really, really wants to die.

Gary told me D found his father – Rada's father; their father – in the woods a mile or so behind their house. We were in the kitchen and Rada had just left for work; D was leaving. I had been talking about how common suicide was. Is. Gary was angry with me. I could tell by the way the muscles tightened in his face and he breathed a little deeper before he spoke. Gary does not believe in shouting. His words became more precise.

He said Rada's father had taken thirty painkillers and slit his wrists. He said it as if he were reading a utility bill. There was blood on the leaves and grass all around him. I said, Why? Not meaning why was there blood on the leaves, but why did he do it? I knew so much less about the subject then. Also, you may recall, I was angry myself. I suppose that what I really meant was: Why hadn't Rada told me this herself? Why had she told *you*? Gary ignored me. He said, There was an empty vodka bottle, a penknife and a smear of cold vomit. I asked how he knew it was cold. Gary sucked air through his teeth. He said D told Rada; Rada had told him. D was seven; Rada was fourteen. There were no pills in the vomit, Gary said. So D said he must have thrown up before he took them. Before he killed himself; which means he would have been drunk when he did it.

I said, You think he never meant to die?

Gary mistook my sarcasm for stupidity. He said that's what D thought; Rada, too.

He turned away. He began carrying plates from the table to the sink. To Gary, the idea of *wanting* to die made no sense at all. There were always more people to help, things to make better. More books to read. But I sensed there might be more to it than that. At work, I checked the file. The autopsy report said there were no pills in the vomit because he had taken them a couple of hours earlier and they had been digested. He had set out to kill himself *before* he began drinking that day. The slit wrists may have been a gesture, an insurance policy, or a fuck-you to the world. As a method of suicide it is rare amongst middle-aged men, mainly because it so rarely works. Rada's father knew what he was doing.

It occurs to me that I could use one of the heavier knives to break a window. Why would I do that? The bars would still be there. But I would have shards of broken glass I could hold to

Kurt's throat the next time he brings me a meal. I could wait behind the door and jump him as he carries the tray. Soup, or sausages, or whatever he has prepared for my supper will go flying all over the room, adding to the stains. He will struggle but I will have the strength of a man possessed. I will cling on to his back while he bucks and thrashes like an unbroken horse, all the while pressing the jagged glass harder against his throat until, eventually, I am forced to draw blood and he calms down, panting. I will smell his sweat and fear as I whisper in his ear that I am going to leave and nothing he can do will stop me.

I shake my head. It will not happen like that. I look again at the knife rack: it is not a lack of weaponry that has held me back. Still. If I broke a window in the front, in the semi-basement bay, I could shout for help.

I have to consider this. I walk back to the bedroom and sit on the chair in the middle of the room. I notice that I have not brought a knife with me. I could shout: Help! I am being held captive! This is something I have always wanted to do. Not *always*, perhaps, but intermittently: you too, no doubt. It would be like saying Follow that cab! to a taxi driver, and meaning it. Such opportunities do not present themselves every day. In life, I find, the secret is to plan nothing, to want nothing, but just to see what happens. What is offered. Such a life requires strength and stealth and is harder than it looks. If I shout, who will hear me? Passers-by? Most likely, they will pass by; it's what they do. If not worse. The Good Samaritan was not the first on the scene. The odds are not good. It is more likely that Kurt will hear. Or that the woman will hear. I don't know her. I may be wrong. But I think she does not go far, if she leaves her flat at all. I have heard noises, from above. When I saw her yesterday – it was yesterday, I am sure, twenty-four hours ago – she had the dilated eyes and helpless, flayed appearance of a subterranean creature suddenly exposed to light. Kurt struck me as a man of more action, a man with things to do. He will not be upstairs all the time. He will not be there now, for instance, in the middle of the afternoon, if it is afternoon. He will have other fish to fry.

So, the woman, then.

If I smash the window and shout for help she will most likely hear me: what will she do? She will not call the police. That much is obvious. Will she come down to the semi-submerged bay and whisper to me through the broken glass? Will she return upstairs and take the key from the hook by the door in her kitchen where Kurt has left it, and slip it to me, or open the door herself and let me flee, after just an awkward, bony hug of gratitude and a single, hasty kiss, while she says I must not worry about her, she can look after herself? Run, Alex, run. I don't think she has it in her. I am not sure I have it in me. I think, in fact, she would wait until Kurt returns from the things he has to do, from the deals he has to cut and the people he has to meet, and she will tell him. She will complain about the noise, and about having to cook an extra meal. Because it strikes me now that Kurt is not a man to make even a sandwich when there is a woman around. When this is all over perhaps I should introduce him to Gary? That might be an education for them both.

When this is all over? I am not sure what I mean by that.

Enough. I have to consider what Kurt will do if the woman – I decide I will call her Beatrice; I don't imagine for a moment that it is her name, but I can't keep calling her just "the woman". I have to consider what Kurt might do if I shout for help and Beatrice hears, and tells him. Will he be angry? Would he take measures to enforce my future silence? Would he wonder how I could do this to him after he has treated me with nothing but courtesy? Might he become tearful and enraged, his judgment clouded by the bitterness of betrayal and might he take the knife that I have used to break the window and plunge it here, into my chest, between the fourth and the fifth rib just to the left of my sternum (to the right as he looks at it)? And as he feels the leathery, elastic resistance of my heart, the muscular repulsion before the tip of the knife pierces the left atrium and my blood begins to gout and spew in earnest, much as Rodkin's must have done when he – Rodkin? Kurt? Likker? – hauled the breadknife across the artery in his throat, would he scream? Or cry with remorse? Strange as it may seem to you, I have not, before now, considered the possibility that Rodkin did not kill himself.

Rodkin is a suicide. Surely? There has to be some point of certainty from which we start. Rodkin killed himself, albeit in a statistically unusual manner. I am not here to question that. I am here to consider and assess the value of his life given the fact of his suicide, from a presumption of damnation. And what do the facts tell me? That Rodkin shared house space with a man who would not think twice about locking me in a basement flat. I realise it is possible, on the contrary, that he thought long and hard about it, but I do not think it likely. For one thing, he would not have known about my arrival before it happened. The quick do not know that we do what we do. That would rather spoil the point, not to mention opening the doors for all kinds of fraudulent malpractice. Imagine it, if you will. You are half way – you hope: the fraction could be greater – through a no more than averagely sinful life. There are things that weigh heavily on your heart – the spouse you deceived, the children whose ambitions you stifled, the parents you disappointed – but you believe, in spite of the evidence, that you are a good person, that you do not deserve to suffer. In this frame of mind you meet, let us say in a pub, or a coffee shop, a man like me – a man younger than you, of working age, and working. You exchange some pleasantry about the drink you have ordered, or about the sporting event being broadcast silently on the giant screen to your left, about which you know nothing at all. You fall into conversation and, in the way of these things, you ask me what it is that I do for a living. I say I am a loss adjuster. And when you ask what that might be, I tell you. Imagine it. You now know that I, or one of my colleagues – Rada, perhaps, or D – a person who does not know you, and, up to this point at least, has had no interest in you whatsoever, will, the moment you die, assess the value of your life. That I, or someone like me, will make a recommendation that, while not binding, will in all likelihood determine the future of your eternal soul, even if you don't believe you have one. Imagine it. That moment would be strange, would it not? Unusual. An opportunity would have arisen. I think, in your shoes, I might be tempted to buy me a drink, and subtly to sound out what my predilections might be. I – that is, you – might be tempted to tempt me, to hint at gratifications that could flow from a commitment to a report that burnishes the better parts of my life until the glow outshines the neglected spouse, the resentful, stunted children and the bitterness of the long-dead parents. Don't you? You would seek to influence me, to bribe me, to corrupt me if you thought you could get away with it. You would. You know you would. A cursory glance at the history of our species will tell you what I say is true. Which is precisely why you've never heard of us, never met us, and why the name we use is false. It would not be fair, on either party, if it were otherwise. That is why there is no sign on our office door, why our business cards give a false name, why you do not know who we are, or even that we are. But Kurt thought I was Lopez and Lopez is one of us, and Kurt should never have heard of him, much less have been expecting him to call at the scene of Rodkin's suicide. Thinking I was Lopez he locked me in here and left me with a rack of knives, one of which I might use to smash the window and call for help although, if I do, the chances are that it will be Kurt himself who comes and, given that he has locked me here it seems unlikely that he would now help me to escape. I will not break the window.

There, that is decided.

I feel a sense of great relief. I feel as if, rather than simply locking the door and bringing me food, Kurt had strapped me to a press, to the sort of apparatus inquisitors use to extract confessions by placing heavy weights upon a board, and the board upon a person, and waiting idly by while the weight presses down upon the person's lungs whenever he or she exhales and, as the muscles weaken, prevents him or her from inhaling until, eventually the suspect suffocates, I feel as if I had been in such a situation and Kurt had, for some reason of his own, relented and lifted the weight before it squeezed the last breath out of me and I have been given another chance to live. I have decided not to try to escape by any action of my own and I feel relieved, grateful even – to Kurt. I will not use a knife to break the window and I will not use a knife to kill him or seek to overpower him or intimidate him into setting me free. I will wait and see what happens. I may try to find out what he knows about Lopez, or I may not.

There is of course another use to which I could put the knives. I could take one of them from the rack and press its point into my own flesh, at the wrist, or the heart or even, like Rodkin, at the throat, my throat, and slash and saw and hack through the pain and fear. I could escape that way.

I stand and walk into the kitchen. Outside the sun is low and the garden is in shade. I choose a knife, a cook's knife with a dimpled metal handle and a faint pattern on the blade like watered silk. I pull up my shirtsleeve and press the flat of the blade to my wrist. My flesh bulges slightly around it. I feel the pressure rise. If I rotate the blade by ninety degrees and pull the edge back towards my body the skin will split and curl slowly back like the crust on a baguette. The blood will seep and well and spoil the beauty of the moment; if I continue, it will gout and spurt and after that I will not see what happens. Possibly. As I say, slashing one's wrists is unreliable. I stand by the window in the kitchen, the knife lying more lightly now upon my arm, for a long time. To the west, to my right, in the tiny corner of the world that I can see, the city will rise up to blot out the sun. It is more probable that I will be bleeding, but alive, when Kurt brings whatever supper it is he intends to bring; I may be slumped to the floor, perhaps, but not dead and not beyond saving. The flowers in the garden will close their blue eyes. The sun will organise ranks of orange, then red, then purple clouds to defend itself, but it will do no good: the city will not be denied. Darkness is its natural state. I relax. I do not need to return to the bedroom, to look at the paper pinned to the cork tiles by the door to recall the words of Isaiah: *I delight not in the blood of bullocks, or of lambs, or of he-goats.* There will be no escape. There will be another sun tomorrow and I will watch it rise. Because even though I tell myself I don't, that it doesn't matter, that one day I won't know and that day might as well be this day as any other, I want to know what happens. Despite myself, I want to see how this turns out.

It is still light when Kurt finally appears. I am lying on the bed and have not turned on the electric light that hangs by a dirty cable in the centre of the room. I am awake, but my eyes are closed. I see Rada, not as she is now, not at work or eating supper in her cycling gear, but as she was in Spain, in a castle where we shared a bed. She was wearing a large, worn, soft T-shirt and plain white panties. Her feet – her toes especially – were larger than I had expected. I am lying now on one side, my left side, my right hand thrust into my trousers. I hear the key in the kitchen door, scratching like a rodent in the walls, and I remember the gap in the skirting, my promise to my unseen friend. I pull my hand from my trousers and sit up. I wonder what food Kurt will bring. Whether he will bring my cigarette lighter. Then I hear Kurt's voice. He asks for your watch, your purse, your mobile phone. He is not alone. I am disappointed, I admit. How could he bring someone else into this? Only now, as he pushes the bedroom door fully open and gestures inside, do I see that it is you.

# 17

WHEN I GET out of the pub it's hot and humid and that doesn't feel right. When you come out of a pub in the late afternoon it should be cold and almost dark, if not actually dark, and raining. It should be raining. But it's not November all the time, and right now it's June, almost July, and the light is bouncing off the moisture in the air, and moving is like swimming through someone else's sweat. Luckily I don't have far to go; luckily I parked right outside the pub and luckily I own the kind of car that has air conditioning and tinted windows. I think: this is why I bought a car with air conditioning. It isn't, of course. You don't buy a car like mine for the fucking ventilation. All the same it would be perfect, now, on an afternoon like this when I've only walked about a metre and a half and already I can feel the sweat beginning to pool, can feel moisture in my eyebrows as if the hairs themselves were starting to perspire, it would be fucking perfect, the air conditioned car, if only Proctorow hadn't chosen such a poxy pub with nowhere to park and I hadn't gone and parked right outside it anyway. Because now I can see – it's impossible not to – a yellow and black plastic warning notice splattered right across my windscreen. The notice tells me not to even try to move my own fucking car. So the air-conditioning is kind of moot. Because although I could run the engine and sit and cool down to my heart's content, it's obvious this thing's going nowhere, and I'm supposed to ring a fucking number and watch some smirking peons who will never ever be able to own a vehicle like this in their wildest dreams, I'm supposed to watch them come and load my beautiful car onto the back of their grubby truck and haul it off to some sad municipal dump while I spend two weeks pleading and begging and bullying a succession of halitosis-breathing jobsworths into accepting my money – *my* money – to let me have my own car back, and frankly – fuck it – I haven't got the time.

I haven't got the time because it wasn't Likker I saw on Proctorow's laptop. It was Lopez. Lopez in the bank on Monday trying to take out Likker's money when Likker had been dead a fortnight. Lopez standing right in front of Rada. Standing even when everyone else – my little sister included – did what they were told to do and got down on the floor. Lopez doing his own thing, even when the man with a gun put the gun against his head, carrying on like the gunman didn't exist, like he wasn't even there. Except that's not quite right. Lopez didn't ignore the gunman. He spoke to him, told him *he'd prefer not* to do what he was told, or some such shit, Rada told us on Monday afternoon when none of us knew what Lopez looked like – or none of us knew we knew, though Rada did, it turns out – and none of us knew that Lopez had anything to do with us, except that we worked for the same organisation, and some of us – me, specifically – didn't even know that. Lopez doing his own thing, which I've got to admit was cool, in its own way, and not something I think I could have pulled off. Or any of us could have, except maybe Theo. I have to give him that.

I probably didn't speak for a minute or two then, when I saw Lopez on Proctorow's laptop. Proctorow just looked at me like I was a dying aunt who'd summoned him to talk about the will. The CCTV footage had ended and my mouth was probably open. There might even have been drool gathering in the corner waiting to abseil down onto the table. Proctorow said, "Pitt? Are you OK?" I said my name wasn't Pitt and I was fine. You can't lie all the time. I told him I had to go, but now I can't go because my car's been clamped and it's all his fucking fault.

I'm looking for something to punch now when I notice that Proctorow has followed me out of the pub, his laptop bag slung across his shoulder pulling him down on one side. He points at my car and says, "That your car?" He keeps his voice flat, but I can hear the joke at the back of it, the sneer, and I'm pretty certain, now, that it's him I'm going to punch. And I'm going to, I've actually drawn my right fist back and I'm leaning in towards the little fucker with my left shoulder, and if I do this right I'll break his nose, I know that, when he says: "Was that Pitt? In the bank?"

And I know it's another stupid Proctorow question, but it triggers something or unhooks something and I feel my arms relax, my shoulders drop. I must shake my head, because Proctorow says, "So who is Pitt, then?"

I say, "I don't know."

Proctorow waits and I say, "It's just a name we use."

He doesn't look convinced, and I'm not sure I do, either. He says, "So who was that in the bank?"

"That was Lopez."

Proctorow waits. He must have learned something in detective school after all, something other than where the shittiest pubs are. We're standing beside my car and I can feel the heat of the afternoon pulsing off the pavement and off the walls of the pub. Proctorow shifts his laptop bag from one shoulder to the other. I am looking for a cab but for some reason, in the middle of the city, at the end of the afternoon when you might just think people would want to get away, there are no cabs. Eventually I say, "Have you got a car?"

"I don't drink and drive."

"That's right," I say. "You don't."

"But I can get us one. Where are we going?"

I think: we? But he's already on the phone.

He's looking at me, now, holding his hand over the speaker on his phone. I say, "Rodkin's." He keeps looking at me. I say, "I don't know. South. We can look it up on the way."

He speaks into the phone again, then hangs up and puts the phone back in his pocket. He says the car will be a while and we might as well not wait out here. We go back in to the pub and I order a couple of whiskies. When I carry them back to the table, Proctorow says: "Who is Rodkin?"

"He's dead. He *was* Likker's solicitor."

Proctorow nods, like this is all beginning to make sense, which I have to say it isn't. He says, "And their deaths are linked?"

Are they? I realise I've just assumed they are, and that they're both linked to Lopez, but I don't know this. I don't know anything at all. Buying time, I say, "Everything is linked."

Proctorow sips his whisky and nods as if this wasn't just hippie bollocks. I get out my own laptop and check Rodkin's address. Proctorow asks what we're looking for and I say: "Do you want a murder or don't you?" And obviously he does.

When the squad car arrives I get in the back and give the plod in the driver's seat Rodkin's address and he says he doesn't go south of the river this time of night, and laughs. Proctorow, to his credit, tells the dickhead to shut the fuck up and drive.

Somewhere just after the river, Proctorow cracks. "OK. Who is Lopez?"

It's a decent question, but I don't have an answer, so I say: "He's the Inquisitor."

Predictably, Proctorow is none the wiser. So I say, "You know how you have cops who don't always, you know, uphold the law, and that?"

Proctorow nods. "I've heard it happens."

"And you know how you have cops who investigate bent cops?"

Procotorow pretends to spit.

"Well Lopez is one of them. At least, he's supposed to be."

Proctorow gestures towards his laptop bag. "But he's on the take himself?"

I say, "Maybe." Because I just don't know. With Lopez I have no idea where I stand. For starters, if Likker knew Lopez, how come Lopez didn't turn up in my research? Which I know is another good question, but the only answer I can come up with is: because he's Lopez.

When we get to Rodkin's, it's still hot. The houses here are four stories high, but the sun is still up above the roofs and it's still hot. There's another police car already pulled up on the pavement.

Proctorow says, "What the fuck?"

I say I'm pretty sure that I can take it from here, but Proctorow, obviously, isn't about to let me shake him off.

I say, "It might just be coincidence. They might be here for something else. Another flat."

But even I don't believe it.

I ring all the bells and a skinny grey-toned woman in a grubby cotton dress opens the door. She doesn't ask who I am and doesn't listen when I say my name is Pitt. She stands back to let us in and says, "They're downstairs."

The stairs take us down and out into a garden full of weeds. The weeds all have tiny blue flowers, the intense violet blue of Rada's eyes. I hope to God she hasn't come here, but I know she has. The back door to Rodkin's flat is unlocked and opens into a kitchen. There's nothing in the kitchen I can see, no food, no kettle, no pots and pans; there's a fridge, but I'm guessing it's empty. There's one of those magnetic racks on the wall over by the sink, with three or four knives on it. I select the boning knife. I know it's a boning knife because Gary has explained these things to me. It's not the biggest and maybe not the sharpest, but if you stick it into someone's chest and it hits a rib it's not going to stop, it's going to bend and keep going. Proctorow is watching me. He tells me to put the knife back. I pause for a moment, then I say, OK and make as if to put it back, but, at the last moment, I slip it up the sleeve of my shirt.

We go through to the bed-sitting room, and it's crowded. There's not a lot of furniture and what there is, is occupied. There's a single bed that's pretty much full of Alex. He's using his jacket as a pillow and his face is turned to the wall. Rada is sitting in the only chair, with Theo standing behind her with his hands on her shoulders. Over by the window there's a big man with no neck who looks like a bouncer in mufti. And over by the door there's two men and a woman I don't know, but Proctorow apparently does.

"Bernie?"

One of the men, short and fat and unshaven, is looking at us with his wet mouth open. On the wall behind him there's a handwritten poster, but I don't get time to really take it in. He nods, "Detective Sergeant Proctorow."

Then Proctorow nods at the woman and says, "Moody."

The woman scowls but doesn't actually say anything.

Proctorow nods at the other man but doesn't say anything.

I feel like none of this is the actual point, because what is absolutely fucking obvious to anyone who's paying attention is that the woman Proctorow called Moody has a gun in her hand, and she's pointing it at Theo's face.

Because Rada is my sister, I say, "Rada? Are you OK?"

I don't bother with Alex because, after all, he's just Alex, and who gives a shit? I'm so busy taking no notice of Alex that it takes a moment before I think: Theo? What the fuck? And by then, he's already talking. He's pretending that there isn't a gun in his face and giving out some shit about how glad he is that I could join them, only I can't tell if he's serious or not. Probably not. Then he's explaining to me that the man with no neck is Kurt and that the two men and the woman, who Proctorow obviously knows, are the bank robbers I might recognise from Rada's report.

I look at the woman and it seems to fit. She's young and her legs look like young women's legs should, even in Doc Martens, but she has a scowl on her face you could scrape paint with. And a gun, of course.

I say to her, "You must be the one who shot the woman in the interview room."

Which doesn't make her look any happier, but doesn't actually get her to say anything, either. I say, "Tell me – because I've been wondering – when you left, was there one dead woman there, or two?"

Moody still doesn't say anything, but Theo does. Smooth as butter, as if the gun really weren't there, in his face, and with one hand on Rada's shoulder, he says, "We've been through that, Dmitry."

"Yeah?"

"Before you arrived."

For a moment I think he's just going to leave it there, i.e. nowhere, but then he says, "Detective Constable Moody assures us that she shot no one."

"And you believe her?"

Theo doesn't answer that, just stands there looking bland and patient.

I say, "I saw the blood, Theo."

"You saw blood, certainly."

"On the carpet. Up the wall."

Theo shrugs, the slightest of movements and I think, not for the first time, that I might just punch him. Which probably isn't fair and which I realise is the second time today I've thought about hitting somebody, but haven't. I know I've either got to actually hit someone or find some other way to calm myself down, because if I go on like this, I'm going to make myself ill. Which isn't right. I'm supposed to be the good guy here. And the woman with the gun is still pointing the gun at Theo's head.

At this point, the woman turns and points the gun at me instead.

The taller man, the one who hasn't said anything yet, now says, "Rachel." Which doesn't really help, as getting onto first name terms isn't my prime objective here.

Theo says, "Please. There's no need for any of this."

Which doesn't help either, because the woman, Moody, says: "Get down on the floor before I blow your fucking head off."

Instinctively, I look at Theo, who makes an almost invisible gesture that I take to mean that I should do what I'm told by a fucking maniac police person with a gun. So I do, even if Theo obviously hasn't. I have to do it carefully, though, on account of there's a knife up my sleeve, and I really don't want it either to fall out at this precise juncture, or to slit my wrist.

The taller man says, "I thought you ditched the guns?"

Still pointing the barrel in my face, Moody says, "This was Bernie's. I ditched yours. Because you fired it. Sir."

I wonder what this has to do with me. The carpet down here is filthy. It feels damp against my cheek, and sticky.

So far Rada hasn't said a word, hasn't moved, or shown

any sign that she's aware of what's going on around her, not even when I asked her if she was all right. I'm looking at Theo, and Theo isn't doing anything. Alex is on the bed, still, facing the wall. Then suddenly Proctorow – I'd forgotten Proctorow – is behind Moody and he's grabbing her right hand, the hand with the gun in it, and pushing it upwards and she's pushing back. She stamps her heel down his shin and onto his foot. He grunts and tugs at her arm and she pulls the trigger.

The noise in the small crowded room is unbelievably loud, and then it's quiet, and then there's another sound, we all hear it, the sound of a woman screaming in pain and shock and probably terror. The sound is muffled, though, because it's coming from the flat above, and we all look up and there's a hole in the ceiling and plaster dust gently falling into Theo's hair, and Rada's.

# 18

TO MY SURPRISE, it was the shorter, fatter, bearded gun/police person, who did not by then appear to have a gun, and whose name and rank were subsequently determined to be Detective Inspector Bernard Jenks, who reacted more quickly than any of the other eight people squeezed into a room that would have been cramped for two or three. I accept now that my surprise may have been based more on on my own prejudices in respect of facial hair and obesity – or, if not actual obesity, which would in this case be inaccurate, or unfair, then at least chubbiness, excessive softness and a pear-shaped physique – than on any actual evidence, but, nonetheless, I was surprised when, with the dust still settling, it was Jenks who stepped forward, revealing the poster, or rather the sheet of cheap plain paper on which had been written in felt marker: *I am full of the burnt offerings of rams and the fat of fed beasts* and grabbed at the gun that the female gun/police person had discharged into the ceiling. At this point the gun/policewoman (whose name and rank were subsequently confirmed as Detective Constable Rachel Moody) fell backwards onto her first assailant, the policeman who had not been a gunman/bank-robber, whose attempt to disarm her had led to the struggle in which the gun was discharged, and who, at that stage was still clinging to her elbow from behind even as she fell backwards on top of him, with Jenks facedown on top of *her*, the three of them grunting and rolling like children in a playground brawl, until, before any of the six other people in the room could intervene, or at least, before any of them, including me, did so intervene, there was a second shot, a little quieter this time, muffled as it was by the close press of bodies. The bullet from this second shot did not penetrate the ceiling but rather pierced the underside of the policeman's chin, the policeman who was not, as far as we know, also a bankrobber, and travelled upwards, severing the trigeminal and oculomotor nerves, before passing through the amygdala, the thalamus and the parietal lobe, shattering the parietal bone, and exiting Detective Sergeant Proctorow's skull before lodging itself harmlessly in the soft antique plaster of the wall above and behind the three bodies, one now dead, on the floor of the basement room.

There are five of us in the office this afternoon. Yesterday was Matthew's birthday. Gary took Matthew and his friends to the cinema. I could not face it. I offered to bake a cake, but Gary had already made one in the shape of a train. Here, real trains rumble by, one floor below our fourth-storey window.

Alex, unusually, interrupts. He says, A classic suicide wound: gun under the jaw, or in the mouth, bullet through the base of the brain. An interesting coincidence, given that it wasn't suicide.

Theo says, Please allow Rada to continue.

I continue.

The hole in the wall was surrounded by a clearly discernible spray pattern of blood and brain and bone fragments from which the angle of impact could easily and accurately have been calculated, had it been necessary to do so, if the lethal shooting had not been witnessed by eight people from a variety of angles and vantage points. Admittedly two of those eight – Alex Corvin and Dmitry Kalenkov had their faces turned to the wall or floor respectively, throughout, and may therefore have limited value as witnesses. Even those, such as myself, who were observing events closely could not, with any degree of confidence, say whose finger had caused the trigger to be pulled, given the way in which the gun and three hands (those of DI Jenks, DS Proctorow and DC Moody) were trapped and obscured from sight between the slim and fat bodies of Detectives Moody/Proctorow and DI Jenks respectively. Nevertheless, none of the eight live people in the room, whether or not they had directly witnessed the shooting, doubted that it had been fatal, even though none, including me, had at this stage actually checked, not one of us had felt for a pulse or held a mirror near the mouth of the presumed corpse or a cigarette lighter up to its eyelids, his eyelids, but we were all, without anyone needing to say so, convinced that the nondescript, non-criminal, non-gun-toting policeman (whose name and rank were subsequently confirmed as Detective Sergeant Edgar Proctorow) was now dead.

I have not described any of this to Gary.

Throughout the struggle and subsequent presumed lethal shooting the sound of wailing/screaming from the room above the basement room had continued; if, as a result of shortness of breath or lessening of the immediate trauma or loss of blood and consequent loss of muscle and/or lung power, the intensity of the wailing/screaming had abated somewhat, it nonetheless redoubled at the sound of the second shot, even though that second shot did not penetrate the ceiling and posed no actual physical threat to the wailer/screamer (which fact may indicate that the wailing/screaming was more the result of shock and fear than of actual injury, although it is of course possible that an initial injury was followed by shock and fear which was subsequently intensified by the sound of a second shot, even though that shot did not, in fact, cause any further injury, at least not to the woman in the room above the basement room from whom it is to be assumed the wailing/screaming emanated). With a shudder the gun/policewoman Moody rolled the corpse of her former professional colleague off her own body and onto the carpeted floor to her right. As she did so the gun slid from her chest, revealing powder burns on her hooded fleece. There were matching burns on the dead Proctorow's shirt. The shorter, fatter gun/policeman, still pinned to the floor beneath DC Moody, tried to pick up the gun but was impeded in this not only by the weight of his former professional and criminal colleague but in fact by the intervention of the taller gun/policeman – who, it turns out, was not in fact a policeman at all in the accepted sense of an officer of the law empowered to arrest malefactors and to keep the peace, not to say to carry arms, but was an accountant whose name and equivalent rank were subsequently determined to be Assistant Chief Constable William Nashe –

Across the table from me now, Nashe nods in acknowledgement.

– who stepped forward and placed his foot upon the pistol, then bent down, picked it up and stowed it in the pocket of his blue summer weight suit jacket, where it bulged and dragged the jacket down on the right hand side. From beneath DC Moody, DI Jenks said, You're under arrest, but it was not clear if he meant it or intended it as a joke or, even, in either case, to whom he referred. No one in the room paid much attention because – presumably coincidentally, but at any rate simultaneously – there came the sound of a *third* gunshot, quieter and more muffled even than the second, but nonetheless distinct and unmistakable. The sound appeared to come from the room directly above the basement room, the room into which it is to be presumed the first bullet had passed and either injured or terrified (or both) the female occupant whose wailing/screaming had been audible ever since (but which now, on the occasion of the third gunshot, abruptly ceased). Six of the nine people in the basement room – including myself, Theo Day and Kurt, whose surname has not been subsequently determined, and who possessed no known rank, and whose house this may or may not have been – but not including Proctorow, who was dead, or Alex Corvin, who was facing the wall or Dmitry Kalenkov (ditto the floor) looked at each other as if to say: what now?

DC Moody – the gun/policewoman who had gone into the interview room behind the public area in the bank during Monday's robbery and had fired the second shot there, after which the terrified wailing/screaming (which terrified wailing/screaming was not dissimilar to that heard during Wednesday's siege/stand-off/shoot-out in the basement flat previously occupied by Matthew Rodkin, and which had just ceased) – began to cry; she tried to hide it, but could not. She was sobbing uncontrollably when the door to the basement room, the door from the cramped hallway that led past the kitchen and to the outer door that itself opened onto the garden where nothing currently grew but weeds, opened.

D says, I wasn't looking at the floor.

Dmitry, please do not interrupt. You will have your opportunity to report.

But I wasn't.

Alex, looking now at the office wall, says, I *was* looking at the wall.

The man is dead, Theo says; as long as there was at least one, it really does not matter how many of us watched him die.

There was a thunderstorm yesterday: Gary and Matthew and his friends were all drenched on the way home from the cinema.

I find my place and continue.

An old man stood in the doorway. He had white hair and

a wooden cane with a silver handle in the shape of an eagle. His shoes were old but well cared for, the thick leather burnished to a deep gloss. He was the man from the bank, or rather from the robbery, the man who had stood in front of me in the queue for the cash dispenser, who had moved slowly and who did not get down on the floor when he was told to, not even when the bank robber, whom we now know to be Assistant Chief Constable William Nashe (here Nashe nods again, less confidently) put a gun to his head, not even when Nashe fired his gun, inadvertently causing the terror/injury of the woman in the adjacent interview room which in turn resulted in wailing/screaming not dissimilar to that which had just ceased to come from the room above Rodkin's basement flat. Theo also recognized the man, and greeted him by name. The man acknowledged Theo's greeting with a slow nod. At the sound of the man's name, Dmitry Kalenkov ceased looking at the floor –

I wasn't looking at the fucking floor.

– and sat up, discovering in doing so that neither DC Moody nor anybody else was now pointing a gun at his head, the gun now being stowed in the pocket of Nashe's blue summer weight suit, where it bulged visibly and made the jacket hang awkwardly, and said, Dmitry Kalenkov that is, said: Lopez?

It was Lopez, the Inquisitor, who said how pleased he was that we were all able to join him this evening and who did have a gun, a Beretta 8000D Cougar similar or possibly identical to that used by the police/gunman Nashe, in his right hand, the hand that wasn't holding the cane with the silver eagle, and who now looked at the short, heavy, stubby gun as if surprised to see it there, in his own hand, although he must have been conscious of its weight, the Beretta not being a light weapon, whatever its other merits, weighing in fact 925 grams factory-shipped and un-adapted, and his surprise must have been staged, affected and, indeed, had the air of a self-conscious theatrical gesture, accompanied as it was by a raising of the eyebrows, a shrug and a shake of the head that seemed designed, if anything, to draw attention to the theatricality of the gesture and to communicate to the nine people in the room, or rather to eight of them (one, Proctorow, being dead and not capable of appreciating or detecting falsely theatrical and ironic gestures, although it is possible that Lopez was not, at that point, aware that Proctorow was dead rather than simply lying, like DC Moody and DI Jenks, on the floor for some unfathomable – to Lopez – reason of his own), that his words were not to be taken at face value. Lopez reached back with his right hand, slipping it under his jacket. When he brought it out again the gun was not there, he must have had some sort of holster on his belt, or perhaps a specially-adapted pocket in the lining of his jacket, he did not appear to be the kind of person who would simply stick a gun into the waistband of his trousers, he looked too elegant, too precise and prepared for that. He said, You must be wondering why I invited you all here this evening. He said it with a sort of one-sided grin and another raising of his eyebrows and a tipping of his head to one side – the right side – that had the same theatrical/ironic effect as the earlier gestures in relation to the gun and which seemed to suggest that we should not take his words at face value, that he in fact wanted us all to know and to be in no doubt that he was teasing us, that what he was saying and doing was absurd, but consciously so, and yet to make us all, individually, wonder if he had in fact, in some way that we could not detect or understand or even begin to grasp, somehow caused us individually and severally to come together in this damp and unprepossessing basement bedsit of a recent suicide which somehow contained nine people – or, rather, eight people and one corpse – who might otherwise struggle to explain why and how they had collectively arrived at this unlikely gathering if it were not in fact the result of the unfathomable machinations of the tenth occupant of the room, *viz*, Lopez himself.

Could he have arranged it?

It is Nashe, the newest member of the team who has spoken, which is in itself surprising, irrespective of what he has said, this being his first ever meeting.

I say, No. It is not credible.

Alex says, I believe it.

D says, Fuck off, you don't.

Theo taps his lacquered fountain pen on the tabletop, calling us to order.

I say that I have always assumed, and that everybody else in the room at the time – with the exception of DS Proctorow, who was dead – would also have assumed, that I was a free agent whose decisions and actions – however misguided – had led me there, to that room, and that the idea that we had all individually and severally, gathered at the instigation of someone, however clever and/or Machiavellian, that most of us had never met, or heard of, even, was as ridiculous as Lopez's own ironic/theatrical gestures suggested it was, even if it did not feel that way at the time.

D smirks. He says, He certainly didn't engineer what happened next.

This is unprofessional. D's part in what happened next being not only central but also controversial, or at least, his continued presence within the team, after what happened, being controversial, representing, some might think, a conflict of interest, or, at the very least, a breach of ethical standards.

Rada, please continue.

It is arguable, of course, that Theo's own position is also somewhat compromised, given that (a) his role in what happened, whilst not by any legitimate standard of judgment as central or fundamental or directly causal or culpable, even, as D's, was nonetheless contributory, at the very least, and (b) that it was his decision that D remain on the team, in the Office, and attend this meeting, and even, when we get to that point in the agenda, report on the incident, rather than, say, being sacked, and/or handed over to the police, or to the Office's own internal security (such as it is, post-Lopez, which may be negligible, or non-existent, the whole question of the capacity, or continued existence, or reality of the Office of Assessment being, in itself, central and fundamental and causal to what happened, in the dead solicitor's basement flat, after Lopez entered, holding a gun and teased us – teased is certainly the appropriate word – about why we were all there, in that fetid basement on a hot, unpleasantly humid Wednesday evening at the end of June).

Lopez ignored the corpse on the floor – or pretended to ignore it, it was hard to tell – and turned to Theo, asking whether he was enjoying the aesthetics of the situation. Theo asked Lopez whether he had yet found Likker's money and, when Lopez only smiled, answered his own question, saying it was clear he hadn't or we wouldn't be here, would we? Lopez was not surprised, at least he did not display surprise – his face and general demeanour remaining calm, untroubled, amused and superior, or patronising, perhaps – but he was not prepared or willing or inclined to respond to Theo's question, or his answer, preferring to ask, instead, a question of his own, *viz:* How was Jackson?

Theo said that he had not seen Jackson in some time.

The Inquisitor smiled, then, or grinned, the corners of his mouth pulling back before Theo had even finished speaking as if he, Lopez, knew what it was that Theo was going to say before he said it (which it is possible that he did, or that he wished to convey the impression he did).

He said, And why is that?

Theo sighed gently, shifting his weight and switching his own silver-headed cane, the cane with the dog's head handle, from his right hand to his left, and said, I think we both know why that is.

Lopez nodded, and Theo nodded and Dmitry, from the floor, where he was still sitting, and where he seemed to be holding his left forearm strangely in his right hand, as if one of the bones, the radius or the ulna, were broken, said, Why is it?

Neither Lopez nor Theo answered, they just looked at each other and neither of them, as far as I could see, looked at D, who now stood up awkwardly, still holding his left forearm with his right hand, as if his wrist were injured and he was wondering how to stop the blood flowing, stood right in front of Theo, right up close, the room wasn't large and was crowded with so many people in it, but still, D stood closer to Theo than he actually, arguably, needed to, and said, Why haven't you seen Jackson?

It was Lopez who said, Because Jackson's dead.

D did not turn away from Theo, did not turn to face or even look at Lopez, but said, instead, to Theo, What about Rivers?

It was Lopez who said, Rivers, too. They've both been dead for years.

Theo didn't say anything.

# 19

IT FELT VERY crowded in my room.

My room? How quickly we acclimatise.

The room was small, there were too many people in it, too much noise. I kept my face to the wall and hoped that they would go away, but I knew that they would not.

Dmitry Kalenkov had always been angry. It is one of those things I knew without knowing I knew, but which became clear the moment the knife emerged from the sleeve of his jacket. The anger is a function of his stupidity, I think. A by-product. When it happened I was surprised it had taken him so long. It made sense.

I wanted a cigarette, still. I wanted to know what had happened to my lighter.

It makes no sense that D is Rada's brother, that they share the same DNA. It must be the mother that makes all the difference.

We cannot blame heredity.

D has to take responsibility for his own stupidity, for the frustration and the rage it causes him, because, to be fair, I think D half-knows he's stupid. I hope he does. I hope a corner of his brain is alive to the inadequacy of the rest. That it listens when he quotes whatever self-help tract he's read this week and laughs. That it says: It surely didn't need to turn out like this? Look at the genetic advantages you had; look at your sister; and now look at you, you pathetic worm.

Maybe there isn't.

Maybe D really is as stupid as he looks, as he sounds, and as he acts. Maybe there is no self-consciousness there at all. Perhaps he really did think that his genius would be recognised? That the Office would spot his talent, would appreciate the true quality of his work and his ideas on Lifetime Value and would take him under its wing. That Jackson, or Rivers, would look down from Riverside House and see that he was good. That they would stop by, one day, to let him know, quietly, that Theo was a great man, of course, a loyal servant for whom we all had the greatest respect, but that it was time for his legacy to pass into the hands of a younger man. A man like D, perhaps . . .

Perhaps he believed that. I had always assumed not. I had assumed his persona was impersonal, an act. That the cars and the gym and the breezy insensitivity were all, somehow, a pretence.

I had to believe that, but it seems that I was wrong. There really is no hope.

When D stabbed Lopez in the throat and Lopez sank to his knees, and then tipped forward, face down on the floor beside Moody, beside Proctorow, I asked whether anyone was going to arrest him. The room was full of police officers, after all. It was just like D, when he finally succumbed to the temptation of serious violent crime, to do so in full view of the law. It was consistent, I thought.

There in my room, in Rodkin's room, I invited the police persons present to do their duty. I became quite animated, despite the warning looks I received from Rada. I appealed to the tallest of the police persons, perhaps instinctively recognizing the authority of height, but he said: I'm not a policeman.

I did my best to look quizzical. It seemed appropriate, and he must have got my gist.

He looked sheepish. I never actually said I was.

No?

Even from the relative disadvantage of my horizontal position, I projected the professional disbelief of the practised cross-examiner.

He said, I'm an accountant.

I was surprised, I have to say.

He said, Until tomorrow, anyway.

The policewoman, the one on the floor who'd pointed her gun at D's head but for some reason had not shot him when she had the opportunity, but who had shot the other policeman instead, said she wasn't arresting anyone. She'd just killed a fellow police officer and had to assume she was suspended from duty. And most likely would be until tomorrow, when she'd be redundant.

I turned to the shorter, fatter, more bearded officer of the law. He was sitting on the floor, his back to the wall opposite me. Just to his right was the gap in the skirting I'd found earlier, and outside which I'd vowed to leave a portion of uneaten cheese, but hadn't. I said, You have a murder, handed to you on a plate. How often does that happen?

I could see he was thinking about it. I could see intelligence there, behind the damp eyes. But still he disappointed me.

He shook his head and said, I work in HR.

Besides, he said, he knew D's father.

It was, I think, the first time I'd ever seen Theo surprised. He said, You knew Pyotr Kalenkov?

The HR-person said, We all knew Pete the Pontiff.

Theo got the look in his eye he sometimes gets when D reports something particularly inane; he said, He was well known to Human Resources?

The HR-person laughed. I wasn't always in HR.

You were a detective?

The HR-person who hadn't always been in HR nodded.

D said, And what was Dad?

Your father . . . your father was useful. To a lot of people.

An informer?

Amongst other things.

Theo stepped towards D. He seemed keen to take control of the conversation, as if he were concerned about what the detective might say next. He said, Your father was many things, Dmitry. Like most of us.

Rada said, But he wasn't Russian?

Across the meeting room table, Rada shuffles the pages of her report. She looks at Theo, appealing for intervention, but Theo says it is what happened. He looks at the table as he says this.

Theo nodded.

The HR/police/gunman said, He worked for Likker. Sometimes.

Rada said, He didn't kill himself, either, did he?

The fat police/HR/gun-man shrugged, his shoulders pulling up into his beard.

Did he?

The coroner said he did.

D said, more loudly than was necessary, I don't believe you. Dad never worked for Likker.

The ex-detective shrugged again. That's how it was.

Then how come he doesn't turn up in Likker's file?

It was obvious that meant nothing to the ex-detective. But the other one, the one who said he was an accountant, Nashe, said, Because he was Likker.

D said, What's that supposed to mean? I've been through his life. That's what we do.

Nashe said, Not Likker. You wouldn't find anything he didn't want you to.

D was getting angry again. He was always angry, but now it was on the surface again. He still had the knife in his hand. He said, That's not the way it works. No one gets to pick and choose.

D, you see, was a believer. That was – is – his problem.

Across the table D makes a noise, deep down in his throat, his chest. If he were a predatory animal, a bear, perhaps, or a dog, you might call it a growl. I ignore him. I am only doing my job. To my right, D's left, Theo is still looking at the table. At least, his head is bowed. His eyes may be closed.

Unchecked, undaunted, I carry on.

Theo spoke up, then, in the basement room, although he spoke softly. To D he said, Nashe is right. Likker was different.

D didn't want to know. He's still dead, he said.

Theo said, It was thanks to Likker that you are here. He certainly knew your father. It was because he knew your father that he asked me to give your sister a job. And, naturally, it was because she asked me, that I gave you a job, Dmitry.

After that there was a lot of shouting on D's part, a lot of stuff I didn't bother to follow, but the gist of which seemed to be that Theo had known all along, known since before D was even born, that Pyotr Kalenkov was no more Russian than I am, that he was a conman and a petty fixer, a go-between, a man who did small jobs for men with more money and more power than he would ever have, but that none of this mattered. D did not appear to agree. He thought it mattered a great deal. It made all the difference, he shouted.

Rada didn't say a word. It was her father, too, but she didn't say a word, then, and, until this afternoon, in the office, reading her report just now, she hasn't said a word since, as far as I know. About her father; not a word.

Meanwhile, D grew louder and louder, his face redder, the knuckles of the fist that grasped the still-bloody knife grew whiter. Spittle flew from his lips and flecked the immaculate herringbone of Theo's suit.

Theo did not move. He did not flinch, much less retreat. The storm of D's rage broke around him.

And still the trigger-happy policewoman did not shoot him and the accountant and the HR-detective declined to intervene.

Which left Proctorow, the policeman who'd been shot, who was an actual policeman, not a bank robber, and could have arrested D, and might have done so, had he not been dead.

And D walks amongst us still, tall and raw and stupid as he ever was.

## 20

So Proctorow, who was a pain, I'd have to say, but who probably, all the same, didn't actually deserve or need to die, was dead. What was left of him lay on the carpet, his blood sprayed up the wall and most of the top of his head not actually on the top of his head. DC Moody and DI Jenks were still there on the floor, too. Jenks had got as far as sitting up, but Moody was lying where she'd fallen, where she'd been when the gun went off and Proctorow died so spectacularly and she'd eventually rolled his body off her own. Nashe was standing over by the wall, near the door, near the poster with the bollocks about he-goats scribbled on it in fat black marker pen. Rada was all right, she was sitting in the only chair, not saying anything. Alex was curled up on the bed like a baby, like he was wishing we'd all go away and leave him in his cot. Kurt was looking from one to another of us like he's wondering what fucking planet we'd all come from and I can't say I blame him, really, because in amongst the blood and brains and madness there were Lopez and Theo facing off across the room in their elegant suits and their hand made brogues and talking all that old man shit where what they said was about a tenth of what they were saying and it was like they didn't really need to talk at all because they each knew what the other was going to say before they even said it. And the rest of us were supposed to be able to fill in the dots, or, if we couldn't, they didn't care because it was just because we're stupid. I'm not stupid but I couldn't be doing with all that any more so I got up, carefully, because whatever they thought they knew, I knew something they didn't know, and I asked, "Why?" And even though I never asked him, even though I was looking at Theo and talking to Theo, Lopez took it upon himself to say, "Because Jackson's dead." It turned out he wasn't the only one. Rivers was dead, too. They'd both been dead for years, apparently, since before I'd joined the Office, Lopez said, perhaps before I was even born. And it was the way he said 'Office' that did it. For once I was pretty fucking sure I was getting the other nine tenths, I still am, and that's when I turned and stepped away from Theo and towards Lopez. I dropped my left hand and let the knife slide down and I already had it in my right hand when Theo said, "Dmitry." But it was too late. Clever as Lopez was, or thought he was, or wanted us to think he was, he wasn't clever enough to see it coming, or sharp enough to move, at any rate.

He had it fucking coming, a fucking long time coming, and now he was dead.

He was as dead as Jackson. Or Rivers. As dead as Rodkin and Likker, as dead as the woman, or women, in the bank, who'd screamed, and then stopped screaming, as dead as the woman upstairs, Kurt's girlfriend, perhaps. As dead as Proctorow, who was a pain, and not the sharpest knife on the rack, and was still there with us, on the floor with his brains all up the wall.

It's quiet in the office when I read this. It's like no one knows what to say or how to look at me, even.

And then Alex, who always was a snotty bastard, and who never liked me, and believe me the feeling was fucking mutual, asked if no one was going to arrest me. But Proctorow was dead and the policewoman wouldn't, and it turned out the other two weren't really plods anyway, they were pen pushers of some sort. But one of them had been a copper once, he said he'd known my father, and it turned out Theo had known Dad, too. And Likker. I mean Theo had known Likker, but also Likker had known my father. It seemed like everyone had. I was half expecting fucking Alex to say he had, too, and I probably would have killed him, I nearly killed Theo. I certainly wanted to kill someone, even though I just had killed Lopez. Lopez knew my father, too, apparently. "Knew him well enough to kill him?" I asked. Because it was as clear as fucking day that he'd killed Rodkin, or had him killed, nobody slits his own throat with a breadknife, Alex was right about that at least, and OK there was nearly thirty years between the two, and no connection, except perhaps Likker, who was the kind of man who killed people, or had them killed. And Theo didn't say yes, but he didn't say no, either.

"Or was it Likker?" I said, because there didn't seem to be any reason for any of this, for anything, for why my Dad wasn't Russian, despite him being more Russian than the fucking Volga, but Likker was the common point, the only common point.

Theo said, "Likker didn't kill your father."

"So who did?"

And Rada asked what did it matter? My sister said that. He was her father, too. But she said it didn't matter, and then she didn't say another fucking word, and hasn't said a word until today, reading her report which like all her reports was unbefuckinglievably tedious and ninety-nine percent totally missing the fucking point.

Yesterday, Sunday, it rained like there was no tomorrow, and it washed away all the flying fucking ants. Theo had given us a couple of days to recover, and to prepare our reports. So now, tomorrow's here, and Rada's still saying nothing and

Alex is still looking at the wall, and Nashe, the new recruit, the ex-accountant-copper, ex-Assistant Chief Constable, ex-bank robber and possible murderer, or killer at least, if we think back as far as only last Monday, Nashe, who's apparently on our team, now (whatever that means after what Lopez let slip and I understood, and maybe – I don't know – maybe everyone knew anyway, everyone but me, I mean, I honestly thought there was an Office of Assessment because, after all, it's been paying my wages every month on the nose, and the money's been real enough, you've only got to see my car to see that,) Nashe says: "So what happened to the money?" And I've got no fucking clue what money he's talking about. But it seems Old Man Theo knows, and even Alex, because Alex says, like it has something to do with whatever it was we are talking about here, "There was a hole, a gap in the skirting," and Theo says, "I expect Mrs Rodkin will be grateful for that, at least." And I still have not one fucking iota of a clue what they're on about, and I'm beginning to wish I still had that knife with me, the boning knife, the one I stuck in Lopez's throat, and I think: breathe. One, two. Breathe.

There's some more talk, some more conversation, then Nashe, the new boy, is giving his report. He's asking if we know what Willie Sutton said, whoever Willie Sutton was, but I'm not listening, I'm breathing and I'm focusing like the book says, focusing on the air passing through my nostrils. I observe the sound of voices, the fact of the sound, I mean, but I do not register what they are saying. I observe myself observing and then I let the observation slip away. And no one else is dead.

When I return to the room, Nashe is saying, "Alex is right: no Book of the Dead shows the heart weighing more than the feather of Maat. There's a reason for that."

I say, "It's not my call, but Lopez should be going down."

Nobody says anything. I can hear the trains rumbling

past the window, behind me, and I look at Nashe, the new boy, and he's looking at Theo. I look at Rada, who's looking down, looking at her papers, straightening the edges of the pile, squeezing her paper clip back into place. I look at Alex and he's looking at the wall.

Nobody says anything.

I say, "What? Isn't that what we're doing here? Making decisions?"

Theo leans back in his chair, settling his shoulders. Alex – fucking bastard Alex, fucking parasitic, soul-sapping, energy-depleting bastard fucking Alex – is still looking at the wall. Nashe – I don't mind Nashe, but I don't know what the fuck he's doing here; after everything that's happened and is obviously going to happen, or not happen, given what Lopez said, like any of us getting paid, or having a job or anything at all, I don't know what Theo thinks he's doing increasing headcount – Nashe is looking from me to Theo to Rada and back to me, but not saying anything. Rada, I have to say, Rada, my sister, the only family I have, my only human contact with the world, when you come to think about it, and I love her, despite her choice of friends, and despite her husband, who, let's face it, is a wanker and doesn't deserve her, or anybody, for that matter, and her kid, my nephew who isn't to blame for any of this, Rada is looking down at her papers on the table in front of her, and fiddling with the fucking paper clip, and saying nothing.

Then Theo, when he's finished settling his shoulders and looking around the table at us all, says, "We make recommendations. Not decisions. That's not our job."

So that's that, then. Apparently we've still got a job.

# Acknowledgements

I AM GRATEFUL TO Felicity Everett, Claire Seeber, Judy McInerney and Phyllice Eddu for their support, encouragement and comments on (very) early drafts.

From the conversations of Nashe and his colleagues it is obvious I owe a debt to *Where the Money Was* (Willlie Sutton with Edward Linn, Broadway Books, New York) which taught me almost as much about the power of myths as it did about the craft of robbing banks.

Everything else I owe to Sophy Miles.